Adventure House
Presents

SECRET AGENT "X"

February 1937

This reprint edition is a facsmile edition. Variations in print and quality are mostly attributable to the rough woodpulp original this reprint edition is based on.

ISBN: 1-59798-142-7
ISBN-13: 978-1-59798-142-2

Published by Adventure House
914 Laredo Road
Silver Spring, Md 20901
www.adventurehouse.com
sales@adventurehouse.com

Vol. 9
No. 4

SECRET AGENT X

G-MAN ACTION ADVENTURES

FEB.
1937

Rose Wyn, Editor

Cover by Wm. E. Luberoff

Published bi-monthly by Periodical House, Inc. Office of publication, 29 Worthington Street, Springfield, Mass. Rose Wyn, President. Editorial and executive offices, 67 West 44th Street, New York, N. Y. Entered as second-class matter December 13, 1933, at Springfield, Mass., under the Act of March 3, 1879. Manuscripts will be handled with care but this magazine assumes no responsibility for their safety. For advertising rates address Ace Fiction Group, 67 West 44th Street, New York City. Twelve Issues, $1.00; Single Copies, Ten Cents.

SECRET AGENT X, an "Ace" Magazine that makes live one of the most dynamic mystery characters in the annals of fiction, gives its readers an unbeatable magazine lineup of the tops in stories: One complete book-length novel of "Secret Agent X," the mystery master, by Brant House, and seven other complete stories of the heroic, blood-racing work of G-men and other government operatives.

Another in the long list of "Ace" Magazines is TEN DETECTIVE ACES, leading variety magazine in the field of crime-adventure stories. Among ten complete, vividly written tales, is a feature novel of another exciting "Moon Man" exploit, "Blackjack Jury," by Frederick C. Davis.

A new "Ace" Magazine of distinctive, human-interest quality comes to America's huge host of fiction readers in SURE-FIRE DETECTIVE, including among a lengthy story bill of fare, "The Cartoon Crimes," unique and suspenseful novelet by Donald G. Cooley.

But that is not all. Here are a few more members of the "Ace" Magazine family:

HEADQUARTERS DETECTIVE
Sensational Lawman Thrillers

WESTERN TRAILS
Salty Cowboy Action Stories

DETECTIVE ROMANCES
Romantic, Vivid Detective Tales

ROMANCE ROUND-UP
Tophand Romantic Western Stories

FLYING ACES
Everything Absorbing in Aviation

GOLDEN WEST
Romances of The Ranch and Range

LOVE FICTION MONTHLY
The Tangles and Triangles of Romance

RED SEAL WESTERN
Two Complete Novels—and Shorts

SECRETS
Has a Vital Story For Everybody

WESTERN ACES
Human Yarns of Range and Owl-Hoot

Death's

The masked man muttered at the cigarette-smoking Agent X: "Keep back—"

One Man Pitted His Wits Against Human Devils who Organized to Destroy Many Souls

Why did those strange human derelicts patronize newsreel-movie showings and immediately leave the theaters with evil, mysterious intent. That was the veiled enigma Agent X had to pierce—while unfathomable gusts of hell's killing cold trapped X and Betty Dale in a murder maelstrom.

Frozen Formula

By Brant House

Author of "City of Madness," "Horror's Handclasp," etc.

"Secret Agent X" Novel

Here was a thrill for the jaded appetites of the dopesters.

CHAPTER I

Death Dance

A RAGGED awning of faded striped stuff fluttered dismally above the doorway of the Juana Diaz Wine Shop. It was bitter cold in the street. In the shop, a guitar whanged a nasal accompaniment to the rich baritone voice that sought to forget the chill of the wind in a song of warmer climes. November was not for the dark-eyed, olive-skinned natives of the Puerto Rican and Spanish quarter just north of Central Park.

A taxi turned off to Fifth Avenue at 111th Street and came to a stop in front of the Juana Diaz. Its fare was a woman. What could be seen of her face and figure indicated that a more searching light might have revealed great beauty.

There was something undefinably strange about the woman—something beside the fact that her stockings, though of the sheerest chiffon, did not match. It was obvious that she had dressed in haste and without a moment's thought. Her jaunty sport hat clashed with the formal sable evening wrap she wore.

The woman had trouble separating one bill from the thick wad in her pocket-book. Finally, she had the driver help himself to his pay and tip. Then her trembling fingers dropped the pocket book on the running board of the taxi.

"You want to hang on to that, lady," said the driver as he picked up the purse.

The woman stared at her purse as though she had never seen it, then clasped it tightly and ran up the street. Halfway up in the next block, she stopped.

From across the street came the sound of music ground harshly from a phonograph. The woman stood on the corner and clung to a steel telegraph post. She uttered a strained, anxious laugh and crossed the street to the somber, gray-fronted dwelling from which the music came. On worn, narrow stone steps she paused.

"Must not forget the mask," she whispered, and then she opened her purse and searched in its depths for a small black packet of silk. This she unrolled to reveal a domino mask to which was attached a length of elastic.

She fastened the mask over her face. She found the bell-pull, gave it a jerk so that the bell within jangled hysterically.

The brass mail flap in the gray door clinked as though cautious eyes had examined the woman on the steps carefully. The door was opened, and the light of an amber-shaded lamp fell upon the exotically beautiful figure of a second woman.

THE woman who sought admittance had dressed without thought or sense of harmony, but the woman in the doorway had omitted nothing from her toilet that would lend her charm. Hers was a dark, secret beauty that warmed to gay colors and daring costumes. Her dark, soft skin had a faint yellowish cast that suggested mixed bloods. Her lips were warm and scarlet, her eyes cold and sea-green.

The woman on the steps swayed slightly forward. "Zerna," she breathed, "I'm desperate. Help me!"

Contempt rather than compassion curved the vivid lips of the woman called Zerna. "Get a grip on yourself, my dear," said she in a strident voice, as she helped the caller into the house.

A man came running down the street, sprang to the narrow steps before the gray-fronted house. He thumped the door furiously and, noticing the bell for the first time, pulled and pushed it until time the woman called Zerna reappeared.

"My wife," the man gasped. "I saw her go in here. I will not have—" He stopped, noticed for the first time that he was speaking to an exceedingly beautiful woman.

Zerna smiled. "Oh, really, haven't you made a mistake? The young lady who just entered has no husband."

The man shook his head. "I beg your pardon. That woman was my wife. I must see her at once. This is a matter of the utmost importance."

A man in the stiff, black garb of a servant appeared directly behind the woman called Zerna. There was something in the dredge-engine cut of his jaw that suggested that his dress was the only humble thing about him.

"This gent making trouble, m'am?" he asked.

Zerna frowned slightly and shook her head. She addressed the anxious man on the steps. "Your name, please."

"Colrich—Mr. Fred Colrich. The woman who just entered this house is Mrs. Colrich. I demand to be taken to my wife at once."

"I am very sorry, Mr. Colrich," said Zerna, "but there is no one here by that name. I know the young woman who just came in very well."

"And that's flat," added the servant. He slammed the door in Colrich's face.

INSIDE the house with the gray door, the phonograph continued to scratch out its music in tireless accompaniment to the shuffling of dancing feet. All the dancers wore small black masks. There were débutantes and wealthy club men. There were street women and potential thugs. It was an odd democracy of the best and the worst in society, joined here by a single link—dope.

Dope stared from the slots of their little black masks, through pupils dilated with cocaine or contracted with morphine. Dope spoke wordlessly from their twitching lips.

Round and round the floor, the couples moved beneath the dim light of tawdry lamps placed on old tables around the sides of the room. And over and above them all hung an aura of indescribable evil. Terror, too, was there, and death; and the darker tragedy of minds going mad, drug-chained to nightmares.

Perhaps the most incongruous couple on the floor was the woman in her sable furs and her partner. Her black mask was spotted with hot, frantic tears and now and again her shoulders would shake with a sniffling sob. Her partner was a withered youth, who whispered to himself, laughed shrilly, smirked continuously.

A man in evening clothes, his face completely masked, stepped from a doorway and spied the weeping woman and her partner. As they wheeled gracelessly within his reach, the man in evening clothes reached out and tapped the woman on the shoulder. She jerked a glance at the man, and instantly her lips twitched into a smile. She all but threw her partner from her, seized the arm of the man in evening clothes, and said: "Thank heaven! I couldn't have lived a moment more!"

The man said nothing. He led the woman in furs across the room and through a small door which he closed after them. The woman in furs jerked off her mask and hat, and with trembling fingers pushed tangled hair back from her waxy brow. Her face was a ghastly mockery of former beauty. She threw herself into a chair, only to spring to her feet a moment later to welcome the exotically beautiful Zerna as the latter entered the room.

"Give it to me, Zerna," she said.

Zerna took the woman coldly by one wrist and forced her back into the chair. "Your husband was here, Mrs. Colrich. That won't do, you know."

The dope-starved woman bit her quivering lower lip. "I couldn't help it. You've got to put me somewhere where my husband can't find me. But you've got to give me a shot first. I'm dying for a shot."

Zerna's green eyes regarded Mrs. Colrich dispassionately. "How does it happen you haven't paid your club dues?"

Mrs. Colrich knotted her fingers. "I haven't the money, I've told you again and again! Oh, why won't you let me have a shot! I can buy that. I've enough in my purse. But I can't get any more money from my husband."

Mrs. Colrich seized Zerna's hand in a tight, desperate fist. "Listen, Zerna," she pleaded in whisper, "I'll do anything. Give me a shot, and I'll try once more to get money from Fred. And if I can't do that, I'll do something else. Isn't there something else I could do? Some work, or something? All those people out there aren't rich, yet they get their stuff regularly." The distracted woman began to weep bitterly.

ZERNA looked incapable of helping anyone but herself. Her green eyes were unflickering. Suddenly she slapped her fingers briskly across Mrs. Colrich's face. "Oh, come out of it!" she said sharply. Then she turned, and with hip-swaying steps, approached the door. She knocked twice.

The man in evening clothes entered the room and looked querulously into

Zerna's now stormy eyes. Zerna tossed a gesture toward the all but hysterical Mrs. Colrich. "She's finished. Sell you the Brooklyn Bridge or her soul for a shot of hop. You'd better write *finis* on her page."

The man in evening clothes had scarcely turned toward the unfortunate Mrs. Colrich before the latter sprang from her chair and threw her arms around the man. She spoke through locked teeth!

"Listen—I don't know who you are. But you've got to give me a shot before I die. I've got money for the shot, but I haven't got the two thousand dollars. I'll—"

The phone on the desk jangled. The man put a hand across Mrs. Colrich's mouth. "Pardon me," he said mockingly. Then, still holding back Mrs. Colrich's hasty words, he raised the phone with the other hand. "Shoot," he said. Then he listened, eyes in his black mask flickering.

After a moment, he uttered a short, dry laugh. "Secret Agent X? Sure, I've heard of him. I heard of Santa Claus, too. Listen, you take a headache pill and quit worrying. One more man on our trail isn't going to make any difference, even if his name is Secret Agent X. We got the whole police force guessing, haven't we? .... Then, ride on the breeze, buddy." He hung up and released Mrs. Colrich.

"Sorry, Ruth Colrich," he said, "but I can't do a thing for you. You don't pay club dues; you don't get in on the club privileges."

For a moment, some of her old strength of character returned to Ruth Colrich. Beneath the pitiful face that dope had made, there was a ghost of her old pride as she said: "I am going to turn myself over to the police. I'm going to tell them everything."

The man in evening clothes lighted a cigarette. "Sure," he said quietly.

Then he went to a door at the other side of the room, threw it wide open. "This way out, Mrs. Colrich."

Ruth Colrich started for the door, only to stop three feet from it. A quivering extended on down through her body. "No," she said tonelessly, "it isn't true. You won't—"

She stopped, locked a scream in her throat by cramming a fist against her lips. The thing that she had seen in the shadows stepped into the room. It was man-height. It was man-shaped. But long black hair covered it from head to foot. Weird, saucerlike eyes stared from its hairy head.

Ruth Colrich's fingers peeled away from her lips. "Wh-what is this?" she stammered. "What does it mean?"

The man in evening clothes laughed. "It means that you or nobody else is going to do any blabbing."

Two long, hairy arms reached out and seized Mrs. Colrich. The woman's face was flattened against a mighty, fur-covered chest so that her screams were stifled. Then the monstrous thing carried the struggling woman into the darkness.

The man in evening clothes shrugged and rejoined the dancers. He sought out Zerna. "Whoop things up a little," he said. "The more noise, the better."

IN an entirely different section of the city, a rather remarkable man paused near the front of the Paragon Theatre and knocked the ashes from the cubical bowl of his pipe. A black overcoat tented shoulders to immense and square that few would have supposed that this man topped six feet in height. The same right angles so much in evidence about his body also governed the shape of his head and face. Atop his square head he had no protection against the chill blast, except his thick, shaggy, black hair. His name was Harvey Bates, and he occupied a unique position among the men who fight the nation's battle against crime. Harvey Bates was chief assistant to that mysterious man of many faces, Secret Agent X.

When he had reloaded his pipe with shag-cut tobacco and tamped it well with a square-ended thumb, he paced by the front of the theatre for perhaps the twentieth time that evening and came to a stop near the mouth of the alley just beyond. There he leaned against the corner of the building and listened to footsteps of some one coming up the alley.

"*His* footsteps?" Bates wondered. Even when he faced Agent X, Bates could not be certain of his identity—not until X spoke in a certain one of his thousand voices.

"Bates!" *The* voice. It was a mere whisper from the tall man whose face was hidden by the shadows of the alley.

Then from the same tall man who stood at Bates' elbow came a second voice, entirely different from the one that just whispered Bates' name: "I beg your pardon, but have you a match?"

Bates produced a box of matches. The man of mystery scratched one into flame and held it at the tip of his cigarette. There was nothing remarkable about his face, or rather the complex combination of plastic makeup material, clever pigments, and hidden face-plates that served him as a face. As he now appeared, Secret Agent X would have been lost in a crowd of three unless you happened to pay particular attention to his eyes. They were the cool gray of steel with a suggestion of compelling, hypnotic power flickering in their depths.

"Anything to report, Bates?" Secret Agent X asked softly as he returned the matches to his lieutenant.

"Yes, sir," Bates clipped. "Certain that in the past ten minutes, five persons entering the theater were drug addicts. They entered only a few minutes before the newsreel." It was a long speech for Bates to make, and he paused a moment before asking: "Why do the hopheads have this unusual appetite for movies, sir? What's the connection?"

Secret Agent X shook his head. "Maybe there is a connection, a dope connection. An usher could pass the stuff out in the dark." The Agent flipped his cigarette toward the gutter. "You may go to the Princess Theatre and check on it in the same manner, Bates. I'm going in here. This begins to look like a rather nasty business."

Agent X walked briskly to the ticket window, obtained a ticket and entered the theatre. His gray eyes darted right and left and centered upon a smartly uniformed usher. Agent X snapped his fingers and beckoned to the usher.

The usher crossed quickly to where X was standing and touched his round, red cap. "Help you, sir?"

A strange sort of smile curled one side of the Agent's mouth. "Very much, I believe," he said quietly. "Will you step into the lavatory just a moment? I really believe you'll do nicely." And he nipped the elbow of the young man and steered him toward the lavatory.

As soon as they were alone, Agent X opened his wallet and produced a twenty-dollar bill. "Will this be sufficient pay for several hours in the arms of Morpheus, my friend?"

The eyes of the young man grew wide. "Beg pardon, sir?"

A chuckle from the Agent. He pressed the twenty dollars into the young man's hand, and at the same time, his left hand removed a cigarette lighter from his vest pocket. "You see this, son?" He held the lighter very close to the young man's nose.

"Yes, sir."

The Agent touched a secret lever on the side of the cigarette lighter. There was a slight hiss. A jet of misty vapor darted from the lighter. The usher's mouth was open, but his cry died in his throat as he pitched forward into the arms of Secret Agent X.*

---

*AUTHOR'S NOTE: Secret Agent X has no use for lethal weapons of any sort. He prefers to rely upon his fists and wits and a few unique defensive weapons, of which the most useful is anaesthetizing gas of his own invention and which is extremely effective at close range. This gas is supplied him in small cartridges, which may be fired from his cigarette lighter, and larger and heavier cartridges which fit his powerful gas pistol. The same gas is contained in the gas bombs he carries, which are capable of rendering a whole roomful of people unconscious.

LESS than five minutes later, a miracle of transformation had taken place. Agent X emerged from the lavatory wearing the usher's natty uniform. It fitted him to perfection, for he had purposely chosen an usher whose figure resembled his own. But what was more remarkable was the amazing change in the Agent's face.

Beneath his deft finger tips, plastic volatile makeup material had been shaped into the exact contours of the usher's face. Coloring had been exactly duplicated.

The agent crossed the foyer, opened the door leading to the center aisle, and glanced across the dark theatre. On the screen, the newsreel had just ended. His eyes as yet unused to the dark, X did not see the man who suddenly bobbed from his seat, near the back of the theatre, and all but knocked the Agent over in his haste to leave.

X turned and followed the man into the foyer. The man glanced anxiously over his shoulder, and X had an opportunity of glimpsing his face. The waxy skin, odd eyes, and twitching facial muscles told the tragic story at once. The man was a dope addict.

Agent X watched the man go on his staggering way, and hardly had the door closed behind him, than a man and woman hurried from the theatre. And there was not the slightest doubt that they too knew the evil pleasures of dope. X was on the point of following them, when a fourth drug disciple came hurrying from the theatre.

This was no mere coincidence. There was definite reason and planning behind the moves of these addicts. Agent X was on the point of stopping this last hophead, when he felt a tug at his elbow. He turned to look down into the face of a mild-eyed, anxious-faced man whose expensively tailored clothes had been badly soiled.

"Usher, you must find Dr. Daniel Wicker for me at once. But for the love of heaven, don't make a fuss about it. He's in the theatre, I know. And you must tell him that Mrs. Colrich needs him immediately."

X regarded the worried man gravely. Only one sort of person ever urgently needed Dr. Daniel Wicker. Dr. Daniel Wicker was the owner of a sanitarium devoted solely to the cure of drug patients.

X bowed slightly. "Certainly, sir. And what name shall I give Dr. Wicker?"

"I am Mr. Fred Colrich. And you must get Dr. Wicker for Mrs. Colrich at once."

All the hypnotic power of X's eyes came into being as he held Colrich's gaze.

"Come this way, please," X said in quiet voice, and led Colrich across the foyer and into a small smoking room. Colrich dropped wearily into a chair.

"Now, Mr. Colrich, something seems to be troubling you. Your wife, eh?" X was speaking very quietly and gazing steadily into Colrich's eyes. "What seems to be the matter?"

"I don't know exactly," Colrich confided. "I followed her tonight. She went to the Princess Theatre just across the street at about eight o'clock. I thought nothing of that. She seems so restless. She left the Princess not ten minutes after she had entered. Then she got into a taxi. I followed her to a particularly unpleasant quarter of the city and to a house, the address of which I have in my pocket." Colrich slapped the breast pocket of his coat. "I can't bring the police in on this, you understand."

Colrich stood up. A bewildered frown furrowed his brow. "Who are you, sir? I seem— Why, you're just an usher—and you've been trying to pry into my affairs."

Colrich's right fist shot unexpectedly to the Agent's chin. It was a feather-weight blow, but it took X completely by surprise. He backed to the wall, leading Colrich in close before he sent a short, jolting left to a point directly above Colrich's heart.

It was a blow that might have killed, had not the Agent's superb muscular control reined it in at exactly the right moment. Colrich's eyes rolled back, and he sagged to the floor.

X glanced quickly around the smoking room. That had been a desperate stroke, entered into with the lightning-like decision that characterized all of the Agent's actions. Here was a rare opportunity to obtain inside information on a dope syndicate that was beginning to assume alarming proportions.

AGENT X had seen in Colrich a possible opening through which to strike at the insidious dope monster. If he could manage an impersonation of Colrich, to gain the confidence of Dr. Wicker, there was a chance that he might learn something about the distributing point of the drug syndicate. For Mrs. Colrich was a drug addict. There could be no other reason for Fred Colrich wanting Dr. Wicker to attend her.

His course decided upon, X hurriedly ripped off the usher's uniform which he had put on over his own clothes. As he moved, he practiced imitating Colrich's voice and characteristic facial expressions. It would be a rather difficult change, for Colrich was a decided blond and the Agent's present makeup simulated a dark complexion.

From the inside pocket of his coat, X took out a compact makeup kit, containing his special plastic volatile compound and basic pigments. He knelt beside Colrich, was studying the man's features intently, when he heard the sound of voices just outside the smoking room door.

"I tell you Dr. Wicker, this investigation will give the Paragon a bad name," came a deep voice from the other side of the door. "I believe that your suspicions are entirely unfounded. Suppose that a few cocaine addicts *have* been seen in the Paragon. There is no possible way in which we can prevent them from entering. We are not medical men, to judge whether or not our patrons use narcotics."

"Er—Mr. Nixon, we of the Anti Vice League are not confining our investigation to any one theatre."

Agent X recognized the slow, thoughtful manner of speaking that characterized Dr. Wicker. But there was absolutely no time for the Secret Agent to eavesdrop. There was no means of leaving the smoking room while Wicker and Nixon, owner of the Paragon Theatre, chose to stand directly outside the door. Nor did the little room offer any place of concealment save a small corner behind an overstuffed chair. Should the two men decide to enter the smoking room . . . .

The rattle of the door knob galvanized Agent X into action. He grabbed his makeup kit and pocketed it. He lifted the unconscious Colrich in his arms, held him upright with one hand while his other hand snatched a scrap of paper from Colrich's breast pocket. Then he lifted Colrich over the back of the large chair in the corner and let him fall to the floor.

X sprang away from the chair and snatched the jet-black toupee, which was part of his disguise as the usher, from his head. His features remained unaltered. Even as the door of the smoking room was opening, X picked up the usher's uniform and threw it into the corner on top of Colrich. Agent X ran his fingers through his own wavy brown hair and turned around.

The first to enter, Dr. Wicker, was a man whose face ran heavily to jowls. His nose was flat and large-pored. His eyes twinkled from pockets of fat. With Dr. Wicker was white-haired, soft-spoken Samuel Arvin, beloved philanthropist and head of the Anti Vice League. His soothing voice and benevolent words were directed at the somewhat ruffled Walter Nixon.

"My dear Mr. Nixon, I sincerely hope we have not given you the impression that your theatre, or its management, has anything to do with this ugly narcotic business."

The teeth of Nixon's undershot lower jaw sought to gnaw his black mustache. "That would be absurd. I am interested simply in what the patrons of this theatre will say if—" Nixon's dark eyes strayed to Agent X.

At that moment, a boisterous voice from the doorway called: "Hold it, gentlemen—and look like three conferees, if you can!"

THERE was the sudden lightning of a flashlight bulb. Nixon's shoulders gave a startled twist. He cursed softly and turned toward the door, as a cherubic-faced young man, wearing a battered hat on the back of his head, walked triumphantly into the room with a camera under his arm. He was followed by a golden-haired, blue-eyed girl, who produced notebook and pencil and immediately attacked Samuel Arvin with a dazzling smile.

"Let's have a story on the dope roundup, Mr. Arvin. Or is this a dope roundup?"

Dr. Wicker cleared his throat noisily. "I thought I told you reporters to stop following us around." His puffy fingers were picking bits of imaginary lint from his vest.

"There isn't any story, Miss Dale," Nixon whipped out angrily. "And if Stien developes that picture he just took, there'll be war."

Stien, the newspaper photographer, chuckled while he mothered his battered camera. "Why not give us the story straight? Who is this gentleman?" He looked directly at Agent X. "Another dope chaser?"

"I could strangle you!" Nixon was muttering as he watched the photographer anxiously.

Agent X had eyes only for the golden-haired Betty Dale who had been so insistent upon getting a story from Samuel Arvin. She was standing in such a position that, with the slightest movement of her eyes to the right, she would be able to see the unconscious Fred Colrich where he lay in a heap behind the chair. If she saw Colrich, she would naturally cry out. And if she cried out, she would unthinkingly betray her best friend.*

Agent X was in a most precarious position, caught in the very act of changing his disguise. He was crushing his black toupee into as small a compass as possible in his right fist. The discovery of the unconscious Fred Colrich would instantly precipitate trouble.

There was only one way in which X could prevent this disaster: he must clearly identify himself to the girl, without revealing himself to the others within the room.

CHAPTER II

THE CHILL OF DEATH

BETTY DALE turned her head. Instantly her eyes fell upon that portion of the unconscious Colrich that was visible from her position, her lips parted and formed a half-uttered word of alarm.

And at that moment, Agent X was seized with a spasm of coughing. All the power in his compelling glance was exerted in attracting Betty Dale's attention. As the girl's wide blue eyes met his steady gaze, he folded his hands, extended his forefingers so that they crossed to form the letter "X".

Sudden realization that she had all but betrayed the very person dearest to her, almost started a cry from Betty's lips. Then she hurried across the room and settled herself in the very chair behind which Colrich was hidden. She leaned far to the right. It was so marked an ef-

***AUTHOR'S NOTE: All followers of the Agent's exploits are familiar with Betty Dale, reporter on the Herald, and X's companion through many perilous adventures. Of all living persons, Betty Dale alone has seen the real face of Secret Agent X. Betty Dale, more than any other person, knows the courage, kindliness, and resourcefulness of the Man of a Thousand Faces.**

fort to hide the Agent's secret, that X feared she would call the attention of everyone present to the hidden man.

Agent X's eyes roved from one to the other of the men in the room. "Which of you is Dr. Wicker?" he asked. "I have a very urgent message for Dr. Wicker."

Wicker cleared his throat. His puffy hands were busy with the upstanding lock of black hair at the back of his head. "I am Dr. Wicker."

X took a step toward the famous doctor, but Walter Nixon detained him a moment, one hand on the Agent's arm. He gnawed his upper lips a moment, looking at X from head to toe. "I beg your pardon, but there is something familiar about you. Who're you?"

"James Nelson," replied X promptly, using the first name that popped into his head. Then he turned to Wicker. "I have a message from Mr. Fred Colrich. It is very important that you see his wife at once. I understand that she is in some sort of trouble at this address." X took out the piece of paper he had slipped from Colrich's pocket. "Colrich followed her and asked me to see you."

Wicker looked at the address and scowled at it. Gordon Stien, the newspaper man, took a hasty glance over Wicker's shoulder. He whistled softly. "Nice neighborhood for people like the Colrichs to be visiting. There's a story around here somewhere."

Agent X was watching the door of the smoking room. It was open a crack. The more he watched the door, the more certain he became that some one was listening.

X took two steps that brought him nearer the door. "Dr. Wicker," he said, "may I urge you not to ignore the message I just gave you?" And as he said that, X reached out and swung open the door of the smoking room. A very surprised and embarrassed man turned scarlet in the face, took one step backwards and began to stammer an apology.

Sam Arvin's eyes lighted up as he observed the hollow-cheeked, blond-haired man in the doorway. "Rister! Come in, won't you?"

THE man in the doorway smiled in a sickly fashion and came forward eagerly to clasp Arvin's extended hand.

"You've met Morgan Rister, haven't you, gentlemen? Dr. Wicker has, I know. Mr. Nixon, I know the name of Rister is familiar to you. He is the manufacturer of commercial oxygen, acetyline, and similar gases of great importance. In addition, he is secretly associated with our Anti Vice League."

"Really, Arvin, you overwhelm me," Rister, keeping his eyes in constant motion. "I really had no idea of meeting you here."

Walter Nixon, who had been staring through the open door, turned suddenly to Agent X. "I've just noticed that one of my ushers is missing, a man who resembles you remarkably."

X smiled. "Unfortunately, the business of lending assistance to Mrs. Colrich prevents me from doubling for your usher, Mr. Nixon, though I must admit a secret yearning to wear one of those dashing uniforms." He backed to the door, sought Dr. Wicker over the heads of the newly arrived Rister and Mr. Arvin. "Doctor, if you will, I really believe that Mr. Colrich would appreciate your coming to see his wife at once."

"Yes, yes," agreed Wicker gruffly. "Coming, Arvin. Er—we may find something that would, er— You understand?"

Arvin nodded. "Coming at once." And, linking arms with Rister, he followed Dr. Wicker from the room.

Betty Dale waited patiently until all were out of the room, then, with a deep sigh, she hastened toward the door. Agent X was there, waiting for her. He stepped into the room and closed the door part way behind him. He slipped one arm about Betty's waist and held her so for a moment, searching the depths of her eyes, marveling at the devotion he saw there.

"Betty," he whispered. "Betty. How can I ever thank you?"

"Thank me? Thank me when I all but gave your plan away? Who is that man behind the chair?"

"The man is Colrich. I was caught, or would have been if it hadn't been for you. I don't know what it means, exactly. This sudden increase in dope traffic is terrible and far reaching. We must stop it. I must warn you that you've put yourself in danger again on my account."

"I love it," she whispered.

"I know. But, Betty, when they find Colrich, they'll know something queer went on here tonight. Nixon has half an idea right now that I am his usher's double. It won't be a very long jump from that to discover that I am Agent X—and that you aided me. I'm not thinking only of the danger this might expose you to from the criminals behind this gigantic scheme, I'm thinking of what the police might do to you if they learned that you are my one close friend."*

"I'll be careful," she said earnestly. "Ill take care of myself."

"Always," he whispered, "take care of yourself for me." And he hurriedly left the smoking room to join Dr. Wicker and Arvin, who were waiting in the foyer.

Dr. Wicker was dangling his watch. "Er—Mr. Nelson, if you will give us that address, I am sure that Mr. Arvin and I can take care of this little matter satisfactorily."

"I am certain of it, Doctor," replied X pleasantly. "However, I have known the Colrich's for years and am quite as anxious to help in this difficulty as you are." This was decidedly untrue, but Wicker and Arvin evidently suspected nothing, for they permitted him to join them without further demur. They left the theatre and crossed the sidewalk to the curb.

A taxi swung in near them. The driver opened the door, so that the brilliant light from the front of the theatre fell across his homely features. His nose was a lean hook, his shoe-button eyes set close together. A cigarette was pasted to his doleful, long upper lip. He stared obliquely at the slip of paper X held out to him.

"Know that address?" X demanded.

"Right!" The taxi driver had a thin, raucous voice. "Took one fare there already tonight."

X sprang into the seat beside Arvin and Dr. Wicker. He glanced through the rear window in time to see Gordon Stien and Betty Dale scrambling into a second cab, undoubtedly with the idea of following them.

The Agent leaned over the driver's seat as the cab started. "Was your other fare a man or a woman?" he asked.

"Woman," replied the driver. "A queer dame. Picked her up in front of the Princess Theatre at about ten after eight."

"What do you mean—queer?" X persisted.

"Oh, dressed funny. Looked like she was gettin' away with some swell dame's fur rigging. She was nervous, too. Dropped her pocketbook, and I could have had the whole works, for all she would have

---

*AUTHOR'S NOTE: The Agent's highly advanced and daring tactics employed in his battle against crime are greatly misunderstood by the police. X has secret sanction from an official of importance in Washington, but because of the very nature of his work, he has never even been able to trust the police with information regarding this official support. So unorthodox are X's methods, so frequently do they carry him outside the law, that he is thought to be a clever criminal. Inspector Burks has accused X of every crime on the calendar and has sworn not to rest until he has seen X strapped to the electric chair.

X shoved the gun against her arm.

It was far wiser to ignore that question. X nudged the taxi driver. "Speed it up, Ham Esler. There's a cab following us. Think you can lose them?"

Esler grunted: "Watch my dust!"

AT that moment, in the room off the dance floor that was a part of the gray-fronted house in the Spanish quarter, the woman called Zerna was standing in front of a mirror retouching her perfect lips with rouge.

The house was silent. Zerna was on the point of leaving when the telephone jangled. Deliberately she stepped to the table and picked up the phone. "Yes?"

A man's voice came over the phone: "Move, Zerna. Secret Agent X is on the way."

"Oh, cool off," Zerna replied insolently. "The guests cleared out five minutes ago, and were plenty satisfied with the brand of hop we hand out. When X gets here, there won't be a thing except the stiff. Not unless—" A look of cunning crept into Zerna's eyes. "Say, chief, why

known. I gives her back the wallet, see. Honest Ham Esler, they call me."

Dr. Wicker leaned forward interestedly. His puffy fingers were fiddling with the brim of his hat. "Furs, you said, driver?"

"Sure—classy furs."

Wicker exploded: "Ruth Colrich has the finest sables in the city! A present from her husband. Poor Fred!" The doctor's twinkling eyes glanced at X. "Where did you leave Fred Colrich?"

don't you tell what you've just told me to Inspector Burks down at police headquarters. Just a tip to the cops on the side, see, and we'll be rid of this X guy for all times."

She replaced the phone, picked up the smoldering butt of a black Puerto Rican cigarette, and ground it out in the ash tray. She glanced once more, critically, at herself in the mirror, and left the house . . . .

The house with the gray front was totally dark when X and his party arrived. Arvin looked anxiously from the cab window. "You're certain this is the place, driver?" he asked timidly.

Esler turned and thumbed at his chest. "Listen, I got a map of New York for a brain. Never-lost Esler! When I say that's your house, why that's your house."

Dr. Wicker thrust a bill into the driver's hand. "You'd better wait," he said, before he joined X and Arvin.

The Secret Agent took the lead, mounted the narrow steps, and took hold of the bell-pull. Its very jangle proclaimed the house empty. He found the door unlocked.

"You're perfectly sure this is all right?" asked Arvin.

"Not at all," said X quietly, thrusting himself in front of Dr. Wicker as the latter would have pushed his way into the house. He flicked on the tiny beam of his pen-size flashlight and sent it darting about the large room into which they had passed. Rugs had been rolled up and furniture pushed back. A phonograph stood at one end of the room.

"Seems to have been some sort of a harmless dance," Wicker suggested.

"Yes," replied X thoughtfully. "Yet a dance closing comparatively early in the evening. A dance held in a private dwelling; yet immediately after the party is over, the house is empty."

He crossed the room that had been used for dancing and pushed open a door to reveal a smaller room adjoining the first. He turned on the light switch.

"Desk, chairs, telephone," X mused aloud. "Air heavy with cigarette smoke." He crossed the room to heavy green curtains that hid another door. He pushed back one side of the curtains and touched the doorknob. "Odd," he muttered. "This knob is icy-cold. Come here, gentlemen."

Arvin pushed Dr. Wicker ahead of him as the pair came nearer to where X was standing. Arvin said: "I suppose you know this amounts to house-breaking, young man?"

X ignored Arvin. "Do you notice a chill draft coming from beneath this door?"

Wicker, nervously fingering the buckle of his overcoat, informed them that it was a chill night. Agent X turned the cold doorknob and opened the door.

"B-r-r-r!" Arvin shuddered. "Feels like a refrigerator."

Agent X found the light switch on the side of the door and pressed it on. There was no visible occupant. Furniture in the room looked as though it was covered with white mold. As X moved around the chilly apartment, his coat sleeve knocked a fountain pen from a small walnut secretary. The pen crumbled to bits as it struck the floor. Soundlessly, the Secret Agent rounded a love seat and came to a stop. Then slowly his lips formed the words: "Look, gentlemen. Here is where the cold comes from."

As Wicker and Arvin were timidly approaching, a merry whistle sounded from another part of the house. Some one boisterously shouted: "The old duffers tried to fox us, Betty. We'll get a story now or tell the cops they're burglarizing."

The cherubic countenance of Gordon Stien appeared in the doorway. Almost at once, his smile faded as he regarded the anxious faces of the three men huddled about the love seat. "Cripes!" he whispered.

Stien hurried forward, took one look over the back of the love seat. His eyes suddenly threatened to pop out on his cheeks.

"And that," said Sam Arvin, like a man in a dream, "was once Ruth Colrich."

THE body of Ruth Colrich, stripped of its furs, was stretched out behind the love seat. The flesh was blue-black, brittle in appearance. And from the body rose a cloud of chill, condensed mist.

"Frozen to death," whispered Dr. Wicker.

"Yes," X added. "Killed with cold. Those fingers— why, a good hard snap would break them off. This is murder."

"Wow, what a picture!" exploded Stien. "Betty, here's a scoop to end scoops!"

Betty Dale, accustomed as she was to horror that came to her in her life as a reporter, turned deathly pale as she viewed the blue-black corpse of Mrs. Colrich. She turned quickly away and centered all of her attention on her notebook.

In the other room, Arvin could be heard phoning the police. Agent X knew that if he was to pick up clues, he must work fast. While Dr. Wicker's eyes were busy in a cursory examination of the body, X picked up Mrs. Colrich's purse and carried it to a table near the door. There, beneath the light of table lamp, he turned the purse inside out.

There was no money. Calling cards engraved with, *Mr. and Mrs. Fred Colrich,* brought a curious, heavy feeling to the Agent's heart as he thought of the helpless husband who must have recently discovered that his wife was heading for the gutter via the dope route. There were also two cheap marihuana cigarettes and an empty hypodermic syringe in the bag. X picked up the hypodermic syringe with his left hand. Closer examination of the instrument might reveal important evidence. X glanced quickly around the room.

Betty Dale was grimly taking notes with a stubby pencil. Stien had just closed his camera with a triumphant snap.

"Could sell these plates to any newspaper in town for five C!" the photographer shouted. "The good old *Herald* ought to give me a raise." He made a dive for the door and was brought to a sudden stop by a ham of a fist that shot out to his face. The big knuckles nipped Stien's nose and pinched until the reporter yelped.

"You're not going any place, picture clicker," said a gruff voice, exceedingly familiar to Agent X. It was the voice of Inspector John Burks of the Homicide Office. Instantly on the defensive, X moved nearer the curtained doorway as the six feet of red beef and brawn that was John Burks came padding into the room.

Burks didn't look toward the corpse. He simply reached out and seized the man nearest him by the chin. And that man was Agent X.

The Agent understood perfectly why Burks had pinched Stien's nose. Burks knew that Secret Agent X, his old enemy, was in that room. And he was determined to find out which of the men was X by a simple method of trial and error. Stien had passed that test—the test that X could not pass.

X's right hand jabbed toward the pocket where he kept his gas pistol. But Burks had been forewarned and was consequently forearmed. The barrel of Burks' gun jammed up just beneath X's chin.

"Move a muscle, and this slug travels up through the roof of your mouth, Agent X. I'm one jump ahead of you this time. A good pinch shows up that putty you use for a face every time!"

Sergeant Keegan and others of

Burks' crew surrounded the Agent. Keegan's deft fingers were going through X's pockets like a vacuum sweeper. Nothing would be left him but his fists and his wits—nothing except the hypodermic needle he had taken from Mrs. Colrich's purse and which he now held in his left hand.

Across the room, X saw Betty Dale, standing very straight, her blue eyes anxious and her notebook clasped close to her breast. Agent X smiled slightly. The game wasn't up yet. One chance in a hundred remained to him . . . .

CHAPTER III

Faceless Horror

INSPECTOR JOHN BURKS had achieved a triumph. He had every advantage, his opponent stripped of all those amazing devices that had so frequently helped him to fool the police. But as he stood in front of the curtained door, his gun muzzle an inch or so from Agent, he unwittingly gave X a powerful weapon. Inspector Burks was too confident. So it was that he did not notice what X's left hand was doing.

At the moment when Burks, face flushed with pride, glanced about the room to make certain that X could not possibly escape, the Agent began the execution of his surprising scheme.

His left arm went up underneath the curtains, so that his hand was directly over the small of the inspector's back. In his left hand, he held the hypodermic syringe, entirely empty, which he had taken from Mrs. Colrich's purse.

X knew perfectly well that the point of a needle might well be mistaken for the point of a knife. He also knew what powerful weapons are suggestion and surprise. To achieve surprise, he simply thrust the hypodermic needle through the curtain and into Burks' back. And for suggestion, a voice actually seemed to come from the room beyond the curtain: "Drop that gun, or I knife you!"

It was ventriloquism, an art in which Agent X was an adept. Never for a moment did X suppose that the courageous inspector would drop his gun.

Burks cursed, sprang forward, wheeled, and fired directly at the non-existent man on the other side of the curtain. And scarcely had the slug roared from the revolver, before X's right hand dropped like a striking falcon to Burks' gun-wrist.

It was all over in a moment—a powerful wrench with his wrist, a knee-kick upward to Burks' arm, and Agent X was in possession of a serviceable accurate police special.

In spite of his dislike for lethal weapons, few persons could shoot with more deadly accuracy than Secret Agent X. The gun was half raised, lying easily in his palm, when Sergeant Keegan drew his gun. The revolver in X's hand bucked, and then there was no longer a gun in Keegan's hand. It had been knocked two feet behind him and had all but taken the sergeant's fingers along with it.

X shouldered the furious Burks away from the door, so that the inspector came under the threatening sweep of the revolver. The Agent was standing, stooped slightly forward, his gray eyes promising certain hell for the man who so much as raised a finger. On his lips was smiling mockery. "It should be written in the police primer, my friends, that it is far more dangerous to park in front of a curtain than a fireplug!" And with that he sprang backwards through the door.

Burks' whistle screamed. There was an instantaneous scuffle outside the front door. X knocked over the lamp in the office, sprang into the dance hall, and shot out the light that burned there—even as the front door opened and police in uniform streamed into the room.

X took to the stairs, ran noisily up half a flight and vaulted over the bannister to land soundlessly at the side of the stairway. Police flashlights pointed toward the steps. There were hoarse orders from Burks. Six coppers started pell-mell up the steps. Several more guarded the front door.

IN the dark, X crept around the stairway and started up the steps a second time, following the footsteps of police, who undoubtedly believed they were following him. X slipped into a closet a moment after a searching police light had explored that closet and found it empty. And when he heard the police thudding down the steps, he slipped out and went to the back of the hall, where a door led out onto an open stairway.

He opened the door cautiously and squeezed out on the stairway. Then he ran down into the back yard to cross it and enter the alley at about the time the police decided they should surround the house.

But there was further trouble in the alley. Three police were jamming one end of it, and there was a car at the other end. X considered the car the lesser of the two dangers.

When he had reached the nose of the car, the headlights suddenly came on and the motor whirred. X sprang just out of line of the searching light beams, leaped to the running board, and shoved the gun against the driver's arm. Suddenly, his right arm went limp. "Well, Betty!" he breathed.

"Hurry!" Betty whispered. "I was going to get this car around in front to pick you up as you came out, but I guess you moved too fast for me. Get in back. I've a slumbering passenger."

"So I see!" X opened the back door of the sedan and got in as Betty threw the car in reverse and backed out of the alley. There was a man in the front seat. His head was all but on Betty's shoulder. X reached over, hooked his hands beneath the arms of the man in the front seat and hauled him into the back seat. He turned the beam of his small flashlight on the man's face.

He was a man about forty years of age, a man with tan, thick-looking skin and faded hair that was graying about the temples. He had a mouth that looked as though it were made for keeping secrets. There was a bruise on his temple.

The Agent's gray eyes twinkled. "Betty! You knocked him out with your slipper. What for?"

"I thought you needed a car. Besides, I don't like him anyway. He's on a rival paper, and he doesn't know the meaning of the word 'ethics'. His name is Steve Wyer. I asked to borrow his car, and he said nothing doing."

"You say his name is Wyer," X puzzled. "Queer. His face is familiar. How long has he been in newspaper work?"

Betty shrugged. "I've known him for at least a year. By the way, where can I drive you?"

"The Paragon Theatre. No, on second thought, I wouldn't dare show up there looking like this. About three blocks north of the theatre would be better. I've a hideout there."*

The Agent turned so that he could see the girl's delicate profile in flashes of passing light. His left arm dropped across her shoulders. "Betty," he said very gravely, "you can't go on like this. You mean far too much to me. I can't have you getting yourself into danger."

***AUTHOR'S NOTE:** In his dangerous work, Agent X requires many hideouts located at strategic points throughout the city. There he keeps complete wardrobes and makeup outfits, as well as compact radio transmitters for communicating with Harvey Bates and other members of his vast group of secret operatives. These hideouts are rented under many aliases, and as long as he is in New York, X is never very far from one of these safety stations.

Beneath his arm, the Agent felt Betty's shoulder muscles tense. A cry of terror screamed from her lips: "That face—"

THE steering wheel twisted from Betty's grasp. The car careened across the street, struck the curb, and stopped with its radiator against a fireplug only because X had had presence of mind enough to drag back on the emergency brake.

"Betty!" X's anxious eyes sought the girl's pale face.

"A—a thing, watching us through the rear window—a black, goggle-eyed monster!"

"Don't move from the car!" he whispered tensely as he kicked open the door.

As he rounded the car, Inspector Burks' gun in his hand, X saw a shadowy form running soundlessly up the street. He raised the revolver and held his fire as the weird shape twisted to the left and plunged into an alley.

The Agent's long legs enabled him to gain yards on the fleeting shadow. He turned the corner of the alley and saw, in the light that passed from a window at the rear of a dwelling, a monstrous shape, a thing of long, thick fur.

X shouted a warning and again raised the gun. This time he shot and then instantly stopped, stood still, and stared, his gun hanging limply at his side.

In the alley, where the hairy monster had been, a swirling cloud of vapor, blue-white in the dim light, spread its ghostly fingers across the alley. The echo of the shot died. The night wind had suddenly become freezing cold, like a blast from the arctic ice fields.

Gradually, the blue-white mist cleared, and Agent X ventured forward toward a tiny black blot in the center of the alley. He turned his flashlight on the black object, and an exclamation whispered from his lips. The huddled, dead thing on the pavement was a black cat. It had been frozen instantly into a furry statue.

X hurried to rejoin Betty, but on gaining the street, he saw a police officer standing beside the all-but-wrecked car. The crash had evidently brought Wyer to his senses, for he was sitting on the running board, rubbing his head and trying to explain something that he didn't know anything about.

Agent X heard a soft whistle from a dark doorway near at hand. He went toward the door and caught a glimpse of Betty's white face. The girl was putting on the slipper she had used so effectively against Wyer and at the same time she was watching Wyer and the policeman.

X stepped into the doorway beside her. "I know that friend of yours. I can't think of his name. Maybe it really is Wyer. But when I saw him last, he was mixed up in a particularly odorous blackmail racket in London."

"I don't like him, anyway," Betty whispered. "I got out of the car when he started coming around. But that monster—what was it?"

Agent X put both hands on her shoulder. "I don't know, yet, Betty. But do you remember, back there in the Paragon Theatre, when I caught a Mr. Morgan Rister snooping at the smoking-room door?"

"Yes. But that—that *thing* wasn't Rister."

"That 'thing,' as you call it, was what killed Mrs. Colrich. What I saw just now brought home to me the terrible gravity of your position. Rister could have easily seen your little act to try and conceal the unconscious Colrich. He didn't leave the theatre when we did. He could quite easily have interpreted your actions as an effort to protect and assist me, as soon as Colrich was discovered. And I am absolutely certain of Rister's connection with this criminal gang."

And while Wyer and the cop were engaged in their argument, X took

Betty by the arm and led her quickly from the doorway. "I've a car in a garage about six blocks up this way," he told her. "Then I'm taking you to your apartment. Watch out for Mr. Wyer. He's in a nice spot to make trouble for you."

Betty shook her golden curls bewilderedly. "And what has the Paragon Theatre to do with this?"

"I wish I knew. Do you realize, Betty, that at least five dope fiends were among the audience at the Paragon tonight and that those dopesters spent their money for ten minutes of newsreel. That's all they were interested in. They left as soon as the newsreel was over. It doesn't make sense."

IT was after eleven o'clock before the Agent had seen Betty safely in her apartment, obtained material for a new disguise, and arrived at the Paragon Theatre. Secret Agent X had become the ruddy-faced, roaring Inspector John Burks himself.*

In Burks' characteristic manner, X stamped into the theatre just as the patrons were leaving. He went to the lounge off the balcony, and from there, to Mr. Nixon's office. He drummed authoritatively on the door with his knuckles, and was immediately admitted by Nixon himself.

X poked a finger at the theatre owner. "Your name's Nixon, isn't it?"

Nixon gnawed at his upper lip and admitted the fact with a nod.

X growled: "What I want to know is if you've a Mr. Colrich here. We just got hold of this notorious Mr. X, who has now admitted knocking Mr. Colrich out and concealing him somewhere in your theatre. Have you found Colrich?"

Nixon smiled and brushed his mustache with a knuckle. "Mr. Colrich is in my private office at this moment, recovering from the attack of this criminal you mentioned. Do you want to see him?"

"Do I?" snorted X. And for an answer, he strode to the door of the office indicated by Nixon.

It was difficult for Agent X to look upon Fred Colrich with anything but sympathetic eyes. Colrich was lolling in one of Nixon's leather chairs, still feeling the influence of the knockout blow X had handed him. Life hadn't been kind to Fred Colrich. The discovery of his wife's vice had probably driven him to desperation. But there was an even greater blow in store for him. As he regarded Colrich, Agent X regretted that he was to be the man to strike that blow.

Colrich blinked with bloodshot eyes at the man whom he doubtless supposed to be Inspector Burks. He sat up a little straighter.

A couple of strides brought X to Colrich's chair. He helped himself from Nixon's cigar humidor and sat down on Nixon's desk.

"What do you want?" asked Colrich.

"Now don't take that attitude," X pleaded. "What I'm trying to do is save a lot of men and women from a hell that somebody's fixing for them." X leaned forward suddenly. "You know what I mean, Colrich," he said hoarsely. "The hell that dope digs! I know you don't want to talk about your wife—but you've got to help us, Colrich. If you've got the slightest idea where your wife has obtained dope, speak up, man. We've got to stop this thing—you and I together!"

Colrich's lips tightened for a moment. Then he said: "I haven't the remotest idea to what you refer. I further object to your mentioning my wife's name in conection with narcotics. My wife has had a nervous breakdown—"

"My eye!" X exploded. "Listen, Colrich, if you don't give a damn for the poor drug-chained devils, you'll

*AUTHOR'S NOTE: Once he has used a disguise, X can duplicate that same disguise without resorting to a living model from which to work. He has impersonated Burks frequently, as well as other important officials of the city. Even the police commissioner himself has not escaped the Agent's marvelous mimicry.

give a damn for your own skin. You'll talk, or I'll take you up on a charge of aiding and abetting your own wife's murder!"

That was the blow X had hated to strike. But it was the only way he could get Colrich to talk.

AT first, the man was completely floored. He seemed to shrink inches. He trembled from head to foot. Then suddenly the lion in him asserted itself. He sprang to his feet, color racing back into his face.

"Damn you!" Colrich shouted, his trembling fists menacing the Agent. "It's the fault of every damned, bungling policeman. You get your murderers soon enough, but you don't take up men like James Starbuck!"

James Starbuck. The name was familiar to X, as well as the character of the man it represented. Starbuck was a worthless, wealthy rounder; a man whose attraction for women had led to the crackup of many a home. In all probability it was Starbuck who had led Mrs. Colrich into dope's dark alleys.

"Murderers, gunmen, you get them all!" Colrich raved. "But when some rotter introduces a man's wife to dope, you sit still and do nothing. And that isn't all; I've been paying out money to keep this thing quiet, and now it will all come out in the papers."

"So you've been paying blackmail, have you?" X prompted.

"Yes. Every other day I would get little printed slips of paper. The whole ghastly mess would be set up in newspaper type and pasted to a letter headed: 'This is how it will look in headlines.' Of course, that was just a threat. The story didn't break into the papers. But now it will."

Little printed slips in newspaper type! X suppressed an exclamation of triumph. Betty Dale's newspaper enemy, the man named Steve Wyer, fitted into the picture perfectly. That was the exact method Wyer had used in London several years ago.

"Listen, Colrich," he said earnestly, "this isn't going to get into the papers if I can prevent it. You help us, and we'll help you. Do you know where your wife got her dope?"

"No, I don't. I only know that she used every pretense to get large sums of money from me—four and five thousand dollars at a clip. Any excuse would do. Sometimes it would be charity of some sort, and then again it would be some sort of a trip which she never took."

X wondered if it could be possible that Wyer had been blackmailing Mrs. Colrich as well as her husband.

The phone on Nixon's desk rang. Agent X scooped it up and immediately a gruff, but carrying voice issued from the receiver: "Is Mr. Nixon there?"

Secret Agent X drew a long breath and put the phone down without saying a word. The voice at the other end of the telephone line was that of Inspector Burks himself. Had X answered in any other voice than that of Burks, he would have immediately given himself away to Colrich. And if he had answered in Burks' voice, he would have simply told Burks that the latter was speaking to Agent X. It was a nerve-wracking situation.

"You tell me about this Starbuck, Colrich," he said. "If he's done anything, we'll put him away where he can't do any more damage."

Colrich shook his head hopelessly. "You can't do anything with Starbuck. He's a slippery lizard. I knew that he had been taking my wife to lunch now and then. I didn't think anything of it; I'm broad minded. I just didn't know Starbuck. But I've learned since then that the man takes dope in one form or another."

The phone rang again. X paid no attention, until the second ringing was suddenly interrupted. Then he knew that some one *had* answered that call. Some one, using an extension to the phone in Nixon's office, was now listening to the voice of Inspector John Burks—Nixon, of course. Nixon was in the outer office.

X picked up the phone in time to hear Burks roar: "The hell I am, Nixon! I know where I am. And if there's another man in your office who looks like me, you hold him until I get there. He's Agent X, and he's all tied up in the most ungodly murder I've run across in a lifetime!"

Agent dropped the phone as though it were hot. He had to move and think with something approaching the speed of light, to get out of this jam. The investigation was taking form. He could see his next move clearly—impersonate Starbuck and force his way in on the dope distribution. If Starbuck took dope, which he undoubtedly did, Starbuck would furnish the link between X and the criminal group. Then there was the blackmail angle. Whether dope and blackmail were connected in this crime, was a question that he might answer soon . . . .

CHAPTER IV

Newsreel Nemesis

SECRET AGENT X lunged toward the door of the office and shouldered it open. "Don't draw that gun, Nixon!" he cried, as he moved like a human projectile across the outer office.

But Nixon had drawn his gun. The phone in one hand, a little automatic in the other, he cried no warning to X, but shot twice in rapid succession. Both of the slugs thudded into X's chest. He fell forward across the desk, to seize Nixon's gun arm and bring it down swiftly against the edge of the desk.

The Agent's bullet-proof vest had stopped the shots, yet their very impact had doubled him over with pain. Even after Nixon had dropped his gun, X clung to the manager's arm. Then he straightened, dragged Nixon halfway across the desk, and slammed a knockout blow to the side of Nixon's head.

X opened the door, slammed it behind him, and hurried from the theatre. Burks had undoubtedly heard most of the scuffle through the phone Nixon had dropped. The police signal system would have the Paragon surrounded in a few minutes—men with orders to arrest anyone who resembled John Burks.

X hurried across the street toward the Princess Theatre, from which Harvey Bates had just emerged. He strode up to his big, square-cut operative. A touch on the arm, and Bates jerked his head around. There was a look of alarm in the big man's black eyes. He never knew when the police were going to connect him with Agent X and take him up for questioning.

The eyes of Agent X were twinkling as he said in one of his voices which was familiar to Bates: "This isn't a pinch, Bates."

There was a long sigh of relief from Harvey Bates. "Fooled me again, sir," he said crisply.

X chuckled. Is your car around here somewhere? Inspector Burks objects strenuously to this sort of masquerading."

"Just around the corner, sir. Learned something at the Princess."

"Let's have it," said X as they strode along toward Bates' car.

"Same thing. Hopheads go there, too. But just for a few minutes."

"Yes. One of them left the Princess Theatre tonight, about ten minutes after eight," X told Bates grimly. "It was a woman. She'll never go again. She was murdered in a particularly horrible fashion."

"Eight-ten," Bates mused. He pulled a scrap of paper from his pocket and glanced at notes scrawled across it. "That was at the end of the newsreel."

"Newsreels again. Bates, there's something about these movies that we're not getting next to. Did you notice anything that could be construed as a dope connection?"

Bates shook his dark, shaggy head.

THE following evening, Mr. James Starbuck lounged in his luxurious apartment overlooking the Hudson. His jaded eyes were on a stack of photographs in the lap of his satin lounging robe. They were photographs of women—women whose hearts beat faster at the sound of his voice or at a glimpse of his handsome face.

James Starbuck was alone, yet he was not startled when he heard the front door of his apartment open softly. Several of his feminine friends were free to come and go as they chose.

The living room door opened slowly. But Starbuck betrayed no sign of alarm, although his visitor was a tall man whose odd, steely eyes so completely dominated his face that Starbuck scarcely noticed his other features. Had Starbuck known them to be the eyes of Secret Agent X, he might have lost some of his composure.

Agent X closed the living-room door behind him. He had entered the apartment, without invitation, by means of one of his master keys. As he faced Starbuck, his right hand was thrust suggestively into his trouser pocket where his powerful gas pistol rested.

"You know why I've come, Starbuck?" he asked in a husky voice that was not his own.

"Haven't the foggiest," replied Starbuck without raising his head. "A holdup, what?"

X shook his head slowly. "I know that you use narcotics, Starbuck. Never mind how I know; it's my business to find out such things. But I haven't found out quite enough; do you understand?"

"Won't do you a particle of good," said Starbuck easily. "I've paid my last bit of blackmail money to your stinkin' organization."

"You're grossly mistaken, Starbuck. I am not here to blackmail you."

"Well, of course not. Call it 'club dues' if you want. It's still blackmail. I'm through, understand?"

"Not with me," said X. "I've come here with one purpose in mind—to get information. Where do you get your dope?"

Starbuck smiled. "Don't use any. If you're trying to under-sell some one, you'd better go elsewhere."

X dropped a hand on Starbuck's —satin-covered shoulder. The ends of his fingers bit deep into Starbuck's flesh. But the man in the chair scarcely winced.

"Listen," said X sternly, "I'm going to find out where you get your dope; where you *got* your dope, since you insist you don't use it now. I'm after the higher-ups who sell the stuff."

Starbuck smiled insolently. "Go to it. I still think you're one of the gang. If you can get me to talk, then —according to your code—you'll have enough evidence to have me murdered. Go on with your blackmail, if that's what you're up to, but spare me your third degree. I won't talk, because I'm not a fool."

The apartment buzzer sounded. Starbuck slid out of his chair. "Excuse me. Some of the people who come here have enough manners to ring before coming through the door."

X followed Starbuck over to where the speaking tube was set in the wall and listened closely while Starbuck lazily answered.

"This is Zerna, Jim," came a strident, feminine voice from the tube. From his position, X could hear every word.

Starbuck glanced at X. "So you're coming in pairs, are you?"

And that gave X his cue for action. If Starbuck believed that X was a member of the gang, then, from what Starbuck had just said, it was a certainty that the woman at the other end of the tube *was* associated with the dope gang.

THE AGENT'S fingers were like hooks of steel as they reached out to clamp over Starbuck's throat. He pulled Starbuck back and put his own lips near the tube. And from those lips came, in perfect impersonation of Starbuck's languid drawl: "Come up in ten minutes, Zerna. Just finished a tub; I'm not quite decent, you know."

He closed the tube, and still gripping Starbuck's throat, forced the man back into the bedroom and threw him on the bed. Starbuck lay flat on his back, fingering his throat. Even Starbuck's icy nerves were shaken by the deadly earnestness of the Agent. For the first time in his life, Starbuck had met a man who was fighting desperately and entirely without a selfish motive.

X slipped a hypodermic needle from a leather case. While his hands were busy with it, his eyes harnessed the man on the bed. But when Starbuck saw the glint of that needle, he uttered an oath and flung himself from the bed.

"I've had enough dope!" Starbuck shouted. At the same time, he tried to knock the syringe from X's hand. His left thumped twice over X's heart, but he might as well have battered at a stone wall.

Once again, X had him by the throat and was forcing his squirming body back to the bed. The point of the hypodermic needle pricked Starbuck's throat. The clubman's struggles stopped almost at once. He sighed, and his whole body relaxed in a harmless, drugged sleep.

X turned to a mirror and opened his pocket makeup kit. He quickly removed plastic material and pigments from his face, and fastened metal plates over his cheek bones before applying new makeup. Thus he simulated Starbuck's prominent cheek bones.

The rest of the work on his face was the sheerest artistry. His slender, graceful fingers pinched and patted the plastic material, while his eyes darted from Starbuck's face to the mirror and back again.

When he was satisfied with the effect, he traded a red toupee for a sleek, black one which, when correctly combed, looked very much like Starbuck's glossy hair. A few drops of a liquid in each eye gave him a darker appearance. Agent X had only to change his coat for Starbuck's dressing gown to be ready to receive the woman to whom he had talked over the speaking tube.

A final glance in the mirror, then he left the bedroom for the living room. Just on the other side of the door, he paused.

A LONG, ivory hand with tapering fingers hung over the arm of one of Starbuck's huge chairs. Those ivory fingers held a slender black cigarette from which a gray wisp of smoke eddied into the air.

"I found the door unlocked and walked in, Jim," said the same strident voice X had heard over the speaking tube. "You don't mind?"

"Not in the least, Zerna," said X, adopting Starbuck's honeyed tone. He sauntered around the chair and looked down at the striking, beautiful ivory-hued face of Zerna. "I am highly delighted."

"Yeah?" Zerna elevated her eyebrows. "Save that honey for some one not so hard to get, Jim. Why haven't you been coming to my parties?"

X smiled Starbuck's half-smile. "Perhaps I haven't been coming because you are so 'hard to get,' as you say."

Zerna laughed harshly. "I am more interested in the fact that you haven't been paying your club dues. Those dues are used in a good cause, you know. They keep certain unpleasant pictures of James Starbuck out of the newspapers. A person does such strange things when he's a little bit hopped, you know."

Zerna stood up, flashing her cold

smile. "That's all, Jim." She started toward the door.

"Just a minute." X caught the woman's hand and found it cold and firm. "I don't want those pictures to get in the papers. What's the price? Do I bring the money to you?"

X knew in asking those questions he was taking a desperate chance. If Starbuck had been paying "club dues," as the blackmail money was evidently called, Starbuck would have known the particulars. But Zerna did not act in the least surprised at X's ignorance.

"You can pay the two thousand dollars tonight and save yourself a penalty charge," she told him. "If you were to step out from the front of the Princess Theatre, in about an hour, and get into a Blue Streak Cab bearing Number Twenty-six on the door, you could drop the money in behind the back seat." And with that she left the apartment.

No sooner had the door closed, than X sprang to the phone and dialed a number. The phone was answered immediately by Harvey Bates, whom X had stationed in a hideout less than a block away.

"Bates, there's a woman coming out of the Crestview—an exotic beauty. Dark hair and eyes, ivory skin, lips you can't miss. She wears a scarlet dress and black furs. Get on her trail, and stick!"

He hung up and hurried into the bedroom to select evening clothes from Starbuck's extensive wardrobe. He was steadily nosing into the fog of mystery. The sale of dope was a secondary importance to the criminals. Once they had introduced a wealthy person into the ways of vice, pictures were evidently taken which could be used for blackmail.

As soon as he had dressed, X left the apartment, walked around the block to the point where he had parked his car. With no minutes to waste, he drove rapidly in the direction of the Princess and Paragon theatres.

THE Secret Agent parked his car about six blocks from the theatre and proceeded on foot the rest of the way, arriving at the Princess about five minutes before the appointed time. In his pocket was a neat package of bills amounting to two thousand dollars, money that he had picked up at the hideout near Starbuck's apartment.*

A moment later, a blue taxi cab pulled up in front of the theatre, and X saw Number 26 lettered in gold on the door. He noticed also the long face and close-set eyes of the driver. The man behind the wheel was Ham Esler, who had driven Mrs. Colrich to her rendezvous with the cold that killed.

X got into the cab and settled back on the right-hand side of the rear seat. Esler turned around and eyed X from beneath the shiny bill of his cap. "Where to, sir?"

"Go to the corner, turn east and go six blocks," X told him, for it was there that he had parked his own car. If Esler was connected with the dope crowd, and there seemed little doubt of that, X intended to follow Esler and see what became of the blackmail money.

As soon as the cab had pulled away from beneath the lights of the theatre, X reached into his coat pocket, produced the pack of twenty hundred-dollar bills, and pushed it down the back seat cushions. A few minutes later, he alighted from the cab, paid his fare, and went across the street to where his own supercharged car was parked.

X waited only long enough for the taxi to swing around the corner. Then he sprang into his car. Esler had started out fast, and might have slipped completely out of sight. But as X swung his car around the corner on two wheels, he had to brake quickly; for Esler's cab was direct-

***AUTHOR'S NOTE: As far as is known, Agent X is not a man of great personal wealth. He has, however, an inexhaustible fund of money, placed at his disposal by certain wealthy and public-spirited men, through the Agent's official sponsor at Washington.**

SAX

ly ahead of him, rolling along at a moderate rate of speed.

Two blocks farther on, Esler's cab pulled to the curb. X turned his into a driveway and watched the cab driver get out and raise the engine hood. X got out of his car and approached quietly on foot to a point where he could watch Esler from behind a clump of evergreens planted at the corner of some one's front yard.

The taxi driver tinkered with something beneath the hood, cursing aloud. Then he went to the back door of the cab, and X could see him taking the back cushion out. All this motor trouble was pretense, then, on Esler's part.

"Well I'll be damned!" X heard Esler explode. The taxi driver sprang from the back of the cab. In his hand was the paper-wrapped package of bills that X had put behind the seat. Esler held the package beneath the front lamps of his cab and ripped off a portion of the paper.

X watched Esler tuck the package of bills under his arm and strike out on foot. X stepped from his hiding place and followed at a discreet distance. Esler rounded the corner and continued briskly along. Directly ahead, X saw the lights of a precinct police station. And then the Secret Agent saw the whole scheme . . . .

STANDING out in front of the precinct station, no doubt trying to look the part of a police reporter was Betty Dale's newspaper rival, Steve Wyer, who was no doubt directing the blackmail scheme. Esler would secretly pass the bills to Wyer. That seemed to be the idea, for Esler was walking toward where Wyer was standing.

But no; Esler passed within five feet of Wyer, ran up the steps, and entered the station. X lengthened his stride, reached the steps, and followed Esler. At the door of the station, he stopped. Inside, he could hear Esler whistling tunelessly. Then he heard Esler say:

"Howdy, Sarge. Honest Ham Esler, that's me. Last night a lady tried to lose her pocket book in my cab, and I give it back to her. Tonight, some swell gent, who looked like he'd put perfume behind his ears, gets into my cab—and what do you think happens? Well, I'd been havin' trouble with my carburetor. When I got out, after takin' this swell to where he wants to go, and went to get pliers to fix that carburetor jet, I finds this under the back seat. It's dough, Sarge!"

For once in his life, Agent X was utterly bewildered. Why had Zerna told him to put the money in Esler's cab, if Esler wasn't the man to collect it? And who could have collected it if not Esler?

X turned and looked back toward the street. Steve Wyer was no longer lounging near the steps. Well, if the ex-blackmailer had anything to do with the crime, now was as good a time as any to find out just what his connection was.

The Agent ran down the steps and looked up and down the street. He saw Wyer walking rapidly. X broke into a run, only to slow down at the corner as Wyer entered the door of a small apartment building. X followed, paused in the vestibule to note Wyer's name on a card above the mailbox assigned to a second floor apartment.

A shrill, unearthly cry knifed the silence. It rose to a quivering pinnacle and died in a short, choked gasp.

But even before it had been silenced, Agent X was legging it up the steps. As he sprang into the upper hall, something lurched out of a door—a white, ghostly thing that seemed to crackle in its joints. The thing fell into the Agent's arms. The very touch of it against his flesh brought burning agony.

X sidestepped and allowed the thing to fall stiffly to the floor. White vapor was condensing in a cloud about the body of a man. That stiff, lifeless, frozen form had been Steve Wyer, not more than five minutes ago. The flesh about Wyer's face looked as though it had been burned, it was that black and crackled. And burned it had been, by a cold so intense as to be actually corrosive to human flesh. Even had a man's body been able to withstand such a temperature, his nervous system could have never stood the shock.

X dragged his eyes from the frozen horror. At the other end of the hall, something was moving, swiftly and quietly. The Agent gripped his gas pistol, wondering what chance it would have against the cold that could kill. He tiptoed down the hall and peered around a right-angle turn. A chill draught waved the curtains in front of an open window. X stepped to the window and looked out on a fire escape. A black and monstrous shape was padding swiftly down the iron steps.

X got out on the fire escape. The black monster was a perfect target, but entirely out of range of the Agent's anæsthetizing gas.

The thing gained the alley pavement. X vaulted over the iron railing of the fire escape, and dropped. Instantly, he was aware that he was followed. He turned his head. Six men were moving swiftly down the alley in his direction.

In the uncertain light from the apartment house windows, X detected the glint of gun steel. Ahead of him, the black monster was hurrying along on soft, animal-like feet. X ignored the men who were closing in behind him. He sprinted after the black, hairy form.

Then, at the opposite end of the alley, the Agent saw another group of men coming toward him. They, too, were armed. Suddenly, X realized why Zerna had showed no surprise at his not knowing the usual method of paying the blackmail money. Somehow, some way, she had known all along that she was addressing Secret Agent X, rather than James Starbuck. Yet his disguise had been perfection itself.

The Agent had been completely outwitted. These men were closing in upon him, were the hop-headed gunmen who served the master brain of the dope gang. They were not out to kill Starbuck, for Starbuck was still blackmail material. They were out to get Secret Agent X.

X understood now why Wyer had been killed. Wyer had been blackmailing Colrich, for the method used was unmistakably Wyer's. The dope gang had resented this muscling in on their prospective victim. So Wyer's death had been scheduled and executed with brilliant daring. And the same master brain that had planned Wyer's death was now out to remove his chief opponent, Secret Agent X.

Not twenty feet ahead of him, X saw the black, hairy monster disappear into a dense pool of darkness. X gripped his gas pistol and stepped into that same shadowy corner, fully expecting to encounter the monster. But the hairy thing was gone.

X's groping fingers encountered a doorknob. Here was a way out of an alley that cleverness had converted into a death trap. But what a choice he must make—beyond the door lurked the thing that killed with cold; out in the alley were slot-eyed, dope-keyed gunmen, ready to riddle him with shot.

Agent X hesitated only a moment. Then he opened the hidden door in front of him.

CHAPTER V

House of the Damned

As soon as he had received the telephone message from Agent X, Harvey Bates had hurried from the apartment where he had been awaiting his chief's orders. He was only about half a block away from the stylish Crestview where James Starbuck lived.

When he had reached the street door, Bates saw the woman in red, who was undoubtedly Zerna, coming toward him and not more than a rod from the door. He proceeded with deliberation, pausing to stuff the square bowl of his pipe and get it glowing before he left the building. He saw Zerna walking rapidly ahead of him. The woman gained the corner, looked both ways, and stopped. She stood at the curb, tapping her foot impatiently.

Bates got into his car, which he had parked in front of the apartment. It was obvious that the woman was waiting for a private auto to come and pick her up, for she completely ignored a taxi that rolled slowly by.

Perhaps two minutes passed before a big green car stopped at the corner. The woman got in beside the driver, and the green car rolled on down Amsterdam Avenue. Bates kicked his motor into life and followed.

Bates kept about a block behind the green car, which continued for a distance of about twelve blocks before it cut to the left and angled for a mile or more deep into the east side of town. The green auto came to a stop in the middle of a rather shabby block. Bates jerked his car around the corner and stopped.

The green conveyance was parked in front of a once-grand brick dwelling. From the corner, Bates watched the woman alight and hurry into the house. The green car rolled on into the night.

Bates proceeded on foot until he was opposite the building Zerna had entered. It was one of those old houses that had been worked over into an apartment building. Without a moment's hesitation, Bates walked slowly up the six stone steps to the door, took hold of the knob, and looked into the shadowy vestibule. His heavy black brows drew together in a scowl.

Just beyond the door, a man lay flat on his face, one arm extended above his head, an automatic loose in his motionless fingers.

Cautiously, Bates opened the door. Had the woman simply stepped over this body? Hardly. It was some sort of a trick.

Bates took a quick stride and planted his heel on the wrist of the man on the floor. The man was suddenly very much alive. He uttered a sharp cry of pain.

"'Possum, eh?" Bates clipped. He stooped to pull the gun from the man's helpless fingers, but he never touched the weapon. The chill nose of a revolver was jammed into the back of Bates' neck. "Don't try it!" a man's voice threatened.

Bates stood up slowly. His eyes shifted slowly around the little room. Two men coming through the outer door held automatics in their hands. There was evidently another directly behind Bates. A fourth armed man and the woman stood in the inner doorway. Bates was completely rimmed by guns. And on Zerna's lips was taunting laughter.

The decoy corpse on the floor got to his feet, picked up his gun, and prodded Bates with the muzzle. "Up the steps, big boy," he growled.

Hands on hips, Zerna jeered: "Sap! How do you like the reception, Mr. Bates? The brains behind our gang think ten jumps ahead of X. They knew X would impersonate Starbuck. Right now, Mr. X is in as tight a fix as he'll ever be. The telephone wires leading from Starbuck's apartment were tapped. When your chief sent out his order for you to follow me, the boys were wise."

Bates growled inwardly as the ring of gunmen closed, forcing him toward the steps and toward he knew not what fate. But greater than the anxiety over his own safety, was his fear that the gang had managed to trap Agent X. Zerna did not appear to be a woman who threatened idly.

ZERNA had not exaggerated when she had said X was in a tight spot. No one knew that better than X as he stepped into the dark where lurked the monster that killed with cold.

Quietly, he closed the door behind him. He listened without breathing for a moment, then took a step forward. Still no sound, no threat of danger. The Agent's hand stole into his vest pocket, where his pen-flashlight was clipped. But before he could pull out the flashlight, a shuffling sound put him instantly on his guard. His right hand dropped toward his gas pistol, but before he had a chance to grasp it, something lurched into him.

Instantly, X found himself caught in a typhoon of bestial fury. The unseen, hairy monster lashed out with arms and legs, kicking and striking, driving the Agent back against the door. Here was blind fighting, with many a wasted blow, when a false move from either man or monster might have decided the victory.

X lashed out with powerhouse blows. Twice his fist sank deep into fur and flesh, without doing any apparent damage. The big, hairy form again pressed him to the wall. Clumsy fingers sought his throat, but got him by the shoulder.

The black monster threw itself suddenly backwards to the floor, bringing X down on top of it. It was like wrestling with a bear that possessed the wit and agility of a man. Once, X was certain that his two hands were locked about the thing's throat. Then, with an unexpected roll to the side, the monster broke that hold and was back on its shuffling feet.

The Secret Agent sprang up, ready for any trouble the black monster might cause—anything but the freezing death. X knew no defense against that. Then something came hurtling out of the darkness and struck X squarely in the chest.

The missile had weight and speed. It caught X off balance, beat the breath out of him, threw him to the floor. As his empty lungs sobbed for breath, a door opened on the other side of the room, and for a moment, X saw the fleeing form of the black monster against the gray light of the night.

X picked himself up, got his flashlight from his pocket, and turned it on the floor. The thing that had been thrown so effectively at him was a metal cylinder a little over a foot in length.

The Agent took the strange weapon and examined it closely. The metal casing seemed for protection. The walls were heavily insulated, and there was an empty glass container inside, not unlike the flask of a vacuum bottle. Some sort of a copper connection had been hastily removed from one end of the cylinder.

Agent X nodded slowly. It was then, as he thought, the weapon that killed with cold was probably gas in the liquid form, compressed until its temperature was something approaching absolute zero. Possibly the stuff was ordinary liquid oxygen, such as is prepared commercially.

Such was the weapon carried by the hairy monster. It accounted for the horrible deaths of Mrs. Colrich and Wyer. It accounted for the death of the unfortunate cat that had appeared in the alley the night before. X understood that, when he had shot at the escaping monster on the previous night, the slug from his gun had struck the tank of liquid gas the monster carried. The gas had been suddenly dissipated, freezing to death anything within its path.

But liquid gas required special equipment for its preparation. It was not cheap stuff. Morgan Rister manufactured commercial gases. He would have the necessary equipment. Definitely, Rister was connected with the gang in some way. The Agent's next move would be to go to Rister and force him, in some manner, to speak.

X crossed the basement room, where he had sought sanctuary from the gunmen in the alley, and went out the same door through which the hairy monster had made his exit. A flight of steps led upward to the street level. X paused a moment to get his bearings.

He was approximately four blocks from one of his hideouts. He would go there at once and get rid of the Starbuck disguise. The disguise seemed actually to have marked him for murder. Some one was thinking ahead of Agent X, anticipating his every move.

As X was passing under a street lamp at the next corner, a crackling voice called: "Jimmy, old boy!"

X turned his head, saw a ragged figure stagger out of a doorway and come toward him with hand outstretched. Mechanically, X shook hands with the giggling, ragged man who seemed so delighted to see him. Then, as the light struck the man's face, X became immediately interested in this apparent intimate of James Starbuck.

The man's face was thin and waxy appearing. His eyes were unmistakably those of a dope addict.

THE man in rags slapped X on the back, linked arms with him, and started to walk him down the street. "How come you haven't been around to any of Zerna's parties, Jimmy?" the dopester asked.

Here was X's chance to pick up information for which he was willing to play the game as far as his limited knowledge would permit. "Didn't know where to go, that's all," he replied.

The ragged man laughed. "Why, don't you go to the movies any more?"

Movies again. X was back to the original question: What had movies, and especially newsreels, to do with the workings of the dope syndicate?

"Tell you what I'll do," the hophead volunteered. "You just come along with me. Zerna's putting on another brawl tonight."

Agent X agreed instantly. Here was a chance to get in on one of Zerna's orgies. As to his disguise, nothing could be more perfect for such a venture than the disguise he was wearing. It had once failed him so obviously that his opponents would never suppose he would try it again. And in the presence of this man, who had been an intimate of Starbuck's, there was no reason in the world why anyone should suppose that X was not the man he appeared to be.

"Is the place very far from here?" X asked.

"Sure—quite a ways. Maybe you can find the price of a taxi, huh?"

"I can do better than a taxi," X told him. "I've got a car up here in a garage."

"Swell! Say, you're a pal!" The hophead staggered up against X and instantly recoiled. "Say, Jimmy," he said seriously, "you ain't packing a rod?"

Evidently the man had felt the gas gun bulking in X's pocket. "Sure," X admitted. "Why not?"

"Why not? Don't you remember, nobody with a weapon can get in? They got some sort of an electric-eye machine sitting at the side of the door. You better get rid of that gat before you try to crash Zerna's joint."

If he entered Zerna's drug depot tonight, he must do so without weapons, or, at least, any metallic weapons that could be detected by an electronic beam. It was a long chance he was taking, he fully realized. But when he thought of the drug-sick man beside him and of the hundreds of other lives that had been ruined, that might yet be ruined, by the insidious syndicate of drug merchants and blackmailers, X decided that the chance he took would be worth it.

IT was shortly after eight o'clock that night when some one beat a rapid tattoo on the door of Betty Dale's apartment. The girl got up from her typewriter where she had been working. Mindful of the warning that Agent X had given her, she opened the door a cautious crack and looked out.

"Oh, Gordon!" she laughed. "Come in. But what's happened to your eye?"

Gordon Stien needed no second invitation. He popped into the room with: "I ran into a door. Have you a nice slice of beef steak?"

Stien went over to a mirror and examined a black and puffy right eye. In the glass, he could see Betty laughing at him. Stien made a face at her. "Cut it out. Get into your going-out rags. Where in hell do you think we're going?"

"I don't know where you're going, but I'm staying here."

Stien pleaded:—"Ah, listen here, Betty, don't let it be said that I got this shiner in vain." He jumped to the door. "I brought the evidence with me. Take a squint into the hall."

Betty went to the door and looked out into the hall. Her rapidly indrawn breath had the ghost of a scream in it. A man lay face down on the floor beside Betty's door. He didn't show any signs of life.

Stien pulled the girl back into the apartment. "I did it with my little hatchet. And what kind of a bird do you think that is out there? A snow bird, by gosh! I mauled all the stuff out of him, see. That's how come the eye. But I got all the stuff out of him about the dope parties. There's a female named Zerna who gives these parties. She moves after each party, as I get it, so the cops can't catch up with her. It's at these parties that the dope is given out."

"Wait a minute," Betty said. "Let me knock out some of this on the typewriter."

Stien grabbed her arm. "Listen, you bit of mellow sweetness, if you think you've got a story now, wait until after tonight. I know where this dope party is being given. I know how we can get in. Everybody wears masks, so I got a couple of masks. I told you I really pulverized that snow bird in the hall. We're set to get in on a real story, if you're game."

"If I'm game!" Betty mocked. "Wait till I change my clothes." And she hurried into the bedroom.

A few minutes later, they were off in Stien's car. At the end of a forty-five minute drive, they entered a shabby, narrow street and Stien slowed down, watching the house numbers carefully. "Here we are, Betty," he said in a whisper. "It's that house we just passed. Get into this mask." He handed the girl a little roll of black silk.

THEY got out of the car and hurried back to a brick dwelling, the identical house to which Harvey Bates had followed Zerna. Stien rang the bell and produced a small card, which he informed Betty, was a pass he had obtained from the dope. The door was opened by a servant who looked like an ex-pug. He glanced at the card in Stien's hand, nodded his head, and allowed them to enter.

They entered a long room that had been cleared for dancing.

A radio was going full blast. Men and women were dancing in a crazy, graceless, abandoned manner. It looked like a drunken brawl to Betty, one in which the cream of society was churned with the bluest of the milk. Hardly had she entered the room before she was seized in the arms of a masked man, who whirled her about the room in a mad, frenzied fashion.

Then a man, sedately clad in evening clothes, cut in, took Betty's arm and led her to the other side of the room. "We want to speak to you, Miss Dale," he said.

Betty saw that this man's face was completely covered, distinguishing him from the others in the room who wore only domino masks. He held her arm in a grip she could not break, led her into a room apart from the noisy dance floor.

There was a number of dope-eyed thugs lounging about the room. The man in evening clothes motioned one

X swung over the sill and dropped to the ground.

of them out of a chair and offered the chair to Betty.

"There is nothing to be alarmed about, Miss Dale," he said gently. "We are simply anxious that you know exactly where you stand. You have the peculiar honor of being a friend of Secret Agent X. This we know, because one of our operatives saw you making an effort, the other night, to aid Mr. X in the smoking room of the Paragon Theatre. Since that time, we have outguessed Mr. X on every occasion. We guessed, for instance, that after he had talked to Colrich, he would impersonate James Starbuck. So, earlier this evening, we arranged a trap for your Secret Agent.

The man in the mask paused, seeming to enjoy the fearful suspense his last statement was creating in the mind of Betty Dale. "Unfortunately," he sighed, "the Agent gave us the slip. Our one fear is that he has managed to crash this party tonight, even as you did. You, who know him, shall point him out to us tonight."

"I—I—" began Betty.

The man held up his hand. "Wait. Will you step this way?" He went to a door at the end of the room and opened it.

Betty glanced around. Two of the doped thugs stood beside her, ready to see that the masked man's demands were carried out. She got somewhat unsteadily to her feet and walked to the door. There she stopped, a scream choking in her throat.

THE room beyond was dimly lighted. Three hairy monsters with great, glassy eyes, sulked in the shadows. In the center of the room sat Harvey Bates. His legs and body were tied to a chair. His hands were held palms up on a wood table by means of straps and staples. Metal supports held curious metal cylinders above each hand.

"You know this man, Miss Dale?" the masked man asked. And when

Betty did not reply, he nodded his head. "Of course you do. His name is Bates, and he is a friend of Agent X. Those cylinders above his hands contain liquid air, a fluid that, when dropped on human flesh, produces far worse burns than acid, and far more pain that hot coals."

One of the black, furry monsters advanced, touched a stop-cock at the bottom of one of the cylinders. A tiny stream of blue-white liquid splashed into the palm of Bates' right hand.

Bates turned deathly pale. He bit his lower lip until his large, square teeth were stained with blood. The liquid gas fumed into misty vapor and was gone, but the palm of Bates' hand was black and stiff.

"Keep lips closed, Betty," Bates said hoarsely.

Betty shook her head. Her blue eyes glistened with compassionate tears. She turned to the masked man. "Stop it. Oh, you can't be so brutal!"

"I think we can," said the masked man. "*You* can stop this torment—if you go into the dance room and point out Agent X."

Betty thought a moment. Unless X so willed it, she had no more chance of pointing him out than the masked man himself. Yet somehow, she must stop this tormenting of Harvey Bates. Without the slightest idea what her next move would be, Betty nodded her agreement.

"Betty," said Bates hoarsely, "you couldn't do a thing like that!"

Betty flashed Bates a quick smile. He was right. She couldn't betray X, even if she wanted to. She did not know, even, that X was in the house.

CHAPTER VI

Mystery Women

BEFORE they entered the house where Zerna's dope party was in full swing, Agent X removed all metallic weapons from his pocket and left them in the car. The same servant who had admitted Gordon Stien and Betty Dale, a few moments before, allowed Agent X and his companion to enter. The Agent's keen eyes compassed the room where the strange dance was being held.

Mingling with the crowd, X saw the hostess, Zerna, in her bizarre and colorful gown. She would dance first into one man's arms and then into another. X saw how deftly she slipped packets of dope into the hands of her partners. There was also a man in the crowd who was handing out dope to the women in the same manner.

It was all very cleverly done. There was nothing to excite police interference. Furthermore, it seemed that these parties were never held twice in the same building.

X was about to choose a partner from among the women, so that he might not appear too conspicuous, when a masked woman all but threw herself into his arms.

"Jimmee! Jimmee, darling!" She seized his arms and pulled them about her slender waist. "Where have you been keeping yourself, naughty boy?"

The Agent searched the dope-dilated eyes revealed through the slots in the mask. This unknown woman was obviously acquainted with James Starbuck—intimately.

X smiled mechanically. "How did you recognize me?" he whispered.

The woman drew a long breath. "Oh, darling, what a question!" She looped the handle of her evening bag over her arm, grasped X's hand, dropped her head upon his shoulder. "How good to feel your arms about me again! Hold me tight, Jimmee." And as they began to dance, the woman was weeping softly.

Agent X had only pity for the woman in his arms. Already her vice had left its tracks upon that portion of her face visible beneath the mask. Whether her evident passion for James Starbuck was real or simply infatuation stimulated by dope, he did not know.

Their dance was not long. Another man seized the woman and dragged her from X's arms to whirl her about the room in dizzy, drunken circles, while she hysterically called out: "Jimmee, dear!"

X was about to search for another partner when he noticed that the mystery woman who had insisted he was Starbuck, had dropped her bag at his feet when she had been dragged from his arms. X picked up the bag, slipped it into his pocket, and turned into a little room at the side of the dance hall.

He closed the door behind him. He hoped that examination of the bag would help him identify the woman, but he dared not risk being caught in the act. There was another door at the opposite side of the room. He crossed to it and opened it a little way. It led into a closet, entirely dark save for a shaft of light that passed through a rough hole in the plaster.

This hole looked out upon the dance hall. Beside it was a camera mounted on a tripod. It was evidently from such a secret place as this that the gang obtained pictures later used to blackmail the wealthy dope addicts.

X returned to a table that centered the room and turned the contents of the bag out on its surface. There was a large wad of bills, a jeweled compact, a card case and a many-folded sheet of paper.

THE card case was empty, but the inner flap of it had been engraved with the name: *Sylvia Rister.*

The Agent's eyes narrowed. Sylvia Rister was Morgan Rister's wife. If Rister was really associated with the gang, surely he wouldn't have permitted his wife to take dope. If he wasn't in with the criminals, where were they obtaining the liquid gas they used for a weapon?

X next turned his attention to the folded piece of paper. On opening it, he discovered that it was a complete metropolitan map of New York.

Why would Mrs. Rister, a resident of the city for years, be carrying a map like this one? X flattened the map out on the table and studied it for a minute.

There were thirty-one circles, all having a common center, drawn on the face of the map in fine lines of India ink.

X folded the map and put it in his pocket. With the idea of returning Mrs. Rister's bag, he left the room and was halfway across the dance floor, when the radio was turned off. The sudden silence fell like a blow upon the drug addicts. They stopped their dancing, clung to their partners, and looked around the room as though they expected something terrible to happen.

"Absolute silence!" Zerna's strident voice demanded.

She was standing at one end of the room, her hard, chill eyes flickering from one masked face to another.

"There is a traitor among you," Zerna said.

Instantly, there arose an excited murmur among the guests, but Zerna stamped her foot and put an end to that. "Because," she said, "there is a traitor here, all must remove their masks at once."

For a moment, no one moved. Zerna repeated her demand. Still, no faces were bared.

The Agent's pulse quickened. Had his deception been discovered? How could his disguise have been penetrated? Then it suddenly occurred to him that there was one bold stroke he might use to divert suspicion from himself.

He quickly raised his right hand and jerked off his mask. Surely, the first man in the group to expose his face would be the last suspected of being the traitor.

One by one masks were removed. The Secret Agent was shocked as he recognized many people from the best families in the city, among other dope addicts. Half the crowd seemed to have come from the wealthy class.

They, no doubt, paid "club dues" to prevent their vice being made public. Others in the group were obviously the lowest in the criminal scale. Probably, their "club dues" were paid in services of unlawful nature.

Zerna looked from one face to another. "We believe that Secret Agent X is among those present," she said. "We have a way of proving this, of course."

She clapped her hands. A door at the side of the room opened, and, to X's horror, Betty Dale was led into the room.

Betty Dale was actually almost beside herself with terror. She knew why she had been brought here. She was to point out Secret Agent X. Actually, she had no more idea which of those present was the Agent. Yet to save Harvey Bates from torture, she had to point. And what if her wild guess should prove correct?

Betty closed her eyes for a moment, bit her lip. Then she raised a trembling forefinger and pointed straight at the back of the man next to her. "That is Secret Agent X," she said firmly.

CHAPTER VII

The Betrayal

BETTY did not raise her eyes to meet those of the man to whom she had pointed, until she heard him curse. There was something so familiar about the ring of his voice that the girl's heart skipped a beat. She looked up quickly, then, into the goggling eyes of Gordon Stien.

"Betty," the newspaper man gasped, "this is a hell of a gag!"

Three men immediately fell upon Gordon Stien. Some one cried: "The girl's giving it to you straight. She came with that guy."

The hophead criminals dragged the struggling, kicking Stien toward the door through which Betty had come. Stien was shouting:

"Of all the rotten deals a man ever got from a woman, this is it! Me, Agent X? What a laugh! Why—"

Then the sound of Stien's voice was muffled by the closing of a door.

It was obvious to Agent X that Betty Dale was on the brink of complete collapse because her grabbing in the dark had resulted in the plight of her fellow reporter. X had no idea what motive had been behind Betty's action, but he greatly feared that she had been tormented in some way.

No sooner had the criminals seized Stien, than X began moving toward the doomed reporter. It was utterly impossible for the Secret Agent to stand back and allow some one else to take punishment that had been designed for him.

Behind the cover of excitement caused by Betty's startling disclosure, Agent X got to the door through which Stien and his guards had passed. When he was certain that no one was watching, he cautiously opened the door and stepped into the room beyond.

The room was dimly lighted. Evidently Stien had been taken to another part of the house. X started across the room, but came to an abrupt stop. Directly in front of him, bound to a chair and table, was the great, square-shouldered form of Harvey Bates. X sprang to his operative. "Have you out in a second, Bates," he rapped in the voice by which Bates could recognize him.

"You, chief!" Bates gasped. "Miss Dale—"

"I know. We must get her out of here. And Stien is on the spot—the spot where I'm supposed to be. Can't have that, you know." The Agent's capable fingers unknotted ropes and loosened straps.

"Any plans, sir?" Bates whispered.

X shook his head. "We'll plan as we move. Here—" X pulled a package of cigarettes from his pocket and shook out three or four on the table together with a paper of matches. "After they've burned about half an inch, a tear-gas cartridge inside the cigarette goes off. Only weapons I have that wouldn't have been detected. Can you manage them with that nasty burn on your hand?"

Bates nodded. "Burn's nothing," he insisted stoutly. "Liquid air."

X held up a warning finger. "Some one coming," he whispered. Hastily, he pulled the straps back over Bates' wrists, but did not hook them. He winked cheerfully at his lieutenant and sprang across the room to crowd himself into a small, open closet.

THE door opened, and Gordon Stien was brought into the room by four of the hophead criminals. The young man had admirable courage. There was a scornful smile forming on his lips as he was taken toward the door of the dance hall.

One of the criminals carried a shiny cylinder, undoubtedly one of the guns used to project the deadly liquid gas. Probably, the criminals had decided to make an example of this man they supposed to be Agent X.

"Better lock that door after you," said one of the hopheads, when Stien and his guards had entered the dance hall.

From his hiding place, X noticed that the key was on the inside of the door. One of the four guards came back into the room for the key. Once he had obtained it and locked the door, X would have no chance of getting to Stien's rescue.

The hophead had his back toward the closet where X hid. The door leading into the dance hall was part-way open. Nothing but quick, silent action could turn aside the fate in store for Stien.

X sprang like a panther. His leap carried him to within two feet of the man at the door. His left arm shot out, his hand slapping over the mouth of the hophead. His right fist pounded up to the back of the man's neck at the base of the brain.

The man went limp, fell into the door with a thumping sound that made X hold his breath. Only the excitement in the dance hall prevented those near the door from noticing the noise.

X pulled the unconscious hophead to one side. Harvey Bates sprang to his chief's aid. Together, they knelt beside the hophead and quickly searched his pockets. X found an automatic and passed it over to Bates.

"I'm going in there and start something," he said grimly. "Stien won't be in any danger after I prove to that mob that he isn't Agent X. I can probably get as far as the middle of the room before they'll even notice me. When I start trouble, you come in to cover the crowd while I get Miss Dale out of this hole. Use tear gas where you can. Shoot only as a last resort."

"Ready for anything," Bates said eagerly.

X stepped to the door and slipped into the dance hall. Two of the doped killers were holding Stien in a chair in the very center of the room. Nearby, stood the man with the gas cylinder. The man in evening clothes, the only one in the room whose face remained covered, was saying: "And as a warning to others in this room, we have decided that you shall all witness the death of this Secret Agent X."

Here was a new thrill for the jaded appetites of the dopesters. Some greeted the announcement with shouts and others with pleasureful shudders.

Betty Dale was terrified beyond speech, beyond tears. Her face was ash gray. Her fingers were knotting and unknotting themselves. Here was murder of her own making. And she knew no way to prevent it.

Agent X calmly jabbed a cigarette between his lips and lit it. With a slight smile on his lips, he walked briskly toward the center of the room. Virtually weaponless, Agent X risked everything to save the life of the man in the chair.

The masked man muttered at the cigarette-smoking Agent X: "Keep back, Starbuck," he growled.

AGENT X's face never changed. The smile seemed frozen there. He moved on until he was directly behind the man with the gas cylinder.

The two hopheads who held Stien never took their eyes from the Agent's face. Then, with a lightning-like motion, X's right hand passed over his face and removed his cigarette, at the same time pressing and twisting the plastic material that covered his face. When his right hand dropped to his side, those quick alterations in his features had told their story—a story that instantly marked him for death.

Fingers, eyes pointed. Then voices exclaimed: "There's Agent X!"

The man with the gas cylinder swung around. The back of his right hand came in contact with the point of X's cigarette. At the same time, X seized the cylinder of gas and wrenched it from the man's grasp.

The two hopheads had released Stien. The reporter was legging for the door. Heedless of the gas cylinder with which X threatened them, the hopheads sprang at Agent X, who squirmed out of their reach and moved toward Betty Dale. His long fingers flipped the smoldering cigarette into the midst of the hopheads. There was a faint pop and white clouds of choking, blinding teargas broke from the cigarette.

Across the room, Harvey Bates appeared. He was moving backwards toward Betty Dale, threatening the mob with his gun. He, too, had one of the tear-gas cigarettes going, and this he flipped into the center of the excited throng.

"Toward the front door, Betty!" X sang out. Then he broke into a run to follow the girl and Bates. Only one man stood in their way—the masked man in evening clothes. He stood directly in front of the door, legs wide spread, an automatic in his hand. The eyes in the slots of his mask met those of X.

"Another inch," he warned, "and I'll kill that girl!"

X dared not count the cost of his next move. There was but one way out for Bates and Betty. The man in the doorway had to be removed, for it was only a matter of moments before the dazed and surprised mob would sufficiently recover from the tear gas to close in. X raised the gas cylinder and stepped directly between Betty and the masked man.

The masked man's gun spouted flame and thunder. Slugs that were like twin battering-rams plumped into X's bullet-proof vest. The Agent's knees felt like jelly. A red cloud of pain filmed his vision. Yet an almost superhuman will kept him upright to shield the body of the girl he loved.

He staggered on, straight into the blazing gat in the man's hand. The gas cylinder hacked down once. The masked man melted to the floor. X tripped over him, fell flat on his face, and lay there a moment, grasping at his wavering senses.

Bates seized X beneath the arms and pulled him to his feet. X saw Betty's pale, anxious face close to his. His lips twisted into a wry grin. "I'm all right," he worked out through clenched teeth. "The bullet-proof vest takes death out of the bullets but leaves the wallop. Let's go. The car's out in front."

Still clinging to the gas cylinder with one hand, X hurried Betty through the front door of the building. From near at hand came the skirl of a police whistle. The sound of the shooting had evidently attracted the cops.

"Move!" X urged. His old strength back again in his well-conditioned body, he lifted Betty in his arms, strode to the car, and put her in the front seat. Bates slipped in under the wheel, kicked over the motor, and as X sprang into the back seat, the car rocketed from the curb.

CHAPTER VIII

SECRET CIRCLES

X LEANED over the front seat, his head between Bates and Betty. "No time for chatter. We're making progress for the first time since this investigation began. These are orders to you, Betty, and to you, Bates."

"Yes?" the girl said eagerly. "What can I do?"

"Keep away from everybody, Betty," X said earnestly. "I mean *everybody*. While this gang exists, you're not safe a minute. These criminals know they can strike at me through you. Our best bet is to trap the whole mob in some way." X drew out the map he had taken from Mrs. Rister's purse, and tossed it into Bates' lap.

"There are thirty-one circles on that map, Bates. You're job, as soon as you have seen Betty safely home, is to find the center of those circles. Communicate with me through G.H.Q." X took hold of the door handle of the car. "Stop in the center of the next block," he ordered.

"What are you going to do?" Betty asked anxiously as X got out in front of the entrance of a gloomy lodging house.

X smiled kindly. "Much, I hope. We've got to wipe this mob out." Then he added beneath his breath: "Before it wipes us out." He hurried into the lodging house, where, on the third floor, he had rented a modest room under one of his many aliases.

In this hideout, he briefly examined the gas cylinder he had taken from the hophead. When at last he put it aside, there was a strange, troubled look in his eyes. As he began working on a change of disguise, he thought back over the evening's adventure. Many things that had been fogged with mystery began to stand out clearly. He understood now that the danger threatening Betty Dale was even greater than he had anticipated.

When he left the hideout a little later, he was a man who looked at home in his shabby surroundings. His face was a hard, vicious mask, with thin lips, a fist-flattened nose, and a killer's squinted eyes.

A rattling old car that looked incapable of the speed he goaded from it, was the conveyance that took him across Manhattan to the beautiful West End Avenue home of Morgan Rister.

A servant informed the Agent that Mr. Rister wasn't at home, and X dealt the man a flat-handed blow to the chest that sent him reeling back from the door. Then X came through the door fast enough to catch the servant by the coat lapel and keep him from falling over backwards.

"I'm goin' to see Rister, yah understand?" he said nasally. "And you ain't stoppin' me, yah understand?"

A door opened, and an anxious voice asked: "What is the trouble, here?"

X looked over the servant's shoulder to see Morgan Rister, his pale hair rumpled, his face colorless above the black satin collar of his dressing gown.

An unpleasant grin spread across the ugly mask of makeup that covered X's face. "Aw, me and James was playin' knock-knock. I gotta little business to transact with you, Rister."

"Very well." Rister's voice became limp. His hand trembled as he opened the door and ushered X into his study.

"Sit down, Rister," X said. "Guess you know why I'm here. It's your lady, again. You wouldn't want it to get out about her and Jim Starbuck and these dope parties, would you?"

Rister said nothing. His eyes had a frightened gleam.

"Sure, you wouldn't, Mr. Rister. Your lady oughtn't to hang out at the joints she does. I seen her tonight with about two shots of dope under her skin. How much for hush?"

"I'm paying you enough," Rister snapped. I've shelled out money to you for the protection of my wife's name. And I've furnished your boss the gas he asked for. I'm through. If I had known you were going to use the stuff for murder, you wouldn't have had it."

"That's fine, Mr. Rister!"

RISTER'S jaw dropped. He stared in utter amazement at the man before him. The voice that had just spoken to him seemed to be that of an entirely different person. Agent X's hand darted into the pocket of his baggy trousers and produced a neatly counterfeited police badge.

Rister slapped his perspiring brow, gasped like a man plunged suddenly into icy water. "I've been talking to a police detective!"

X came nearer and put his hand on Rister's shoulder. "That's the idea. We knew down at headquarters about your wife. We had an idea that the liquid gas the gang used to freeze Mrs. Colrich came from your plant. We just wanted to be sure."

"Wh-what are you going to do with me?" asked Rister.

"Well, I could take you down to headquarters as an accessory to the Ruth Colrich murder. You tell me all you know about the gang, who runs it, and where they get their dope—and maybe I'll give you a break."

Rister shook his head and stared blankly at the wall. "I can't help you. I know nothing of these people. They simply had some pictures of my wife. Not very pleasant pictures. They had been blackmailing her with them. Then they turned on me. I didn't actually give them the gas. I made it easy for them to steal it."

X had been studying Rister closely. The unfortunate man was perfectly sincere, he was certain. Probably, his eavesdropping at the door of the smoking room in the Paragon Theatre had been an effort to hear if Wicker and Arvin were talking about his wife in conjunction with the dope parties.

X took Rister's hand in his own and gave it a grasp that seemed to transmit new energy into the man's body. "Good-night, Rister—and good luck!"

Agent X left the Rister home and drove for several blocks until he came to a drug store. He went in, found a telephone pay station, and called a number that was listed in no telephone book. It was the telephone of Harvey Bates' office, the general headquarters for the Agent's crime-fighting machine.

To his surprise, it was Bates himself who answered the phone. The Agent's voice at once slipped to the familiar tone that Bates would recognize.

"Any results from the map, Bates?" And as he listened to what Bates told him, his brow became deeply furrowed. "Impossible! Have you made those measurements carefully?" He was silent for a moment, staring thoughtfully at the wall of the telephone booth. Finally, he said: "Meet me at the office of A. J. Martin in one hour. Bring the map." *

Though it was after midnight and traffic had thinned out, it was nearly an hour before X arrived at the office he maintained in the name of A. J. Martin. He had not changed his disguise.

Bates as usual was punctual. As soon as he had arrived and had stopped marveling at his chief's present appearance, he brought out the map, a flexible steel rule, and drafting instruments.

"Want you to check my measurements, sir. Think I'm right. Be glad to find out," Bates clipped.

X spread the map on the top of the desk. There were thumb-tack marks in the extreme corners. He measured the distance between these. Then, with the rule and instruments,

---

*AUTHOR'S NOTE: A. J. Martin, representative of the Associated Press, is the Agent's most useful alias. Under that name he maintains a downtown office where many of his secret records are kept. His press credentials are genuine, giving him the privilege of entering many doors that would otherwise be closed to him.

he found the common centers of the circles. He nodded his head slowly.

"You're a hundred per cent right. The center of those circles is in the estate of Samuel Arvin, head of the Anti-Vice League. But before we accuse Arvin of anything, we ought to take another look at newsreels. Arvin may have nothing to do with this business, but newsreels and this map have. I'm going to the movies tomorrow. And before you go, Bates, here's something to think about. The gas cylinder I picked up tonight contained nothing more potent than ice water."

Bates frowned. "Something colder than that was used on me," he said with a shudder.

"Yes!" X smiled. "Used on *you*. Think it over. It's important."

AGENT X attended the first matinee at the Paragon Theatre the following afternoon. He was disguised as a well-known member of the narcotic squad, a guise that brought Walter Nixon, the operator of the theatre, across the lobby with a troubled frown on his forehead. Just as X was about to enter the aisle, Nixon tapped him on the arm.

"Will you step over here a moment, sergeant?" he whispered.

X was agreeable. "What's on your mind, Nixon?" he asked.

Nixon gnawed his lip and said nothing until he had drawn X away from the patrons who were entering the theatre. Then he said irritably: "How long is this going to keep up? It seems to me that there are police or members of the Anti Vice League here at every performance. I think the patrons are beginning to notice it. I demand to know just what you expect to find here at the Paragon."

"We're looking for dope," X said. "The reason the investigation continues is that we have been unable to find any dope here or at other theatres. You should be thankful of that, Nixon, instead of crabbing about it."

"It's very annoying," Nixon persisted.

When he left the theatre, ten minutes later, Agent X thought he was on the track of an important discovery. He had seen only the newsreel, and while his eyes had not left the screen, in the darkness his hands had been busy with pencil and paper. He went immediately from the Paragon to the Princess Theatre directly across the street.

Again, he left as soon as the newsreel had been shown, and his heart was pounding madly with excitement, because of his discovery. While he was as certain about it all as he was about tomorrow's sunrise, he nevertheless went to one of the downtown theatres and once again checked on the newsreel. Then he went directly to the office of A. J. Martin, phoned Harvey Bates and Jim Hobart.*

It was, of course, as A. J. Martin that he welcomed redheaded Jim Hobart and Harvey Bates. Though the two friends of the Agent had met, they had never worked together on a case before; and both were a bit reticent, fearful, no doubt, of betraying some of the Agent's secrets.

X SPREAD the map he had found in Mrs. Rister's bag out on the desk once more, and beside it he put a narrow slip of paper on which he had scribbled an odd list of letters and numbers. His gray eyes were twinkling, his lean lips smiling as he asked: "Did either of you ever see that particular newsreel known as 'Photo-News'?"

Bates nodded.

Hobart said: "Sure, Mr. Martin—a lot of times."

"Then I need not go into detail as to how the title, 'Photo-News' is

***AUTHOR'S NOTE: Jim Hobart, famous director of the Hobart Detective Agency is an old friend of Agent X whom he knows only as A. J. Martin. It was the helpful assistance of A. J. Martin that had established Hobart in his successful business and Hobart is devoted to his mentor, willing to fill strange requests at once and without asking too many questions.**

thrown on the screen. You will remember that the word 'news' is spread pretty well across the screen, three stars separating each letter. Now, for just a scrap of history. I'm sure you both know the origin of the word 'news'?"

Hobart said: "It came from the directions, north, east, west, and south as represented by their abbreviations, N, E, W, and S. Isn't that right?"

"Exactly right. And when I found a slight, apparent flaw in the film, which cast a black mark on the screen above the letter 'S' in the trade-mark, and found that same flaw on every Photo-News film shown at every theatre I visited today, I began to think it meant something. And so it does."

Harvey Bates grunted. The Agent looked at him and smiled. "What's on your mind, Bates?" he asked.

"A direction. I noticed that flaw on the film before. It was in a different place, though. Never paid any attention to it."

"No one would pay any attention to it," X went on, "for without this map, it means nothing. However, if we take a rule and a compass, get the directions down on the map, then draw a line from the center of the thirty-one circles in the direction indicated so subtlely by the newsreel, that line will intersect all of the thirty-one circles."

"Now, which circle are we going to use? Simply pick out the day of the month, is my guess. This is the ninth, so we consider the ninth circle. Note that a line passing through the circles due south from the common point, which we know to be Arvin's back yard, intersects circle nine at East Eighteenth Street and at just about the place where Zerna held her dope party last night."

"I'm still in the dark, Mr. Martin," said Hobart, his freckled face screwed into a puzzled mask.

"It is simply a subtle way of informing the dopesters where they will meet and obtain their dope ration," X explained. "Serial numbers, faked on the film, indicate the exact time and exact address. All a dope addict has to do to establish his connection is to drop into any theatre showing Photo-News, get the direction, draw a line on his map, and go to the proper address at the proper time.

"It's no wonder the police have made no headway. The whole dope syndicate is constantly on the move. Zerna throws parties in houses or apartments that she rents. But is it Zerna who figured all this out? I doubt it. She's hardly that brainy.

"The point I'm making is this: now that we know how it is done, we can direct that mob into a trap of our own making!"

"Right, sir!" Bates clipped. His square face beamed in absolute admiration of his chief.

"Pull on a moment," said the more skeptical Hobart. "How's that to be done?"

"I've learned," X said, "that the Eastern Film Agency distributes next week's Photo-News films tomorrow morning. Tonight, with the aid of one of Bates' staff photographers, we tamper with those films so as to direct the whole gang into our trap. I'll need you and Bates, and some of your best men, to watch the film agency. See that no one else tampers with those films after we have made our changes. That clear?"

Bates and Hobart nodded.

"Then at midnight tonight, you'll be on Forty-ninth Street near the film agency. I have a little job to attend to before then."

The "little job" X had mentioned, concerned Mr. Hamilton Esler of the Blue Streak Cab Company. "Honest Ham", Esler might be—and certainly appeared to be, after turning over the money which X, as Starbuck, had placed in the back of Esler's cab. But after all, if Esler was associated with the blackmail dope-gang, he would have known ahead of time that the supposed Starbuck was really Agent X. It would have been well worth the money he had turned over to the police to be alibied in the eyes of Secret Agent X.

SHORTLY after Bates and Hobart had left the A. J. Martin office, X walked in the door of the office of the Blue Streak Cab Company. Esler, owner of the small string of cabs, was sitting with his feet on the desk. A commonplace man in appearance was Mr. A. J. Martin, yet Esler's black eyes examined his visitor searchingly.

Agent X pulled out his card, which represented him as a member of the Associated Press. "Looking for a little human interest angle on the recent death of Mrs. Colrich," he said to Esler. "I understand that you were the man who drove her to the quarter where she was murdered. Suppose you give me a line on how she was dressed and how she acted."

"Why, sure, Mr. Martin," Esler agreed. "You see a lot of funny stuff, driving around in a cab. Wonder to me some of you newshawks don't go in for taxi-wheeling. It was like this. . . ."

For the next ten minutes, X apparently listened to Esler's accurate account concerning Mrs. Colrich. Actually, his eyes were busy, roving around the office. His gaze got as far as Esler's desk, and there it stopped. There were thumb-tack marks on the surface of the desk—marks that immediately awakened the Agent's interest.

A few minutes later, when Esler excused himself to go out to the curb to give a message to one of his drivers, X slipped a steel tape measure from his pocket and calculated the distance between the four groups of thumb-tack marks which roughly represented the four corners of a square. A fifth group of pricks was somewhere near the center of this square. X reeled his tape and put it into his pocket. Then he went out to the curb where Esler stood.

"Do you know where Montgomery Mansion is?" he asked.

Esler thought a moment. "Oh, that old wreck of a stone building in the north end? You can hardly see over the weeds in the yard in the summer. Sure, I know that joint."

X took a roll of bills from his pocket and peeled out a twenty. "This will convince you I really want to go there," he said quietly.

HALF an hour later, the cab stopped in front of a dark, deserted house of stone that rambled across several unkept lots. Montgomery Mansion was a once-grand manor where Agent X had hidden one of the most complete crime laboratories in the country.

"You must be going to call on the rats, mister," Esler said, as he regarded the old house distastefully.

"Yes? Well, I brought the rat with me," X said quietly. At the same time, he pressed the muzzle of his gas gun into Esler's back. "Get out," he said. "And take it easy. My nerves are just a little unstrung tonight."

"What the hell?" gasped Esler. "Is this a stickup?"

"Oh, no, this is a finish. It's about the last thing that happens to a man of your stamp before they turn on the juice in the electric chair."

And across the sunken flags and through the old doorway, Agent X prodded the taxi driver. Through rooms of darkness, across creaking floors, X guided Esler. He forced the man down basement steps. He unlocked a steel door that looked as though it belonged on a bank vault. He thrust Esler into a room beyond, switched on lights, and followed. He closed and locked the heavy door behind them.

"You've got fox-brains," said X. But when you drew thirty-one circles on a lot of maps of this city, the thumb tacks, in the corners of the maps, left their marks on your desk.

The needle point of the drawing compass used to make the circles, also left marks. Knowing the measurements of the maps, and also where the center of those thirty-one circles was, I simply compared the known measurements with those indicated by the marks on your desk. Hamilton Esler, the maps which drug addicts carry in order to locate their dope connections, were fixed up by you in your office!"

"Who are you?" Esler asked hoarsely.

X smiled grimly. "I am the man you've always managed to keep two jumps ahead of."

"Secret Agent X," Esler pronounced slowly, fearfully.

"As good a guess as anyone will ever make," X admitted. "I am the man who looked like James Starbuck the other night when I rode in your taxi. You knew I wasn't Starbuck that night, for Zerna had no doubt warned you that I was simply impersonating Starbuck. My death was scheduled for that night. Your mob followed the cab, intending to kill me. But it seems I bear a charmed life. Even you were afraid I might escape. So you arranged a perfect alibi.

"Acting my part as Starbuck, as yet ignorant of the fact that my disguise had been penetrated, I put a stack of supposed blackmail money under the seat of your taxi. Knowing that I would watch to see what became of the money, you handed it over to the police. Thus you squashed any theories I might have had concerning your tie-up with your organization."

X slipped a black leather case from his pocket, snapped it open with one hand, and took out a loaded hypodermic syringe.

"What are you going to do?" Esler's voice was no longer steady.

"I am going to turn out your light for a time, my friend," X said. "Your day as a field general is over."

Step by step, Esler moved back toward the wall of the room. His eyes flitted from the hypodermic syringe to the Agent's gas pistol. When his back touched the wall, he lunged suddenly forward in an insane effort to jump the Agent's gun.

The hypodermic needle darted out like the fang of a serpent and buried itself in the flesh of Esler's throat. Esler's arms fanned the air wildly, feebly. Then, with a long sigh, he melted to the floor.

X was beside him in a moment, his keen eyes intent upon Esler's face. He nodded his head slowly. How could he better direct the dope gang into a snare than by disguising himself as the criminals' leader? He took out his pocket makeup kit and opened it on the floor. Henceforth, until the entire gang was behind bars, he resolved to look and act the part of Hamilton Esler.

CHAPTER IX

Triple-Trap Summons

It was in the disguise of Hamilton Esler that Agent X set out to meet Bates' photographic expert that night. In this disguise, there was always a chance that he might run into some members of Esler's gang who would unknowingly drop important information.

At exactly midnight, X and the photographic expert approached the film distributing office. As they entered the alley at the corner of the building, X held up an arm, checking the man at his side.

"Wait," he whispered. "Some one is at the back door of the place. It may be a janitor or a watchman." Or, he thought to himself, it might be one of the gang, coming to make changes in the newsreels in order to inform his servants of their next meeting place. It was a ticklish situation. If he tried to hold the prowler up with a gun and the man turned out to be a watchman, it would be necessary to knock the man out The watchman's absence would simply attract attention, not only to the police but also to the criminals.

The man beside X was a photographer, unused to night prowling of this sort. He was ill at ease, certainly, or at that moment he would not have lurched into an ash can.

Immediately, there was a scuffling of feet in the alley near the back door of the building. Agent X's right hand shot down to his trouser pocket and pulled out a small, round ball. He threw it with all his strength at the corner of the building. It was a magnesium flash bomb, such as X had frequently employed to create a moment of surprise when making some of his daring escapes. Tonight, he employed it with a different objective in mind.

The bomb struck the side of the building and burst. For an instant, the vicinity of the back door of the building was illuminated in the lightning-like flash. But the illumination lasted only for an instant, and X had not succeeded in seeing the running man's face. However, there was something about his back, the sudden jerk of his shoulders, that was familiar. Agent X immediately broke into a run in a desperate effort to overtake the man.

But the prowler had a long lead. At the mouth of the alley, a car was waiting, its motor idling. The fleeing man sprang into the car, which accelerated down the street. X shrank back into the shadows. The men in the car must not see his face.

A moment later, X had rejoined the photographer. They entered the building together and quickly located the files where the newsreels that were to be distributed on the morrow were kept. Agent X spread a sheet of paper out on a table. On the paper, he had drawn an excellent facsimile of the trade-mark of Photo-News, and the flaws he wanted inserted between the "N" and "E" were clearly indicated, as well as the alterations in serial numbers.

He did not bother to explain the purpose of these alterations to the expert. Actually, these changes would direct the dopesters to a large, deserted warehouse near the Oak Point railway yards on the river front.

As soon as he had made his instructions clear, X left the man to his work. Near the corner of the building, he was met by Harvey Bates who was awaiting orders.

"Surround the place, Bates," X directed. "The alterations are being made, and your man must not be interrupted. The criminals may send a man to try and make changes, understand, since films go out to the theatres in the morning. Needless to say, you've got to prevent this. Our scheme may go haywire, but we've got to try it."

"Sure—everything will be okeh, sir," Bates said.

But Agent X, walking off alone in the dark, was not so optimistic.

X SPENT the following day in Esler's taxi-cab office, actually living the part of his disguise. But it was a day of anxiety and disappointment. The trap had been set for midnight that night. Had it a chance of succeeding? Had some master brain discovered his designs?

Hamilton Esler, he knew, was but one of the men behind the huge vice machine. Others, whom X suspected, were still at large.

Late that night, X left the taxi office and went to a pay telephone station, from which he called Betty Dale's apartment; but there was no answer to his ringing. He called the office of the *Herald* and learned that Betty Dale had gone with Gordon Stien, early that morning, to cover an out-of-town assignment.

X slammed up the receiver and left the booth. Why hadn't Betty heeded his warning? And it was not like her to leave town without leaving word with him.

In desperation, he took Esler's cab and drove to her apartment, hoping to find a note there from the girl. But there was nothing except a cold emptiness about the place.

His plan, his trap—it *had* to work now. Some sixth sense warned him that Betty was actually in the gang's power. Only by capturing a part of that pack of human wolves could he hope to pick up the trail of the girl.

Ten minutes before midnight, X slewed the taxi around the corner at Cabot and Oak Point Avenue. Instinctively, he knew that the shadows around the nearby warehouse were peopled with masked, hop-headed killers. As he brought the cab to a halt, he sensed motion all about him—men slinking in the shadows. Was he to lead them into the warehouse where Bates, Hobart and their men waited to subdue the gang with threatening guns and tear gas, or was he caught in his own web?

X got out of the cab. A man came shuffling along the sidewalk, head lowered and hands in his pockets. X waited. The man came up and flicked the beam of a flashlight on X's face. X saw that the man with the light was masked. But he was a dope fiend, no doubt of that. Had the others, the real leaders of the gang obeyed his newsreel summons?

"What's the job, chief?" the man whispered.

X commanded: "Bring the rest of the boys. We're going into that warehouse. There're some crated silks and furs inside. I got the whole job mapped out. There ain't a copper for blocks around here."

The masked man put his fingers to his lips and sounded a soft, owl-like whistle.

They came out of the darkness, the masked men with killer's eyes. There were perhaps a score of them. They surrounded the Agent, waiting impatiently for his directions.

"Don't draw no gats," X whispered. "This is a cinch, I says."

He led the way to the door of the warehouse and took hold of the latch. Was it merely imagination, or was that metal latch colder than the air that surrounded it? After all, it was a cold night. He lifted the latch.

THE door swung suddenly out of X's hands. He sprang back, reached for his gas gun. But his hand remained poised in mid-air as a stiffened form pitched forward to his feet. A cold draft, like that from an immense refrigerator came from the door of the warehouse.

"Cripes!" a man at X's elbow whispered. "The freezing death! Who is this guy?" and he pointed at the frozen man on the ground.

X took but one glance at the man on the ground. The man was one of Harvey Bates' best operatives. Then Bates and Hobart, inside the warehouse. . . .

"Hey, Ham!" came Zerna's strident voice. She was elbowing through the crowd of criminals behind Agent X. "Ham, you gotta do something. They got no right to treat a woman that way!" Zerna reached X, seized his arm and shook him.

"What woman?" X demanded, his heart drumming dully against his ribs.

"Why, Betty Dale!" And at that instant, Zerna flashed the brilliant beam of a flashlight on X's face.

X knew he was caught. While his lips quickly said, "Why the hell should I care what they do with Betty Dale," he had been counting on the darkness to mask the anxiety that must have showed in his eyes. Zerna had been expecting something of the sort, and for that reason had flashed on her light at that moment.

But if Zerna had noticed that pained expression on the Agent's face, she concealed her knowledge cleverly. "Maybe you don't, Ham, but when I see those devils makin' a dope fiend out of an innocent girl like her, I get mad."

"Where is this girl you're so anxious about?" asked X. He was walking into a trap. He wanted to walk into a trap.

"Out on the yacht," Zerna said. "They're going to make a hop-head out of her. I'll take you out in the launch."

In spite of pangs of fear for Betty Dale that knifed his heart, X managed to comply to Zerna's request without the slightest indication of anxiety. There was no doubt in his mind but that Zerna had spoken the truth for the first time in a long while. Betty Dale *was* in the hands of the criminals. And they would use the Agent's love for her as a powerful weapon to gain their own ends.

CHAPTER X

Two Minutes to Death

AGENT X left the masked dopesters, without a word of explanation, and followed Zerna down to the river front and out onto the pier to join the woman, where a motor launch was tied. Zerna pushed ahead of him, climbed down the ladder, and got in under the wheel of the boat. X untied the painter, and as the motor started, sprang from the pier.

Zerna handled the speedy craft well, while X pretended to relax on the leather-upholstered seat beside her. Once away into midstream, Zerna pushed the throttle to the limit, and the boat seemed to skim along on the mist that pressed close to the surface of the water.

Zerna's green eyes seemed to possess catlike ability to see in darkness. She handled the boat with a recklessness born of desperation. But X knew that she was desperate, not because of any feeling for Betty Dale, but because she knew she was utterly alone with her worst enemy—Secret Agent X.

They had passed Fort Schuyler and had entered the deeper waters of the Sound. Zerna cut the speed of the craft somewhat and piped a shrill blast on the whistle. Her signal was immediately answered by a deeper note coming from near at hand. A little farther on, X made out the white, ghostly form of a steam yacht riding at anchor with a smaller gasoline cruiser in tow.

The right hand of Agent X had been busy in his pocket. He drew it out now as the steam yacht signaled again. Zerna's hand went out to touch the button that operated the electrical whistle of the launch, but the Agent's left hand darted forward and closed over her wrist. It seemed almost that he could feel her pulse jump as his fingers touched her.

"No," said X softly. And as he spoke, his right hand, holding a hypodermic syringe, joined its mate.

A frightened oath whispered across Zerna's lips as the needle entered her flesh. She struggled briefly against the hold the powerful narcotic was taking, then subsided in the Agent's arms.

X cut the ignition switch and allowed the boat to drift in the direction of the yacht. Then he climbed over the cockpit and slipped silently into the icy water.

Long, powerful strokes brought Agent X to the stern of the boat. He caught the rope that towed the gasoline cruiser and climbed hand over hand up the rail of the yacht. In another moment, he was moving along the dark deck, his water-soaked clothing making a tell-tale swishing sound.

A FLASHLIGHT cut a clean swath through the darkness and centered on the Agent's face. X staggered forward to fall, from pretended exhaustion, into a man's arms.

"Agent X!" X whispered hoarsely. "Is he here? He's impersonating me. He rounded up the gang some way, I think. I just escaped, swam out here to warn you guys."

A masked man came within the rays of the flashlight held in the hands of the man who was supporting X. "Yes," said the masked man quietly, "Agent X is here; right on deck, as a matter of fact. One of the crew picked out Zerna's launch with the searchlight. It's drifting at the stern. Zerna seems to be sleeping in it!"

X pulled quickly from the grasp of the man who had been supporting him. His hand started toward the pocket where his gas was concealed, but stopped halfway. In the dim light, black monstrous shapes loomed menacingly, surrounded the Agent with gleaming cylinders of the cold that killed.

"Don't move, Secret Agent X," said the masked man. "We prefer not to kill you at the present moment." The masked man came through the circle of hairy monsters, stepped boldly up to X and began to search his pockets. But his grasping fingers never reached the Agent's gas pistol.

X's left fist cracked up to the point of the masked face's chin, while his right snatched out his gas gun. It was a certainty that the cold-killers would not open up their deadly liquid gas as long as one of their own bosses would have shared the same fate as Agent X. As the masked man collapsed on the deck, the ring of hairy monsters closed in. Yet as long as X kept near the unconscious masked man, he knew that he was safe from the killing cold.

He fired the full charge of his gas pistol at the heads of those monster men. But, evidently, because they were amply protected against the effects of their own weapon, the Agent's anæsthetizing gas seemed to have little effect. It was a hand to hand scuffle from there on.

The hairy men tried to smash X's skull half a dozen times with hasty blows from the metal cylinders in their hands. But their weapons were too heavy to easily follow the weaving, bobbing form of Agent X as every one of his supple muscles was brought into play in swift, deft dodges and in lightning bolt punches that flattened two of the hairy forms on the deck before the fight was well started.

Suddenly, a door in the wall of the cabin opened. The blaze of unexpected light caused X to glance toward it. A hoarse, pained cry ripped from his throat as he saw within the cabin something that made him immediately unconscious of personal danger.

Lying on a bunk in the cabin, her clothes twisted and wrinkled from continual tossing, her golden hair disheveled and snarled, was Betty Dale. Muscles of her arms and legs twitched convulsively. Her lips moved, whispering, babbling about the nightmare-things that peopled a dope dream.

Instantly, the Agent's arms were pinned behind him by the furry monsters that had taken immediate advantage of his shock. Hands rifled his pockets, removed all his special devises and tossed them over the rail. A man stepped from the cabin where Betty Dale lay. He, too, wore a mask over his face.

"Miss Dale's future is not a particularly bright one," said the masked man. "Our dealings with dope have taught us that no matter how fine a character a woman may be before she acquires the habit, she eventually ends in the gutter. It is our hope that your affection is so great that you will not permit this thing to go farther."

THE heart of Agent X seemed encased in ice. Better far that they had killed Betty outright than that they should subject her to slow degradation of body and soul in this manner.

"Name your price," he said dully.

"Very well," said the man in the mask. "First of all, let me compliment you on discovering our secret communication method depending upon newsreels and Esler's map. The trap you designed for us was a failure only because of one tiny error; you made the mistake of supposing that Hamilton Esler was the only leader of our organization. Naturally, when we discovered that the newsreel had been altered, we suspected you of doing the tampering, because our *real* director had not changed the films.

"Our killers arrived at the warehouse long before your men. And under the threat of the killing cold, they surrendered—after our men had made an example of one of your men. Both the redheaded detective, and the big, square-shouldered man named Bates, are locked in the hold of this boat, together with their eleven living operatives. The presence of Bates told us that you were the man behind the trap, since we were already familiar with Bates because of our eavesdropping on the orders you gave him when you were in James Starbuck's apartment."

"Get to the point," said X.

"Very well. You and your men are to die. There is no alternative. But it is within your power to save Betty Dale from a life that is worse than death. You seem to be a man of great financial resources. You may purchase Betty Dale's life for a check made payable to Hamilton Esler in the amount of fifty thousand dollars. In addition, you will tell us where you have hidden Esler. Betty Dale will be liberated immediately when the check is paid. *But,* if you do not pay, I swear to drag her through every hell conceivable."

"I see," said X. "Nevertheless, I should like some time to think this over."

"Certainly," the masked man agreed. To the fur-clad men: "Lock him in the hold until he decides."

A MINUTE later, X found himself in a cramped little room in the hold of the boat, chained by the left wrist to the steel wall. Just outside the door of the room, one of the fur-clad killers was on guard.

A look at these black hairy monsters beneath electric light showed the Agent that they were men wearing fur suits, hoods, and masks which evidently protected them from the freezing death they dealt. A small opening at the bottom of the masks enabled them to speak, but could be immediately closed when they went to work with their gas. These masks not only protected their faces, but also their lungs. Too much oxygen, such as was rapidly liberated from the frigid, liquid air, was quite as harmful as too little; it was actually capable of burning up the lungs, if breathed in too great quantities.

X had not required time to think over the ultimatum he had been handed by the criminals. He would have gladly paid the price they asked to save Betty Dale. He had been simply stalling for time in hope of seeing some way to save Bates, Hobart and their companions as well.

No sooner had he found himself alone than his right hand pulled out his watch and snapped the gold chain attached to it. Then he put the watch behind him, pressed it against the wall, and opened the back of the case with his thumb nail. Though his watch was the size of an ordinary pocket watch, the actual movement was no larger than that of a lady's wrist watch. The rest of the room in the case was occupied by a coiled ribbon-saw of the finest steel.

With this keen tool in his possession, X went to work on the chain attached to his left wrist. The softer metal yielded quickly before the tiny teeth of the saw and twenty minutes later, he was free. He then dropped watch and saw on the floor and called to his guard.

The fur-clad men came into the room and approached X fearlessly, for the Agent held his left arm behind him as though it were still chained to the wall. Through the thick glass lenses in the man's mask, X saw his little black eyes, the pupils constricted to mere needle points. As he had expected, these servants of the gang were kept kill-crazy with liberal rations of dope. The man would make an excellent tool in the clever plan that was rapidly forming in X's brain.

"How much money would it take to buy you?" X asked. "Would a couple of grand fix things up so I could get away from here?"

The man laughed harshly through the mouth opening in the fur mask. "Don't act crazy! I know the guys I'm working for, see. They'd dope-starve me, see? I'd go nuts."

X had asked this question for but one purpose, to hear the man's voice. Suddenly he lunged forward from the wall. The fingers of his right hand were talons of steel, striking at the man's throat. At the same time his left arm swung around in a powerful haymaker, the single remaining iron link on his wrist catching the guard at the side of his fur-clad head. In spite of the protection his headgear offered, the guard dropped to the floor with scarcely a groan.

X dropped at the man's side, quickly found the fasteners that buckled the fur garment in place. He removed the suit, hood, mask and heavy, gauntlet gloves and laid them aside. Then he slipped out of the taxi driver's uniform that was part of his disguise as Esler, put on the fur suit and hood, and then dressed the unconscious guard in Esler's uniform.

Taking the makeup material from his own face was a task that required time and steady nerves, for he wanted to remove it and at the same time keep it as nearly intact as possible. For a moment, the light saw what no living person save Betty Dale had seen—the real face of Agent X, hidden, a moment later, by the fur mask that was part of the guard's uniform. Then, with infinite care, he replaced the plastic makeup material on the face of the guard, shaping it to conform with new facial contours.

The guard did not now resemble Hamilton Esler as closely as X had, but after all, that was not what X had tried to achieve. He wanted to be able to pass the guard off as Secret Agent X.

THE man already showed signs of reviving, and X braced him against the wall, held his head between his two hands, and stared steadily at the man's eyes. Never had the tremendous will-power of the Agent been called upon for a greater test of hypnotism.*

As the guard's eyes met those of X, the Agent repeated in a soft, compelling voice: "You are Agent X. You are Agent X. When anyone asks you who you are, you will tell them that you are Agent X. But you are also Elisha Pond because Agent X is Elisha Pond. When you sign a check you will sign it with the name Elisha Pond. Why?"

"Because," repeated the man mechanically, "I am Agent X. And when I sign a check, I sign it Elisha Pond."**

X smiled to himself. The plastic mind of the dope fiend was completely in his possession. As long as he remained in the same room with the man, he would be able to dictate his every action.

As soon as he was sure of his subject, X got to his feet, went to the door, where, in the voice of the guard, he shouted for help at the top of his lungs. As soon as he heard footsteps on the steel stairs leading down into the hold, he pivoted, went back to the guard, and lifted the helpless man in his arms—only to throw him down again as soon as he was certain that some one had entered the room behind him.

X turned around. Two men wearing black masks, several members of the crew, and three of the fur-clad cold-killers had crowded into the room. X pointed to the man on the floor. Through the opening in the

*AUTHOR'S NOTE: As has often been stated, Agent X is a master of hypnotism. Science tells us that drug addicts are excellent subjects for hypnosis because their habit greatly lowers their resistance to suggestion from a more powerful mind. The daring plan which X put into execution at this critical moment would not have been possible had his hypnotic subject not been a slave to drugs.

**AUTHOR'S NOTE: It is in the name of Elisha Pond that Agent X draws upon the huge fund of money placed at his disposal for use in his war against crime.

fur mask he wore, he said: "The devil tried a getaway, chief. Look, he had a saw in his watch. He cut clear through the chain and tried to rush me."

One of the masked men nodded his head. "He was just stalling for time. He'll make his decision at once." He pulled a check and fountain pen from his pocket. The check was made out for $50,000 and lacked only the signature. The masked man held the check out to the hypnotized guard. "Will you sign this?"

The guard's dopey eyes were glued on those of Agent X. "I will sign it," he said tonelessly. "I will sign it with the name Elisha Pond."

"Why?" demanded the masked man. "Elisha Pond is an old coot with plenty of dough, but you're Agent X."

"I am Agent X," repeated the guard. "But I sign checks Elisha Pond. Agent X is Elisha Pond."

"Sure," said the other masked man, "that makes sense. You wouldn't expect Agent X to sign his own name to a check would you? He'd be spotted by all the police in New York if he did. This Pond guy must be just one of the Agent's phoney names."

The other masked man was inclined to be skeptical. "Maybe you're right; but how come Agent X's voice sounds just like the voice of this guy?" And he indicated the real Agent X who masqueraded in the guard's fur uniform.

"Sure, boss, don't cha get it?" X hurriedly filled in. "X can talk like anybody. Wasn't he talkin' just like Esler when he came aboard?"

The masked man nodded. "You're right. What's the difference, just so he signs the check." He handed check and pen to the guard. The masked man would soon discover the difference if he ever had the opportunity of trying to cash that check. The handwriting in the signature would certainly not be that of Elisha Pond.

X slipped unnoticed from the room and hurried up to the cabin above, passing members of the crew unnoticed because of the fur garb he wore.

BETTY'S cabin door was a flimsy thing beneath the bucking shoulder of Agent X. As he rushed headlong into the cabin, the girl awoke suddenly from her drugged sleep, saw the Agent's fur-clad form, and opened her mouth to scream.

X clapped a furry glove over her mouth. "Betty!" he whispered tensely in the voice by which she knew him. And as recognition gleamed in the girl's eyes, his hand dropped from her mouth.

"You! Darling!" she fairly shouted. The drug had excited her to such an extent that she had lost all sense of restraint. She threw her arms about the Agent and sobbed hysterically.

"Betty, you must control yourself," he whispered and took hold of her shoulders and shook her. She stopped her laughing and crying, and stared at him with strange, wondering eyes. "Betty, there isn't a moment to lose. You must think straight!"

Betty's lips quivered as she complained: "Y—you're so cross!"

X shook his head sadly. The poor girl had lost all sense of proportion. "Listen, dear," and his voice became infinitely tender, "there's a motor boat drifting astern. There's an unconscious woman in it. I want you to get into that boat. I'll help you down to the water and you'll have to swim to it. Can you do that?"

Betty laughed. "With you I can do anything."

"No. I can't go with you. Bates and Hobart and the others are locked in the hold."

"I won't leave, then. You can't send me away, because I won't leave!" she all but screamed. And again came a fit of hysterical weeping.

There was nothing to do, X knew,

but take her into the hold with him. He quieted her, promising that she should go wherever he went. "But you must be quiet, do you understand?"

"Still as a mouse," she agreed, nestling her head on his shoulder.

X went to the door of the cabin and looked out. The deck was clear. He beckoned Betty to join him. Together they tiptoed toward the companionway leading down into the hold. The Agent's heart was in his mouth. At any moment Betty might do something impulsive that would spoil their every chance.

At the bottom of the steps, X could hear the masked men questioning the guard whom they evidently still believed to be Agent X. They were demanding that he tell them where Esler could be found. The hoax could not last for much longer. But still, the hold would be the last place they would look for AgentX.

X held Betty in his arms, keeping his gloved hand over her mouth to prevent her from uttering so much as a whisper as they stole past the door of the room where X had been confined. Then they were again in the friendly darkness, moving quietly along toward a yellow spark of light. They passed the door of the engine room. Then, directly ahead X saw that the light came from a globe screwed above a door. In front of that door, one of the fur-clad men mounted guard.

Still holding Betty tightly, X approached the guard. "The boss wants the girl down here with the others," he said.

The guard at the door asked no questions, but produced a key and fitted it into the lock. He swung the door open. X, standing directly behind the man, raised his left foot and planted a powerful kick in the small of the man's back, so that he sprawled head first into the room. And before the man could utter a cry, X landed directly on top of him, seized him by the throat, and choked him into silence.

X looked around the room. Harvey Bates, Jim Hobart and their eleven men were in the center of the room, lashed into a huge bundle around a wooden post that rose from the floor to the ceiling. X drew Betty into the room, closed the door, and set to work on the ropes and gags that held the men in motionless silence.

A THIRD masked man had joined the other two in the cabin where the criminals were impatiently questioning the man they supposed to be Secret Agent X. It was this man that X had knocked out almost as soon as he had boarded the yacht. He looked on a moment while his companions shook the supposed X by the shoulders and roared:

"You've not told us where to find Esler! Where's Esler?"

The dull-witted guard, still under the influence of the hypnotic trance, merely shook his head. "I am Agent X," he said. "I sign my name Elisha Pond."

The third masked man snarled an oath. "The man's crazy. How sure are you he's Agent X?"

He went over to the supposed X and gouged makeup material from the man's face.

"Why, you poor fools, he's tricked you. This is Jeris, one of our own men. Agent X has escaped, hell knows how!"

"Search the boat!" cried one. "Up on deck. He'll be with the girl." And they raced pell-mell for the companionway. On deck, they turned out the entire crew in a frantic search.

For five frantic minutes, they searched. Then the three masked men met at the stern of the boat. "Listen," one of them whispered, "the engineer says there isn't a guard down there where we had Bates and the others. Agent X and the girl must both be down in the hold, trying to get the others free. Our best move is to wipe out the whole group."

X darted for Zerna with the needle.

"That's the stuff," one of the others agreed. "Pump liquid air at 'em.

"Sure. Get down through the hatch at the stern. The one at the prow is locked, and the key's been lost for months. Bottle them up with the cold that kills."

DOWN in the hold, Agent X's deft fingers were flying, untying knots and pulling gags. Betty, too, worked with furious, dope-keyed energy. She gnawed at knots with her teeth, skinned her fingers on the coarse hemp.

"Not a word," X cautioned as he liberated Bates. "Everyone quiet. We're outnumbered by about three to one. You free the others, Bates." He turned to Betty. "Wait here. I'll be back in a moment. I'm just going to look out the door."

The Agent left the room and went back along the way he had come, but at the end of the companionway he stopped. There was a man on the steps—one of the fur-clad killers. Another man was passing down cylinders of deadly liquid gas.

It was impossible to mistake the purpose of the fur-clad killers. They held the vantage point that X had hoped to hold—the companionway. They had corked the one opening in the bottle.

X turned and ran quietly back to join the others. Not great need for quiet. All the gang members, and the crew, had been called out of the hold, which belonged to fourteen men and one woman—and death.

As soon as he gained the prison room, X called Hobart and Bates to the door.

"What are the chances?" Hobart asked eagerly.

The Agent shook his head slightly. "None, that way," he whispered.

"There's a stairway leading up to a hatch at the other end of the room where we were tied," Hobart told him.

"Locked," Bates clipped. "Don't think it's guarded."

"One of my men is an ex-burglar," Hobart said. "If we weren't so damned empty-handed—"

X interrupted: "Where is he?"

Hobart called one of his operatives over to the door, and X addressed the man:

"How long would it take you to noiselessly open that hatch, if you had tools?"

The man grinned. "Sort of out of practice at that sort of thing. I could do it in ten minutes before Mr. Hobart sort of reformed me."

"Come. There ought to be something in the engine room you can use."

X hurried the man back to the engine room, there to hurriedly pick up a center punch, cold chisel, hammer and pliers. X found a jar of matches and some oil-soaked waste. These he stuffed into his pockets. Then he picked up all the pipe wrenches he could see. Good weapons, too—these. . . .

Thus equipped, the Agent and the ex-burglar hurried back toward the room where they were to make their last stand against the doped killers. Even as they reached the door, they could hear shuffling footsteps coming along the passage behind them. X closed the door of the room. It locked only from the outside, but by main force they might be able to hold it for a while.

"Talk, everybody," X urged. "Move around and make a lot of noise. We've got to cover the sound of the man working on the lock of the other hatch. If the gang gets wise, it will be just as easy for them to attack us from that point also."

He went to the door and opened it just a crack, so that he could look out. One of the black-clad killers was in sight, saw the door open, and raised his deadly cylinder. A stream of the hissing, blue-white liquid slapped against the door. Only the fur suit the Agent wore protected him. Some of the liquid got in under the door, and the temperature of the room dropped degrees almost at once.

For a slow torturing death, the mob had only to turn their weapon on the door. Half of the danger of the stuff lay in the fact that it could make the air in the room too rich in oxygen, actually burning up tender lung cells.

"How much longer to break that lock?" X called huskily.

"Two minutes, that's all."

THE killers were massing outside the door. It would take just two seconds for them to break into the room, and less than thirty seconds to turn everyone in the room into frozen statues of horror.

X turned to Bates. "Promise me," he whispered, "to guard Betty Dale with your life."

"Of course. But what are you going to do, sir?"

"Never mind," X said sternly. "Protect that girl."

Secret Agent X reached into his pocket and took out the ball of oil-soaked cotton waste and the jar of matches. He had obtained these in the engine room, knowing that in a case of emergency one man could hold back the cold that killed, could destroy it—at a price. Agent X was ready to pay that price.

The liquid, oxygen gas was in itself uninflammable. But since all combustion depended upon the presence of oxygen, that combustion was much more rapid and intense when the surrounding space was saturated with oxygen. In his own laboratory, X had seen a heated piece of iron burst into white hot flames in the presence of a small quantity of liquid oxygen. He was ready to repeat that experiment tonight on a larger scale with human lives at stake.

He had only to carry the fire to the very origin of the freezing death to turn that portion of the ship's hold into a veritable blast furnace. It would cut off the criminal advance with a sheet of flame. It would rob the killing cold of its teeth by uniting the oxygen with combustible materials. And when the blast came—Agent X pushed the ugly thought from his mind.

Behind the furry mask, he smiled. Betty Dale, Hobart, Bates and the others would have their chance. That thought alone spurred him on to do what he must do.

CHAPTER XI

Invitation to Hell

BETTY DALE had seen Bates and the Agent talking near the door. As X took the ball of waste from his pocket, she came forward to join him. "What are you going to do?" she asked anxiously.

X did not look at the girl. He dared not to risk the pangs of a final good-bye. Instead, he answered her cheerfully: "I am going to plug up a little opening, that's all."

X raised his hand and closed the furry mouth-opening of his mask. Then he opened the door a crack. Outside, some twenty feet from the door, were half a dozen of the fur-clad killers. Each held a cylinder of freezing death in his gloved hands. Then, at a signal from their leader, they moved suddenly forward toward the door.

Agent X sprang out to meet them. His surprise appearance brought the line of killers at a momentary stop. But even as they released six solid streams of the blue-white, hissing stuff, X struck a match and lit the waste. Holding the flaming stuff at arm's length, he rushed headlong toward the killers and flung the burning waste into their very midst.

There was a dull roar, and white-hot flame rose in an all-consuming sheet from floor to ceiling.

Betty Dale screamed, sprang toward the door. But the strong hands of Harvey Bates seized her.

"Let me go!" she screamed. She turned, beat at Bates' chest with her small fists. Bates' arms were like bands of steel about her. He scarcely saw the desperate fury in her face as she struggled to throw herself into that white-hot inferno. Bates' eyes were dimmed. He was never to forget that heroic figure, silhouetted against that wall of flame.

Almost the first thing the blast had touched had been the fur-clad form of Agent X. Bates had seen that mighty figure flung backwards. He had seen the Agent's arms fly upwards to shield his eyes from the stunning brilliance of the fire. He had seen that figure lurch forward into the fire, a figure that was itself a wreathing mass of flame.

Had he been able to project his sight beyond the searing curtain of fire that blocked the criminal attack, he would have seen that same flaming figure, fighting its way toward the companionway, staggering up the steps to reach the deck rail. Then he would have seen a human meteor dive from the side of the boat to be immediately extinguished as the black water closed over it, leaving only a little cloud of steam to mark the spot where Agent X had disappeared.

A TRIUMPHANT shout from Jim Hobart: "The lock's broken. Come on! Up on deck. Grab a wrench, you. Let's move!"

Bates held the struggling, sobbing girl in his arms as he moved back toward the steps with the others.

"He'll be all right," he muttered in the girl's ear. But Bates could not lend the ring of conviction to his words.

He lifted the girl in his arms as they gained the deck. The flames had sought out the wood framework of the central portion of the cabin, and the surface of the water was tinged blood-red by the tongues of fire.

A group of criminals, taken entirely by surprise, came around the corner of the cabin. But they had scarcely time to draw their guns before Hobart's men were upon them, beating them to the deck with lusty blows from their pipe wrenches.

Vigilant patrol boats and other craft were looming out of the rose-tinted fog, coming to the aid of the burning vessel. Some of the criminals were deserting in a life boat. Others fought with Hobart's men for the possession of a second life boat. But Bates had all he could do to hold Betty Dale. Help was so near that before the fire on the yacht began to creep their way, they would all be safely away. It was escape that the courage and quick-thinking of a single man had provided. But at what a price!

Thinking only of Betty's safety, Bates carried the girl as far away from the actual fighting as possible. But as he reached the other corner of the cabin, a fear-mad killer almost bumped into him. The man had a gun. He raised it, laughed insanely. Instinctively, Bates threw Betty behind him.

A bullet from the mad killer's gun lanced through Bates' left arm. Bates' big right hand closed on the man's gun-wrist, and with a powerful twist, brought the man's right arm up almost to his shoulder blades in a hammer-lock hold that brought a shriek of agony from the killer. The man dropped his gun, slipped from Bates' grasp, and dived for the rail.

Bates never noticed whether that crazy killer went over the rail or not. He turned around. To his horror, he found that Betty was gone.

THE girl who loved Secret Agent X had taken the opportunity offered by the criminal's attack, to slip from behind Bates' shielding body. Free from his protection, she had run swiftly down the deck, past the blazing cabin, and to the other end of the boat. She had but one objective—get to Agent X.

Golden hair flying, eyesight blurred from clouds of smoke through which she had passed, Betty seized the arm of the first man she met.

"Where is he?" she gasped out. "I must find Agent X. Where is he?"

The man laughed harshly as he tore out of her grasp. "Gone to hell, where the rest of us will go, if we don't get off this damned tub. He dived over the rail in a mass of flames, sister. I'd look for a new man if I were you!"

Blindly, her hands found the rail. She stared fixedly at the flame-tinged water. She blinked back tears to see three shadowy forms drop one at a time into the gasoline cruiser tied to the stern. A flare of ruddy light found the face of one of the men. That face was covered by a black mask.

Not far from the cruiser, Zerna's small launch drifted. Betty looked from the cruiser to the launch. Her two fists clenched. In her slim body a new strength was born. She would carry on the great work that *he* had been unable to finish. . . .

In the forty-foot cruiser, one of the three masked men untied the rope that connected the smaller boat to the yacht. Another tinkered with the engine.

"It couldn't have ended better," said the third man. "We can make a clean getaway. We have realized nearly a million dollars in the racket."

"We needn't quit," said the man in the prow as he cast off from the yacht. "I have some of the best blackmail pictures in the lot right here in my pocket." He took a leather case from the inside of his pocket, patted it affectionately, and returned it to his pocket.

The engine popped, broke into a steady murmur. One of the masked men took the wheel, reversed the screen, and backed the cruiser away from the burning yacht. Then he turned the prow of the boat due east across the Sound. They had not gone a hundred feet before they sighted a motor launch coming straight toward them.

"It's Zerna," said one of the men. "She's following us."

"Take her aboard," replied one of the others. "After all, she's been on the level with us."

The man at the wheel cut down on the throttle a little. "It looks as though she were trying to ram us. No, she switched off the motor. She's going to bump. Stand by to give her a hand."

A small anchor at the end of a line was flung from the launch to land in the cockpit of the cruiser. The masked man who was leaning forward to steady Zerna's boat, muttered an oath. "Zerna didn't throw that anchor. Zerna's doubled over in the cockpit. Looks like another woman."

They saw the woman beside Zerna stand upright, step to the edge of the cockpit, and spring to the deck of the cruiser.

"Look out!" cried one of the men. "She's got a gun."

"Put up your hands, gentlemen," said Betty Dale, her voice as steady as Zerna's gun in her hand. "Agent X taught me to shoot straight."

Three pairs of hands stretched above three masked faces. Betty nodded her approval. "Move just a little closer together, please, so that I will have less trouble shooting you if it comes to that. I am going to signal the police."

But Betty was watching their hands, when she should have been watching the feet of the man to her left. He braced the sole of his shoe against the anchor Betty had tossed aboard. With a suddenness that took the girl completely by surprise, he sent the anchor sliding across the deck. Betty saw it coming, tried to jump aside, tangled with the rope attached to the anchor, and fell to the deck.

They were upon her in a moment. Cruel hands wrested the gun from her. Cruel fingers shackled her wrists together. A hand clamped over her mouth.

"Now, Betty Dale," one of the masked men whispered, "you wanted to be with Agent X. You'll get your chance! Get that anchor and rope, one of you fellows. The girl goes over the rail, see?"

ANOTHER masked man reached for the rope and started to pull it over the rail into the cruiser. It seemed to be stuck on something. The man went to the edge of the deck, knelt to untangle the rope. But for two ticks of a watch he was unable to move.

Sticking out of the water, clinging to the rope that reached from Zerna's launch to the cruiser, was a black, withered-looking hand. Then a black, gleaming, goggle-eyed head bobbed to the surface.

The man at the rail uttered an alarmed oath, tried to scramble backwards from the rail and at the same time drew his gun. But the black monster from the water jerked itself to their deck and rolled into the masked man. There was a frantic tangling of arms and legs. The masked man raised his gun toward the monster's black head. But instantly that withered-looking hand clamped over the man's wrist and turned the muzzle of the gun skyward.

The black talon of the monster from the water wrested the weapon free. His grotesque head turned slightly. His goggling eyes saw the other two masked men forcing Betty Dale back toward the rail. The monster raised the gun, fired once.

The single shot clipped one of the masked men in the leg. He tumbled to the deck. The other released the girl and stepped back toward the tiny cabin of the cruiser.

Betty Dale, from where she crouched near the rail, watched the dripping, grotesque figure herd the three masked men into the cabin of the cruiser and follow them to the hatch. The girl got to her feet and came timidly toward the strange man who had saved her. What if *he* had not died?

A police-boat siren wailed, and the bright beam of its searchlight slit the blackness.

"Cruiser ahoy!" came the cry from the patrol boat. "What's going on there?"

The strange man with the gun turned his head and called back: "This is Detective Sergeant Keegan of the Homicide Office. Come alongside!"

Betty's arm, half-raised to touch the man in the strange garb, dropped limply to her side. She backed to the stern as the police cruiser swept along side. As Keegan entered the cabin, he called out to the men getting from the patrol boat:

"Get that girl out of that launch this cruiser is towing. It's Zerna, the dope peddler. Some of you come in here while I talk with these mugs. Miss Dale, you stick around for a story."

KEEGAN stepped to where the three masked men were backed against the wall. Silently he frisked them. He produced the flat leather case from the pocket of one of the men and flipped it open. He nodded his hooded head. "This is good evidence of the blackmail racket, Mr. Gordon Stien!"

The masked man thus addressed shrank back against the wall. Keegan reached out his gloved hand and pulled aside the mask that had covered Stien's pop-eyed, chubby face.

"Just as Esler handled the field work of the gang," he said, "Stien snapped indecent pictures of the doped victims with hidden cameras set up at Zerna's dope parties." Keegan handed the folder of pictures to one of the cops from the boat. "Give those to Burks."

His goggle-covered eyes turned on Stien. "The other night at Zerna's party, you were to be killed because Miss Dale had pointed you out as Agent X. Actually, this was not only an opportunity for you to alibi yourself, but also you knew that Agent X would never stand by and see an innocent man suffer for his own deeds. By appealing to his human qualities, you hoped to force X to reveal himself. The gas cylinder which was to be used for your 'execution', contained nothing but water. You were taking no chances. Agent X discovered that and understood at once that you were associated with the gang. It was you, Stien, who were responsible for Betty Dale's capture by the dope gang, for she trusted you. She was later drugged in an effort to extort money from Agent X."

"But who are the other two birds?" asked a patrolman.

"One at a time," was the reply. "The man next to Stien is Dr. Samuel Wicker. Just pull off the mask, won't you?"

The patrolman jerked off the mask of the second of the two villains. Dr. Wicker's jowls wobbled with wrath. "A damned lie!" he roared.

"The lying was on your side, Wicker. You pretended to cure dope addicts while you actually supplied the gang with drugs from your own pharmacy. Dope legitimately supplied to the Wicker Sanitarium for the tapering-off type of dope cure, was resold to the addicts who were victims of this gang's scheming.

"We now have three points to a compass, do you see? Esler might represent the east; Stien, the south; Wicker, the west. I really believe that they got their idea for their clever method of communicating from the

SAX

fact that their own initials could be found at the four points of the compass. Esler did the field work, Stien was chief blackmailer, and Wicker supplied the dope. But there had to be a head man. Behind that remaining mask, you will find the handsome visage of Mr. Walter Nixon!"

Nixon jerked off his own mask. His small black mustache was bristling. "All right. Let's hear some more of that wild tale, Sergeant Keegan. And you might explain why you're wearing that crazy garb!"

"Later, perhaps. Mr. Nixon was not a difficult person to spot. He has a strange peculiarity. Whenever a flashlight picture is taken, he twitches his shoulders as though some one had lammed him across the back. The other night, when Secret Agent X saw Nixon trying to enter the film distributing office, he tossed a simple flash bomb in Nixon's direction. Though he did not see Nixon's face, X noticed that peculiar twitching of the shoulders as Nixon ran down the alley.

"Then again, it was Nixon who kept thinking one jump ahead of Agent X. When Agent X made alterations in the news films in order to attempt to direct the gang into a trap, Nixon got wise almost at once. Why? Simply because Nixon himself was the man who altered those films, and he knew there was trickery somewhere. Again, when Agent X was impersonating Inspector Burks, and questioning Mr. Colrich in Nixon's office, Nixon was the only one who could have overheard what Colrich said about Starbuck having led Mrs. Colrich astray. A moment later, when he picked up a phone call from the real Inspector Burks, he knew the Burks in his office was Agent X and that X's next logical step would be to go to Starbuck and question him in regard to Mrs. Colrich's murder.

"So Nixon had the wires to Starbuck's apartment tapped, sent Zerna to do spy duty. When Agent X impersonated Starbuck, the whole gang was all set to kill Agent X."

Nixon sneered. "That's very clever, but how is it that you know all this?"

"Agent X told me this before he died."

"That's a lie!" Nixon whipped out. He pointed a finger at the accusing figure in front of him. "I'll tell you how he knows all that. He's Secret Agent X. That garb he's wearing is one of the cold protection suits our men wore—" Nixon stopped, turned deathly pale. "I mean. I—I—"

"Yeah," said one of the cops, "we get exactly what you mean. You've just let yourself in for the chair and dragged your buddies right along with you. Every cop in the city knows that Mrs. Colrich and Steve Wyer were killed with liquid air. Now, you've just admitted the job. Maybe this guy is Agent X. We'll take him up if he is, but that isn't going to help you any, Nixon. If this guy is Agent X, he's done a sweet job of rounding up a mob of worse than murderers." The cop turned to his men. "Handcuffs for three. No, make it four. Agent X, after a job like that, I don't care about taking you in, but duty is duty."

NEAR the door, Betty Dale was quivering like a leaf. Was there a chance that this strange man, who wore one of the cold-killer's fur garments with the hair singed off, was really Agent X? Could he have gotten through that wall of flame, even though that protecting garment was on fire, and plunged into the Sound?

Keegan's harsh voice laughed at them all. "Don't be nuts! Agent X is dead. I saw him burned. He just gave me the information, that's all."

Nixon gesticulated wildly with his handcuffed hands. "Take off that hood. You'll see! He's got his face covered with that mask to hide it. All his makeup material is gone. I threw it into the Sound myself together with his weapons."

Hoping against hope, Betty Dale

crowded her way into the group of police surrounding the man in the black garb and his three captives. The officer in charge of the patrol boat reached out and unfastened the black leather hood of the man who insisted he was Sergeant Keegan. Then he pulled off the leather mask with its thick-lensed goggles. Betty uttered a pitiful little scream and buried her face in her hands.

Sure enough, behind the mask was the face of Detective Sergeant Keegan.

Keegan grinned triumphantly at the men about him. He gestured at the three captives. "The arrest was made on your territory," he told the cop. "You're responsible for delivering them safely, together with the evidence. They're dangerous. When a dope addict got to the point where he or she was of no further service to the gang, that addict was disposed of. That was why they killed Ruth Colrich. Of course, Steve Wyer was killed because he was muscling-in on the blackmail racket by sticking Colrich on the grounds of theartening to reveal Mrs. Colrich's vice."

Keegan started back on deck, stopped in the doorway, and added: "If you see Burks before I do, tell him I'll deliver Mr. Esler, the fourth member of the gang tomorrow morning. I'm a little tired, and I'm sure Miss Dale is. Maybe, if she'll let me take her back in Zerna's launch, I can give her more details about the story she'll write for the paper."

"Thanks," Betty husked. "You're very kind." She allowed the detective to lead her to the deck where the unconscious Zerna was stretched out. Keegan pulled Zerna's launch near the cruiser and helped the girl in. Then he cast off and started the motor.

Betty sat silently in the cockpit beside him, looking steadily at the cruel, black water. She felt Sergeant Keegan's arm drop about her shoulder. "Please don't," she said huskily. But the arm remained just where it was, pressing her a little closer. She heard Keegan's voice talking, but she didn't look at him. He was saying:

"It was cruel, wasn't it, to stand there and talk about Agent X's death."

"You—you knew then?"

"I've known for a long time what Agent X thought of you, Betty. That's why I said it was cruel to stand there and talk about his death. I couldn't help it. You understand, don't you? Or have you forgotten that, in a little compartment in the heel of his shoe, Secret Agent X always carries a tiny tube of makeup material big enough for an emergency disguise?

"Agent X didn't die, Betty. The fire couldn't quite burn through that suit of fur before he struck the water. And Agent X is quite a swimmer. He clung to the side of the cruiser long enough to remove that little tube of makeup from the compartment in his heel. Then he did a quick, but quite convincing, job of making himself look like Keegan."

"Oh, darling—" And if Betty had anything else to say, the words were lost in joyous sobs as she clung close.

The lips of Agent X were very close to her ear whispering: "Agent X couldn't die, knowing that you were waiting for him, dear. . . ."

In the prow of one of the patrol boats that had picked up the doped killers of the criminal crew, as well as the operatives of Agent X, Harvey Bates stood looking out across the water. The burning yacht cast ruddy reflections upon the water. Police searchlights created strange, gargantuan shadows. He was listening intently, and there was a tight feeling in his throat as he heard a weird, eerie whistle from somewhere in the darkness.

"Thank heaven!" Bates choked out. For he knew that whistle could have come from the lips of but one person. It was the mysterious musical signature of the mysterious Secret Agent himself.

Justice Borrows Bullets

By

Roger Torrey

The tragic, cowardly finish of his pal's career, and the spirit of a small boy who might some day meet a like fate, lashed Special Agent John Archer on to follow a microscope hunch that could earn him a fool's name or death—or both.

JOHN ARCHER had left a growing law practice to join the Federal Bureau of Investigation, solely because he'd thought there'd be excitement in that branch of the government service. He'd found very little. He was young, only twenty-seven, and lusty and full-blooded; and he had the young lusty man's conviction that definite and decided action would solve all trouble. He argued to Evan Dykes:

"We're going at this wrong, Evan. The thing to do is force a show-down and stamp them out. While we spend time checking their books, kids are going hungry."

Dykes was directly opposite to Archer in every respect, save that of working for the same government service. He was fifty-six, twice and ten years as old. He was thin, pale, white-headed. He was a former accountant and had all that profession's respect for the exact truth, in either figures or fact. He shook his head, said:

"You're wrong, John. You're very wrong. You're a lawyer; you know we haven't proof that'll stand up in court."

Archer said stubbornly: "Milk in this town used to be ten cents a bottle; it's fourteen, now. We know the producers get no more for it. We know the storekeepers make no more profit on sales. The jobber is taking the difference. It's a racket. Heber's books show big payments to cash. Put on the screws, and make him say to whom. I'm willing to bet they're made to Mike Tovar; he's got a finger in every other racket in town."

"We can't prove that, John."

"We can stick him for income-tax evasion."

"But we're working on this milk racket."

They argued about it until they came opposite their hotel, where they stepped from the walk, Dykes in the lead. Archer looked up to the right, saw two cars coming but still a safe distance away. Dykes apparently didn't think so because he halted, turned his head to speak.

Then Archer saw the second of the two cars pick up speed and swing out to pass the first. He heard the whine of gears as the driver shifted into second for more pick up, saw the car surge ahead and swing out and toward them.

He cried out, jumped ahead in an attempt to clutch Dykes, who twisted his head at the same time and saw the car come surging at him. He jumped back, but not in time.

Even in that instant of flashing action, Archer knew it was no accident. While he hadn't been watching the car particularly, he had the impression that it had been parked just beyond their hotel. He got a glimpse of the license plate as the car sped away. Then he ran to Dykes.

THE sedan had struck and whirled the white-headed man in such fashion that he'd fallen under the car. One of the rear wheels had passed over his legs, and from the twisted way he was lying, Archer knew they were both broken. He'd fallen to the pavement with tremendous force, because, even over the hiss of screaming tire rubber, Archer had heard the thud he'd made. He was unconscious now, with blood streaming from his nose and mouth, and from one lacerated cheek.

Archer heard a traffic policeman's whistle shrill out, and heard the man come pounding up as he lifted Dykes to the curbing. The policeman said:

"The dirty rats! Hit and run!"

Archer didn't turn his head. He was straightening Dykes' twisted legs, holding Dykes' broken and bleeding head clear of the pavement. He said:

"Call an ambulance! Quick!"

"I got that license number, bud!"

"So did I. Call an ambulance!"

The policeman lumbered away toward a call-box, and Archer held Dykes while a crowd gathered. Then the policeman came back, said, "They're on their way," and cleared the crowd from the still unconscious man. He said to Archer: "Is he your father, bud?"

"A friend—the best I've got."

"That's tough, bud—that's tough."

Archer said: "It's going to be tough for somebody. That driver went twenty feet out of his way to hit him."

The license number of the hit-and-run car was 5-D4-587, and Archer noted this down while he rode the ambulance to the hospital. He watched them carry Dykes to the operating room, then went to the phone and called the police station. He got Joe Denny, Bunco Squad Captain, gave him the license number and said:

"Check it, will you, captain. The car's a small sedan, if that helps. And keep it quiet."

Denny said he'd do this, asked: "How's Dykes?"

"If he isn't hurt internally the doctor thinks he'll live. He's got a fractured skull but not too bad. One leg's going to have to be taken off. It's crushed too badly to do anything else with."

He heard Denny whistle softly, then Denny said: "If they catch that hit-and-runner, he'll get life."

Archer said: "He should get the chair. It was deliberate."

He waited four hours before he could see Dykes—four hours of torturing thoughts of the year he and Dykes had worked together, of Dykes' unfailing kindnesses and help, of Dykes' loyalty and burden-taking ways, of his almost fatherly counsel. He finally saw him, just before they took off the crushed leg, and Dykes managed to smile a little and whisper:

"I *thought* you'd be around to see the old man, John."

Archer had difficulty in saying, "You'll be a new man, Evan, when they get through with you," because he wanted this to sound bright and cheerful—and couldn't. He very apparently failed, because Dykes muttered:

"You don't mean a *new* man, John. You mean *half* a man. Keep on with those books—the answer's there in those cash payments."

Archer said he would.

Dykes warned weakly: "Work slow, John. Keep away from Mike Tovar until you've got proof. You're alone on this, unless they send somebody to give you a hand. Work slow, and play safe. They mean business."

Archer watched them wheel him away toward the operating table—and the loss of one leg—and decided Dykes was right about the milk profiteers meaning business. And he thought of Dykes, still worrying about the job at hand, and decided to mean business himself. He had gone with the F.B.I. because of a love of honest excitement and an equally honest hatred of crooks. Working for the Government had been an impersonal sort of thing, for a while, but this feeling had gradually changed.

The personal feeling had been creeping in since Archer had started this case. First it was children being robbed of life-giving milk. Seeing Dykes, his friend and partner, deliberately run down and maimed was the final thing needed to make Archer run amuck—but with his head controlling the running....

JOE DENNY was still checking on the hit-and-run car when Archer went into his office. He said:

"That's tough about Evan Dykes, Archer. Anything I can do?"

Archer said it was all being done. Denny looked at his tight, hard-drawn face, his tight, hard-bitten lips, and said:

"And I take it you'll do what's needed. I'm having that car checked now." He broke off as a clerk came in the room and handed him a slip of paper, then said:

"Here it is now—a Hurz sedan. License is 5-D4-587. Registered to William Heber. That's Heber, who runs the Dairy Products Incorporated. His place is on Front Street."

Archer said: "You should tell me. We've been checking his books, captain. We were coming from there to the hotel, when it happened."

Denny looked curious. "How'd you get at his books? Find anything?"

"We're supposed to be checking his income-tax reports. There've been a lot of big cash payments made that don't look right. Heber's been acting nervous about us, too. It ties up, all right."

Denny said thoughtfully: "Heber's supposed to be square. I don't know. I know you fellows are checking this milk racket, and I'm glad of it. We can't do anything, unless there's a complaint made. You can. If we can help, we will. You know that."

Archer leaned over the desk, said: "I'm going out after Heber, now. When I get him, I'm going to charge him with attempted murder and try to break him on the racket payoff at the same time. You know the local people—and I'll ask favors if I need them."

Denny said he'd be glad to help in any way, and added: "I don't know about the attempted murder charge. A hit-and-run driver isn't planning murder, when he does it."

Archer said grimly: "*This* one was. It'll be a first-degree charge, if Dykes dies. If not, it'll be attempted murder."

Denny said: "You know best. They're supposed to teach you things like that, I understand."

"They do," Archer told him. "I'm going out and grab Heber before he knows about us tracing his car."

HEBER'S home was a fair-sized, comfortable house, set in a respectable but far from wealthy neighborhood. The yard was big, well-kept, but didn't have the spick and span effect a hired gardener gives to a place.

Two boys, tinkering with a bicycle on the front porch, looked up as Archer came up the walk, and one of them volunteered:

"Just ring the bell, mister. Mom's inside."

Archer did this, asked: "Your dad home yet?"

The boy said his dad wasn't, and then the door opened, and Archer faced a buxom, matronly woman, who looked as though she'd be at home in a farm kitchen. He started to speak, but the woman turned and called:

"Marian! It's Mr. Sproat!"

Archer said: "I beg your pardon, but my name is Archer. Is Mr. Heber expected soon?"

The lady said: "At any time. I'm *Mrs.* Heber." Then she laughed, as though she and Archer shared a joke, and confided: "I thought you were my daughter Marian's friend. She's been expecting him. Won't you come in and wait for Mr. Heber?"

Archer said he would and followed her into a comfortable, though worn hall, and from there into an equally worn parlor. Mrs. Heber and the house reminded him of his own mother and the mid-west farmhouse in which he had grown to manhood. He said:

"I'm sorry to intrude, but it's necessary that I see Mr. Heber at once."

Mrs. Heber said her husband was always home between five and six, and then to a girl who came hurrying into the room:

"I'm sorry, Marian! It was Mr. Archer, here, wanting to see your father. It wasn't Mr. Sproat, after all. This is my daughter Marian, Mr. Archer."

Archer said he was very glad to meet Miss Marian and meant it—and felt sick at the errand that had brought him to the house. He liked Mrs. Heber and thought that "like" was too weak a word for what he could feel for Marian. She was small and he liked small girls.

She wore little makeup, and he didn't care much for painted cheeks. She was dark, with big blue eyes, and Archer admired honesty more than any single thing in the world. Altogether, he thought Miss Marian quite a girl. She said:

"I'm sure dad will be home right away, Mr. Archer."

Archer talked vaguely about the weather and was suddenly conscious of a slight bristle on his cheeks and that his shoes were dull instead of glossy. The bell rang, and the girl left the room to answer it, and Mrs. Heber said comfortably:

"I declare, since we've moved to town, that bell's worn out by young men ringing to see Marian. First it's one and then another. Why—"

She broke off as Marian brought a tall, thin-faced man into the room, and said:

"Mother, this is Mr. Sproat. Mr. Archer; Mr. Sproat."

Archer shook hands with Sproat and decided he didn't like him and never would. He didn't like smooth and soft young men, and Sproat was both. And he got a curious impression of Sproat at the same time. Sproat seemed to be watching him and studying him—and Archer felt as though Sproat knew his errand there. Then the man proved this by saying:

"Rather an odd way to make an arrest, isn't it, Mr. Archer?"

Sproat's voice was so smooth and silky that for a moment Archer didn't realize what had been said. Then he flushed as Sproat turned to the girl and said:

"I'm sorry, Marian, but your father's in trouble. He had an accident with his car, and this man is here to arrest him."

The girl faced Archer, head up, and demanded: "Is this true?"

Archer said nothing for a moment, and Mrs. Heber said: "I can't believe it. If it was an accident, why should Will be arrested?"

Sproat said: "I'm afraid he was excited. The police will call it hit-and-run driving because he didn't stop at the time."

"Is this true?" the girl asked again.

Archer said miserably: "I'm afraid it is. These things happen."

He walked toward the door, said: "I'm sorry about it. Believe me, really I am."

She taunted: "And I thought you were a *friend* of Dad's!"

THE boy with the bicycle was still on the porch, but was alone. He looked up as Archer came out the door, said:

"Will you give me a lift on this, mister? I got to have somebody hold this chain while I tighten the sprocket." He pointed at the bicycle, and Archer bent to help him.

Then the girl said icily, from behind him: "That will do, Tommy. Let Mr. Archer go."

Archer straightened and went down the walk, leaving the staring Tommy. He called Denny, the Bunco Squad Captain, from a corner drug store, said:

"Heber's not home yet, and I can't wait for him. Will you send out a couple of men and stake the house for me? You might put out a general order to pick him up on sight."

Joe Denny said he would, then: "Where you going to be? When we get hold of him, you'll want to be called, won't you?"

Archer said: "I've got something to do, but I'll be at my hotel after that. Call me there if there's news."

Denny said he understood, and Archer called a cab.

The books they had been checking in Heber's store suddenly loomed in importance. After all, Dykes had said the answer was there, and Archer thought Dykes might be right. He would take time to procure; knew that in that time the books might be altered or missing. So he decided to take a short-cut, though he knew Dykes would not approve of this.

The cab let him out on Front Street, at the corner where Heber's dairy and food store was located. Archer paid the driver, told him not to wait, and watched the cab roll away. He saw another car parked a few feet down the street, decided this meant nothing, and turned into the entry of the store. When he tried the door, he knew something was wrong.

It was open, standing slightly ajar, and Archer remembered Dykes telling him that Heber had watchman service to guard against a thing like that happening. He drew the gun from under his arm, took the vest-pocket flash he always carried, and stepped inside.

He flashed the torch; heard a hurried scramble, and his light picked a man running toward the back. He raced after this man, shouting:

"Stop, you!" and as he did, another man shot at him from the side of the store. He flinched from the crashing report and dropped his light. The same man shot again, and he fired in return. He heard more noise from the back of the store, heard men run out from that direction, and then saw a side door open to show a patch of gray against the dead blackness.

Archer shot twice at the figures huddling through the door, then raced to the door after them in time to see a sedan start down the street, with two men hanging on the running board. The sedan's lights flashed on, showing the license plate, and he saw the sedan was Heber's; that the license number was 5-D4-587, then saw a uniformed policeman running up the walk toward the car.

The car pulled past the policeman, and one of the men on the running board leaned away from the car and fired directly at him. The policeman turned and ran into the wall by him, and Archer, aiming carefully, fired the remaining three shells in his gun at the disappearing car, then ran to the policeman.

The cop looked up at him, groaned, then said: "What's it all about?"

Archer thought he knew the answer, but didn't tell the man. Instead he asked:

"Where you hit?"

"In the leg—high up."

"Where's the nearest call-box?"

"Half a block that way."

The policeman pointed the direction, twisted his wounded leg in the effort, and groaned again, and fainted. Archer ran toward the call-box, deciding that Heber's books were as important as Dykes thought they were. And then he waited for the ambulance and police cars to come—and had one of the last carry Heber's books to his hotel.

MIKE TOVAR was an easy man to find, but a hard man to see. He lived in a neighborhood that didn't want him, but was afraid to say it didn't; lived in a house that looked like a motion-picture parody of a gangster's castle. And Mike could well have played the gangster part in the picture.

He was big, broad, burly. Hair grew low on his forehead and high on his cheeks, and his little pig-eyes were sunk in rolls of fat.

Archer, following an armed guard into the room, found him with his big frame sunk in a chair that seemed too small to hold him. He looked up, said in a voice that tried to sound friendly:

"Hi, man! What's on your mind? Sit down."

Archer didn't accept the invitation. He turned, looked at the man who'd admitted him, and Tovar took the hint and said:

"Okay, Jack. If this guy wants to take me out of here, I'd go. He's got the law back of him, I hear."

Jack, the guard, went away. Archer said: "So you know who I am?"

Tovar admitted readily: "Sure! You're one of these tax guys who go around saying people ain't paid enough. You was lined before you was in town an hour."

"Little scared of this tax business, aren't you, Mike?"

"Hell, no!" Tovar said. He tried to make this convincing, but his eyes showed worry. "I got lawyers and bookkeepers to figure it out for me. They know their stuff."

"You paid none last year."

Tovar muttered something about bad investments.

Archer said: "Of course, you list all the money you *do* make, Mike."

Tovar said his bookkeepers did, and looked more than a little worried. Then Archer said:

"Okay! What's this money Heber's been paying you listed under. Tell me *that* one."

He was watching Tovar's eyes when he asked this, and it seemed to him that some of the worry faded with the question.

Tovar laughed, said: "So that's it, huh? Well, see here—I had a few trucks left over from the old days; trucks made to haul—uh—well, say milk. You get it? I sold 'em to Heber, and he's been paying for 'em. That's all."

"In cash?"

Tovar looked puzzled. "Hell, no—check, of course. I got a record of them in my books."

"You ever around Heber's store?"

"Well—uh— Say, what the hell *is* this?"

Archer said evenly: "It's this, Tovar! Heber ran into my partner today and almost killed him. We're looking for him now. There's been a robbery at Heber's store this evening—after that—and I'm checking up."

Tovar said: "I get it! Listen—I been down there, of course—seeing Heber about the truck payments. But I wasn't there tonight, and I can prove it."

Archer said, "You may have to," and started for the door. Tovar got up, went over and stopped him just as he got there, however. Tovar then leaned close said:

"Now get this; I don't monkey with stuff the man with the whiskers says I shouldn't monkey with. Get that? No federal man's got a thing on me—and won't *get* a thing on me. That plain?"

Archer said, in the same even tone: "I could take that as a threat. Is that what you mean?"

Tovar's face reddened. "Take it the way you want to. I mean, I won't be framed."

Archer tapped the big man on the chest with one stiff forefinger. He said: "Now, *you* get this. We don't frame a man; we don't have to frame a man. And if we get something on him, we take him. Is *that* plain?"

He turned then and walked out, leaving Tovar staring after him.

THE telephone awakened him, just as it turned daylight. He fumbled for it, grumbled, "Yeah—Archer speaking," and heard in return:

"Joe Denny at the station. We've found your man Heber."

Archer came wide awake in that second. He said: "I'll be down—right away. Hold him."

"Don't hurry," Denny said dryly. "He'll stay here."

"What d'ya mean by that?"

"He was found in the car he hit Dykes with, out along the Middle Road—off the road and against a tree. His car's wrecked completely."

"What about him?"

Denny said: "Well, he's not smashed so bad we can't tell who he is, but that's about all I can say. The crash happened about three, and the medical examiner says death was instantaneous."

Archer put the phone down slowly. In a way, the news was what he'd wanted to hear—the man who had maimed Evan Dykes had paid for it in one sense. Killed by the same instrument he'd used to make Dykes a helpless cripple for the rest of his life. Archer rather liked this idea, but the thought of Heber's family—of Marian, of Mrs. Heber, of the boy with the bicycle—took away this sense of justice rendered. It wasn't their fault, and he knew the burden of grief would fall on them. He dressed, half hoping the identification would be at fault and that the man in the wrecked car wouldn't be Heber . . . .

The Medical Examiner was small, brisk, paunchy. He rubbed his hands briskly together, studied the card Archer showed him, then said:

"Well, a Government man! We hear much about them, but rarely see them."

Archer said: "We keep out of sight—most of the time. What killed Heber?"

The M. E. said briskly: "Fractured skull and crushed torso—instantaneous. The skull structure was broken in badly. And here's something odd."

He led Archer to a morgue slab, pulled back a covering sheet to show the body of a middle-aged man, and said:

"I can assure you this business of mine is full of surprises. Look at this."

He pointed, explained: "The wrists are lacerated. Neither hand is injured in the slightest, but look at those wrists."

Archer looked and saw lacerated flesh on both the dead Heber's wrists. He was still dressed, though his coat and shirt had been cut away from his chest, and Archer saw where blood had stained the shirt cuffs. In addition they were dirty, discolored. He said slowly:

"I suppose you have a microscope?"

"Naturally I have—one of the best. I use it in post-mortem work."

He brought a complicated brass affair over, said with pride: "If you'll tell me what it is you want to know, I'd be glad to assist you. Microscopic study is rather a technical thing."

Archer stated dryly: "That's one of the things they taught us in school, doctor. Thank you just the same."

He scraped at the dead man's sleeve, put this scraping on a slide, and did the same with one of the dead man's wrists. He studied both these slides through the scope, carefully, then stepped aside and asked:

"What do you make of this, doctor?"

The medical examiner peered, said: "Why, sir, I'd call it fibre of some kind. Rather coarse fibre, I'd say."

Archer smiled grimly and said: "I'd call it the same. Thanks."

He walked toward the door, and the pursy little doctor called after him: "And—yes, I'd say it was very dirty fibre as well."

Archer nodded agreement and kept on going. He had to see Joe Denny, and he wanted him in a hurry.

THE government man found Denny in the bunco-detail room, feet propped on a desk, and snoring loudly. He shook him and Denny woke up, peered at him and grumbled:

"I been up all night. Thought I'd take a nap for myself."

Archer said: "When you put that call out to pick up Heber, how was it done?"

"The regular way." Denny looked surprised. "When you called in and wanted his house staked, I put it out to the radio cars and over the station system. One of the boys in the radio cars saw the wreck along the road and called in. Just routine."

Archer said: "Thanks, captain. I'll tell his folks, or have them told."

Denny looked relieved and said he didn't envy any one that job.

Archer said: "It's got to be done, and it might as well be done now. They'll be over it that much sooner."

"How's poor Dykes getting along?"

"As well as can be expected. He's going to feel a lot better when I tell him this thing is cleared up."

Denny yawned, said, "Well, you got the guy that hit him, anyway," and Archer rejoined:

"I've got the answer to a lot of things, I think. Listen, captain—there're two things I want you to do. You know the local setup, and you can give me a hand." He leaned over the desk, talked persuasively, and Denny finally said:

"It's okay, but you take the blame if it falls through. I'm going to live here, after you're gone, you know."

He called a clerk, said: "Dig up one of the print men. I've got a job for him to do," and, when the clerk had gone: "Do you want the medical examiner now, too?"

Archer said: "Bring him with you, when you come. That's time enough."

Denny nodded, and Archer picked up the phone. He called Guy Sproat's house, got Sproat and said:

"This is John Archer. Mr. Heber has been killed in an accident, and I thought it might be best if you broke the news to his family." He listened a moment, said:

"I took it for granted you were their friend, is all. You'll do this at once then, is that right? Thank you." He said to Denny then:

"He's going to do it right now, as soon as he dresses. He seems to think it's too early in the morning to be called for a job like that, but after all, we've got our work to do."

Denny grinned, said: "Yeah! Early in the morning's a good time to be doing it, too. Up with the milk-men, after the milk racketeers."

Archer phoned again before he left Denny's office, and Mike Tovar was dressed and waiting for him when he stopped by Tovar's house. The big man said:

"What is it now?"

"I want you to take a ride with me and look at some things."

"Is it a pinch? You got a warrant?"

Archer didn't like the big racketeer, and this showed in his voice when he said:

"No—but if you make a point of it, I can probably get one. You've got your fingers in too many pies, Mike, to make an issue of a warrant."

The big man said sullenly, "It's just I don't want a frame hung on me," and climbed in the car. Archer drove to Front Street and to Heber's store, and when they pulled up in front, Tovar blurted out:

"Hey! You trying to pin this on me?"

Archer said: "Listen — that's enough. If you want to come in here with me and answer some questions, all right; if not, all right. I'll just take you in."

"You can't pull this third-degree stuff on me."

Archer said, "Okay, you're asking for it," and climbed from the car and into the street. Tovar got out, as hurriedly, said:

"Okay—I'll go in with you."

Archer said, "That's better," and led the way into the store.

A FINGERPRINT man from the station, Joe Denny, and the pursy little medical examiner, were waiting for them. Denny said:

"Joe, here—" he pointed at the print man—"has found plenty of prints, and I've found this." He held up a piece of stained rope, added:

"It was on one of those bales there. It had been pulled out and cut off."

Archer said, "That's all we need," and went to the store phone. He called Heber's house, asked for Sproat, then said:

"Mr. Sproat? . . . . This is Archer, again. Do you suppose you can come down to the store. There are some things here I'd like either one of the family, or a friend of the family, to see, and I suppose they're too broken up over Mr. Heber's death to be available." He listened a moment, hung up the phone and said:

"He's coming right away."

Tovar asked: "Now what *is* this?"

Archer blazed out at him: "It's this. There're prints here, and we're going to check to see if your prints match them. There's a piece of rope here that ties in with this, and that's going to come into the picture. If you told me the truth last night, all right; if not, I'm going to find it out—and right now."

Tovar shut up, and Denny said: "Those calls ought to be coming through pretty soon. I put a crew on the job."

Archer replied: "That's fine. Here comes Sproat."

Sproat came into the store, solemn-faced, said to Archer and Denny: "It's a terrible thing, this Heber matter—terrible."

Archer said: "Yeah—all of that. I wanted you here to tell you what I've found, Mr. Sproat. The situation is this—when Mr. Dykes and I checked Heber's books, we found records of cash payments, though no record of who they were made to. Then Dykes was run down and maimed. Naturally we suspected Heber, as Heber's car was used. Then the picture changed a great deal."

Sproat looked interested, said: "Indeed!"

"As I see it now, somebody tied Heber up and used his car to run down Dykes. The same person wanted Heber blamed for the accident, so he kept him tied up for a while and then killed him."

Sproat looked thoughtful and said he didn't quite get the last. Archer explained:

"It's simple. If Heber had been killed before his car was used to run down Dykes, the medical examiner would have known it from the condition of the body. It was important that he be kept alive."

Sproat nodded. Tovar looked interested and kept his eyes flashing from Sproat to Denny and then to Archer. Archer went on with:

"This same man then wrecked Heber's car, with Heber's body in it, and so it would look as though Heber had been killed in the accident. The books at the store here might have led to something—and an attempt was made to steal them. I got them instead."

Tovar blurted out: "That don't mean a thing to me. My books'll check with 'em on those truck payments."

Archer started to answer, but the phone rang, and he answered this instead. He listened a long moment, said, "Thanks," and then hung up.

He came back, said to Tovar: "Let that print man take your prints. Denny, you help your man on that, if he needs it."

Then he nodded at the medical examiner, and that man brought out his microscope and put it on a stand.

Archer said to Sproat: "Okay, guy. I want to see your hands."

Sproat said: "I don't understand. What for?"

TOVAR had straightened and was staring at them, as was Captain Denny and the print man. Only the medical examiner seemed to understand what was going on. Archer said then, spacing his words:

"Because that microscope will show parts of rope fibre ground in your hands—rope that was used to tie Heber's wrists while you used his car to run down my partner. That's why! You made a mistake, Sproat, when you told Heber's family I was waiting to arrest Heber for hit-and-run driving. That's what put me on you."

Sproat turned his head, looked at Denny, then turned back to Archer. He said:

"I heard the police were looking for him."

Archer moved toward him, snapped: "That's odd. I didn't have the police look for him until after you'd told the family I was there to arrest him. *How did you know?*"

Sproat didn't answer. Archer reached out to take him by the wrist, said at the same time:

"Another thing—Captain Denny's men just searched your place and found a notebook with notations of cash received on the same dates Heber paid it out. They did the same at Tovar's—and found nothing. That clears Tovar and cinches you. That's why I took both of you out of your places. Let's see those hands of yours. The microscope will tell us the truth."

Sproat suddenly whirled away and grabbed for Denny's belt. Denny carried his gun there, police fashion, and Sproat managed to snatch this clear as Archer closed with him. There was a brief flurry, then the gun boomed out in an oddly muffled way, and Sproat crumpled to the floor. Archer stepped back, breathing hard, said:

"That's what he wanted it for. He knew he'd burn for Heber's murder and he took this way out. He's dead."

Big Mike Tovar said: "Well, I guess that let's *me* out!"

Archer shook his head. "Just for this, Mike, we're going to take your prints, just the same. There are other things we'll be talking to you about, and we might as well do it now and save time."

He watched the sullen Tovar being printed, then took the microscope and knelt by Sproat. In a moment he looked up and said:

"It's as I thought. That rope-ground fibre into his palms when he pulled it away from the bale. Look, doctor."

The medical examiner looked and agreed that this was right. Archer said:

"That's fine. In our business, we can't leave any loose ends."

ARCHER faced the girl and her brother in their parlor, again. He said slowly:

"I'm very sorry about it, Miss Heber. It should make you feel better to know your father was innocent. It should make you feel better to know that, through him, we've got this milk racket in hand. It's just a question of time before the men who worked with Sproat in the racket are arrested and jailed. Your father helped on that. We're going to get Mike Tovar on this same deal—the trucks he sold your father were used to haul whiskey, and he never paid a tax on the profit he made that way."

The girl said: "Poor dad! I knew he didn't do anything like that."

"He was probably forced into it; Sproat probably told him he'd kidnap you or the lad here. A threat like that will frighten any man. Through him, we've broken the racket."

"That doesn't bring him back."

Archer said it didn't and that he was sorry. He started toward the door, and the boy blurted out:

"Say—are you a G-man?"

Archer said he was. The boy said: "I'm going to be one when I grow up."

Archer thought of Dykes, in the hospital for following his duty, and said:

"I don't know, lad. It's a tough business."

Then the girl said: "Come and tell me how it comes out, Mr. Archer."

Archer felt rather glad he was in that business. After all, he'd done his job; he'd gotten justice for Dykes and the girl's dead father; rough justice perhaps, but still justice—G-man justice.

STATEMENT OF THE OWNERSHIP, MANAGEMENT, CIRCULATION, ETC., REQUIRED BY THE ACTS OF CONGRESS OF AUGUST 24, 1912, AND MARCH 3, 1933

Of Secret Agent X, published bi-monthly at Springfield, Mass. for October 1, 1936

State of New York }
County of New York } ss.

Before me, a Notary Public in and for the State and county of New York, personally appeared Rose Wyn, who having been duly sworn according to law, deposes and says that she is the editor of the Secret Agent X, and that the following is, to the best of her knowledge and belief, a true statement of the ownership, management (and if a daily paper, the circulation), etc., of the aforesaid publication for the date shown in the above caption, required by the Act of August 24, 1912, as amended by the Act of March 3, 1933, embodied in section 537, Postal Laws and Regulations, printed on the reverse of this form, to wit:

1. That the names and addresses of the publisher, editor, managing editor, and business manager are: Publisher, A. A. Wyn, Larchmont, N. Y.; Editor, Rose Wyn, Larchmont, N. Y.; Managing Editor, None; Business Manager, A. A. Wyn, Larchmont, N. Y.

2. That the owner is: (If owned by a corporation, its name and address must be stated and also immediately thereunder the names and addresses of stockholders owning or holding one per cent or more of total amount of stock. If not owned by a corporation, the names and addresses of the individual owners must be given. If owned by a firm, company, or other unincorporated concern, its name and address, as well as those of each individual member, must be given.) Periodical House, Inc., 67 W. 44th St., New York, N. Y.; Rose Wyn, Larchmont, New York; Magazine Publishers, Inc., 67 W. 44th St., New York, N. Y.; C. A. Publishing Company, Mount Morris, Ill.

3. That the known bondholders, mortgagees, and other security holders owning or holding 1 per cent or more of total amount of bonds, mortgages, or other securities are: (If there are none, so state.) None.

4. That the two paragraphs next above, giving the names of the owners, stockholders, and security holders, if any, contain not only the list of stockholders and security holders as they appear upon the books of the company but also, in cases where the stockholder or security holder appears upon the books of the company as trustee or in any other fiduciary relation, the name of the person or corporation for whom such trustee is acting, is given; also that the said two paragraphs contain statements embracing affiant's full knowledge and belief as to the circumstances and conditions under which stockholders and security holders who do not appear upon the books of the company as trustees, hold stock and securities in a capacity other than that of a bona fide owner; and this affiant has no reason to believe that any other person, association, or corporation has any interest direct or indirect in the said stock, bonds, or other securities than as so stated by her.

5. That the average number of copies of each issue of this publication sold or distributed, through the mails or otherwise, to paid subscribers during the months preceding the date shown above is (This information is required from daily publications only).

ROSE WYN, Editor

Sworn to and subscribed before me this 21st day of September, 1936.

EDWARD H. ZINSER,
Notary Public
Queens Co. Clk's No. 2976, Reg. No. 3095
N.Y. Co. Clk's No. 100, Reg. No. 6-Z-66
Commission expires March 30, 1938.

Undercover Checkmate

Fast-Action Story of a Coast Guard Sleuth's Lone Courage

Holtz' code was to kill his snatch victim if cornered

By Steve Fisher

Wounded, swimming in the cold, black sea, Lieutenant Ted Tay could summon Coast Guard aid with his magnesium flares. But on the Lady Death kidnap craft was little Martha Mason, the child movie star, who would be murdered at the first boom of Navy guns.

IT was the dimmest corner, and the dirtiest. Tay had chosen it because of that, and he sat now, slumped in his chair and gazing at the pony of ten-cent whiskey in front of him. Through the open door he could see the rotting wood of the San Pedro fish docks. The smell of long-dead mackerel, blended with the fetid odor of the barroom, put a stench in his nostrils that he did not like. He gulped the whiskey and shook his head.

The woman was still watching him. It would be a woman who would recognize him like this: unshaven, wearing dungaree trousers, an old leather jacket, and his blue service cap, minus the Coast Guard insignia. His eyes were dark, smoldering bitterly. He wiped his mouth, and ignoring her, called for another drink.

The barkeep brought the whiskey, and Tay tried to concentrate his gaze on it, but he was uncomfortable. He wanted to get up and leave, and he would have, except that he was aware that it would only make him more conspicuous.

She had a vivid, purple-checked skirt, a navy-blue slip-over sweater, and skin as white as thin milk. Her eyes were blue, but a little watery; she had a pert nose, and a mouth that was a curved slash of crimson. Crimson to contrast the chalky white of her face, and the hay-wig effect of her bleached hair. Yet, with all this, there was a hard beauty about her; and when she smiled she did not show dirty teeth as one might have expected; they were white and glistening, so that her smile captivated.

She was with two men but they did not look at Tay, and when he ordered his third drink, she got up from her table and went to the bar. She leaned on the bar and smiled over at him. Tay nodded, but there wasn't a flicker of emotion on his face. At last she strolled over.

"Mind if I sit down?"

His voice was a little hoarse: "Not at all."

When she was seated, her manner changed. She said: "Listen, mister, this isn't a game." She took a clipping from her purse and pushed it across the table to him. "That's you, isn't it?"

He glanced at it. It was from yesterday's San Pedro *News*. There was a picture of him in his junior-lieutenant uniform, a story beneath:

LIEUTENANT TED TAY DISMISSED FROM COAST GUARD

Officer Once Called "Trigger" Tay, Hero of Sea Battles, Accused of Accepting Bribes from Smugglers.

San Pedro, March 13:—Lieutenant Ted Tay, one-time hero of the Coast Guard, who figured in several thrilling conflicts at sea with smugglers and aliens, was dismissed today from the United States Service when a court-martial, trying him for bribery, failed to find him guilty on the grounds of insufficient evidence.

Had he been found guilty, Tay would be on his way to Alcatraz; as it is, the one-time pride of the Pacific Coast Guard is on the "beach." He maintained his innocence during the court-martial and, when interviewed by reporters this morning, stuck to his story.

TAY did not finish reading the lengthy article. He pushed it back to the hay-blonde. He lifted his thin eyebrows and looked at her with burning black eyes.

"If it *is* me, what of it?"

"If it is you," the blonde repeated slowly, "I want to make your acquaintance. My name is Sandra Poynter."

Tay only nodded and drank his drink.

Sandra went on hurriedly, casting glances at the men from whose table she had come: "You got pretty rotten pay in the Coast Guard, didn't you?"

Tay smiled without humor. "They brought that out in the trial as my motive for accepting bribes."

"A man who doesn't take money when he has the chance is a fool," Sandra stated. "Don't you agree?"

"More to the point," Tay replied soberly, "is, are you offering any?"

She looked at him sharply for a moment, then said: "Yes. We need a man like Trigger Tay on the *Lady Death.*"

He asked: "Rum?"

There was a strange look in her watery-blue eyes. "Better than that,

Tay, and more dangerous—not that you'd mind."

He asked: "Narcotics?"

"Maybe," she answered. "Want to try out for a week, with a thousand dollars in the pay envelope on Saturday?"

He looked around, fingered his empty whiskey pony. The men at the other table were watching him now. He looked back at Sandra. He didn't know why, but his heart was in his throat, beating like the pulse of a man with fever.

"It's a deal," he said softly.

The *Lady Death* docked not at a wharf, but underneath it. A high, old-fashioned wharf which was falling to pieces, and on which stood a galvanized tin warehouse that had long ago been condemned and out of use. There was a float under the wharf, and a gangplank from it up into the warehouse. An ingenious, if not a neat, arrangement.

The *Lady Death* was by no means so ancient. It had been a pleasure yacht, but was stripped in both lines and engines for high speed. Although it was no longer than forty feet, the compartments were compact, and guns could be rigged in four of the portholes, either starboard or port, in less than a minute. Added to that was the three-incher on the forecastle, which, in daylight sailing, was disguised as a winch covered by canvas. The *Lady Death* was not unlike a minute replica of the navy's vest-pocket cruisers.

Tay sat in the bridge, on a chart table, smoking a cigarette. He had shaved, so that his bronze face was smooth and hard, like velvet stretched over steel. He wore his blue cap pushed back on his head.

"Isn't it about time you told me what the racket is?" he asked quietly.

A big, red-haired man turned toward him, brown eyes glittery. He had said his name was Holtz, and that he was the boss—otherwise the captain.

"Never mind, Mr. Trigger Tay," he said; "you'll find out."

Tay arched his eyebrows, replied, "I suppose," and tossed his cigarette out the bridge window.

At that moment there was a rumbling sound overhead on the wharf, the sound of a car's motor, which presently died. Holtz straightened up, grew tense.

"Wait here," he snapped. "Signal the engine room to start the motors. We're getting underway at once. You'll take the helm, I'll con."

Tay said dully: "Okay."

But his blood was racing, and when Holtz rushed from the bridge out on deck, Tay got up and went to the enunciators. He signaled the engines, walked over to the gyro and glanced at it. He knew the harbor, from Wilmington through the Pedro channel, right out into the breakwater, by heart.

THE engines started and the bulkheads of the *Lady Death* throbbed and quivered as the deep, steady purr droned up from the lower decks. Holtz rushed back into the bridge, very excited. He signaled the engine room "ahead full." Tay took the wheel, started ahead of him and wondered at the advisability of speeding through the busy harbor.

The powerful little boat lunged forward suddenly, roared out from beneath the wharf and skimmed like a comet across the water. Tay had his hands full dodging the dim lights of the inner channel freighters and smaller vessels.

"Give me hard spotlights and a hand on the whistle," he snapped.

"I'll take care of the whistle," Holtz growled.

They zoomed around a sailboat coming in under its auxiliary motor, headed straight down past the San Pedro Fifth Street landing, where navy motor launches tied up. From now on, the channel would be thick with shore boats, going to and fro

SAX

from battleships, and navy gigs and launches.

"Don't you think we should take it easy?" Tay asked.

"Easy, hell. Not with our cargo."

Ted Tay's black eyes flickered. He kept his hands hard on the wheel, spoke out of the side of his mouth: "Where aweigh when we hit the breakwater?" He was thinking: a coast guard boat would play hell chasing *this* craft!

"We'll veer south," Holtz replied. "Shoot right in between the battleships *California* and *Idaho* and set a course for the San Clemente Islands."

Water was slicing from the sharp bow, the *Lady Death* lay first port, then starboard, sweeping around the shore boats and launches.

Tay spoke: "San Clemente Islands our destination? They're pretty bleak and barren."

"No, that's not where we end up," Holtz said; "but that's where we lose anybody smart that tries to follow. We dart in and out through the islands, then shoot to open sea and head for Mexico."

Tay grinned tightly, pointing the bow of the *Lady Death* between two battleships to race through the breakwater. "I've followed you as far as Clemente myself, and we've been lost there," he said. "We looked into every rocky crevice out there and found nothing. That's why I asked."

At that moment Sandra Poynter came on the bridge.

"Take the wheel, Holtz," she said, "the big shot wants to see our new man."

The shift was made at top speed, which was another rule of navigation that Tay had never before broken. He followed the girl down the narrow deck to a lighted cabin. When he entered, his lips tightened, and his face became inscrutably hard. Lou Landers, whom every G-man in the country had a finger on, but never a hand, sat behind an oak desk. On the deck behind him was something in a gunny sack.

Landers had a narrow, crafty face, dark-complexioned skin, and high cheekbones. His eyes were narrow, an odd color of slate. His forehead was high, and he had dark, patent-leather hair. His lips were thin, cruel. He wore a neat blue suit. An automatic lay on the desk in front of him.

"Sit down, Tay," he said coldly.

Tay sat down, never taking his eyes from Landers. Lou Landers leaned back, lit a cigarette. When his thin lips parted, Tay could see a gold tooth.

"I guess you know why we hired you," Landers went on softly. "Not because of your seamanship. Seamen come a dime a dozen these days." He paused, then: "You're feeling a little bitter about the Coast Guard, aren't you?"

Tay grinned tightly. "That's right," he said. "I need this job. I didn't have any money saved. I can tell you about the service and maybe keep you out of the way of the cutters. They *are* after the *Lady Death*."

Lou Landers' eyes were bright flames. "Are they?"

Tay nodded. "But your boat is too fast, and your route too tricky. I don't think you've any worries on that score."

Landers leaned forward. "What business do they think we're in?"

"Dope."

The criminal's facial muscles relaxed a little. "Do they know that *I* am the power behind the activities of the *Lady Death?*

"No," Tay answered soberly; "else they would have put barbed wires across the channel."

LOU LANDERS smiled this time, a crooked smile. It was evident that he felt much better. He pulled out a bottle of Scotch and, setting down three ponies, poured drinks. Sandra reached over and took hers, gulping it down.

Tay said: "I don't touch the stuff when I'm on board ship."

Lou Landers replied: "Go ahead, it's the best there is. It will do you good. So the service gave you a dirty deal, eh? Maybe it's a good thing, Tay. We'll treat you right on the *Lady Death.* The Coast Guard has been all wrong. We don't deal in anything so petty as dope."

"No?" Tay's thin eyebrows were arched.

Landers got up, went to the gunny sack, and jerking the cord from the top of it, shook the object inside. Sandra rushed over, her face white.

"Be careful," she rasped, "you'll hurt her. You promised me if I came you wouldn't hurt her, Lou. You—"

"Shut up," he snapped. "She's all right!"

Tay's eyes dilated as he stared down at the trussed up figure of a little girl. She was very little, but very famous. Tay recognized her golden curls and big brown eyes at once. She was terribly frightened.

"Martha Mason, the child star," Landers said. "You see, we—"

His words stopped short. Tay had taken the automatic from the table and was holding it on Landers and Sandra. His words were short, clipped:

"There's more than one way of bagging a rat! This is one of the unconventional ways—getting the San Pedro *News* to publish a fake story about an officer named Tay being court-martialed and dismissed so the opposition will take him in."

Lou Landers' teeth closed tightly. "Unconventional but old," he snapped. "Just like the trick of the unloaded gun on the table as a test for double-crossers."

Landers' jerked a gun from his shoulder-holster. Tay's rage, when he had seen the helpless little child star, had made him give way to the hysteria of falling for the gun trick. He jerked the trigger of the automatic. It clicked empty. As Landers' weapon roared, Tay sprang forward, the automatic reversed in his hand.

He had spun out of the way of the bullet, and now he slashed the gun down on the kidnaper's head. Landers stumbled back, still firing; but firing wildly, blindly. Blood was streaking down his face.

At that moment a shot rang out from another quarter. A hot slug caught Tay in the shoulder, spun him around and slammed him up against a bulkhead. One hand on his bleeding wound, he stared with hot eyes at the pearl-handled revolver in the hand of Sandra Poynter.

Landers' shots had stopped. He rubbed his eyes now, shook his head. Then he pointed his gun straight at Ted Tay's heart. The Coast Guard sailor hurtled the desk, came toward the swarthy crook. But a roaring shot caught him in the side.

Weak, fighting for consciousness, he stumbled toward the door of the cabin and jerked it open. A shot followed him, biting into the panel of the door. Tay turned, an unholy light burning in his black eyes. He hurled the empty automatic at Lou Landers, then moved through the door and out on deck before Sandra's next shot could touch him.

Men were coming on the run from both the forecastle and aft. The *Lady Death* was cutting through the water at 45 knots, a streak of white in the murk of the night. Shots roared red from the deck, screaming past Tay's ears.

Then the outnumbered coast guardsman was hurtling the rail of the speeding vessel.

He landed in the water, and in the next instant the *Lady Death* was gone, and he was alone. He bit hard on his lip. The wounds in his shoulder and thigh stung with the bite of the salt. The sea was cold, and black.

Treading, Tay at last took off his blue cap, reached in and drew out four small metal objects. He pulled the cap from the first and released it from his grip. A red flare shot up like a rocket. In a few minutes Tay let go the second flare.

The fourth and last flare had just died down when a sweeping searchlight rippled across the water, found him and steadied its gleam on his bobbing figure.

LIEUTENANT TREVOR, in charge of the coast-guard cutter was a man who had a face the color of a ripe tomato—sharp blue eyes and a thick lipped mouth. His eyes were blue, and at times, sardonic. His hair was iron gray.

"We followed as soon as we saw the *Lady Death* speeding through the breakwater," he said, "but at the speed they were going, we could hardly keep her course. I didn't expect you to go overboard so soon, Tay."

"I didn't expect to," Tay clipped, slipping on a dry pair of blue trousers, and quickly buttoning up his shirt. He put on his tunic, strapped a holster belt around his waist and put a loaded service automatic in it. "Naturally, we were trying to get a lead on the craft because we thought they smuggled dope. But when I saw that poor little kid—Martha Mason—met Lou Landers himself, and realized what the racket really was, I sort of went crazy. I fell for his gun gag. Although he had enough faith in me to let out quite a lot, he still had the trick up his sleeve."

"So it's Landers and his Hollywood kidnap crew," Lieutenant Trevor breathed.

Tay nodded: "The same mob that cleaned up three hundred thousand last month for Ronald Hunter's snatch, then returned Hunter all cut up because the money had been marked and not in the denominations they had specified. The case practically every G-man on the coast is trying to crack."

Trevor's red face was hard. "The other Coast Guard cutter is standing by, Tay. Between the two of us, *we'll* crack this case and crack Landers too. The trouble is—"

"There's no trouble," Tay snapped, "except that we've got to work fast, and we've a helluva sweet battle facing us."

"What's the schedule?"

Tay grinned. "Holtz, their skipper, gave me a cock-and-bull story about shooting around Clemente and heading for Mexico. But I happened to get a look at the charts on the bridge. They go in the direction opposite Mexico. There were lines marking the navigation shoals around Seagull Island; that's their spot. Thirty miles east of Catalina in what is probably the most dangerous water for boats there is!"

"Think we can beat them there?"

Tay shook his head. "Not a chance in the world. They're probably halfway already, and their craft can run circles around us. It wouldn't do any good to catch them, anyway—though we couldn't attack, so long as that little girl is aboard with them. It's too dangerous."

Captain Trevor asked: "Then what's the plan?"

Tay's eyes were hot. "What they'll do is deposite Martha Mason on the island with that woman who is in charge of her, and a couple of men—for safe keeping. They've been doing this on every case, which is probably the reason they haven't been caught yet. But, the *Lady Death*, with some of the gang's lieutenants aboard, will return to the mainland to write the notes and collect the ransom. That's also part of their system. If they get caught, they figure they can refuse to tell where the kid is—unless they're released.

"What we have to do is figure as nearly as possible the straightest compass line between Seagull Island and Pedro harbor, then lay off on their course and wait for the *Lady Death* to return. With the two cutters, and a good stiff battle, we should be able to take them."

"We will," Trevor snapped.

"Sure, and after that I'll go ashore from the *Lady Death,* disguised as one of the crooks returning for something, take them by surprise, and get the little kid back."

"Great!" Trevor ejaculated, "great!" His voice quieted. "But it isn't going to be easy," he added.

MIDNIGHT water, and two Coast Guard cutters lying quietly waiting. Trevor stood on the bridge of one, with his binoculars in hand. Below him, on deck in charge of the gun crew, was Ted Tay.

Presently the other cutter flashed a short signal. Trevor bellowed orders for full steam on the engine. Tay snapped to the sailors: "Ready—on the guns!"

The *Lady Death* came then, like a white ghost flying over the water. The cutter nosed directly into her path. The other cutter lay off. *Lady Death* veered violently to the starboard, tipping forty-five degrees in the turn.

"Load—fire!" Tay yelled.

The gun from the deck of the cutter let go a blast that whirled across the water, caught the *Lady Death* under the bow. The ship kept going, however, and Trevor called the command for the cutter to take the chase. The other Coast Guard vessel let go a salvo at the *Lady Death* immediately following Tay's.

Wham . . . .

The kidnap power boat lurched in the water as it took the chunk of steel in the fan tail.

Trevor's cutter was right behind the *Lady Death* now, speeding in her wake. Tay wished they could go faster. In a moment the crook boat would be out of range. He called his orders to the men:

"Slam breech . . . . Mark—*fire!*"

Red flashed in a hideous glow, and a salvo—which could travel faster than any boat—whirled through the air, straight into the butt of the *Lady Death.* The kidnap yacht seemed to be slowing. Tay could see the cutter was gaining. The other cutter was coming up very quickly.

"Mark—fire . . . ."

The roar of the deck gun . . . . the sweating, tense sailors leaping back as flame burst from the muzzle —then opening the hot breech, stuffing in another charge, slamming the breech again . . . . Pointer and setter turned their wheels to get the muzzle on the target. Tay's shrill voice again:

"Mark—fire!"

He could have yelled for joy now. The *Lady Death* was swinging about, reversing her course. She headed back between the two cutters, picking up speed as she came. The cutter across the water from Tay bravely maneuvered into *Lady Death's* path. The kidnap cruiser veered, slashing through the water, to avoid collision. The side of their vessel faced the cutter that had blocked their course, and Ted Tay saw—with sudden horror—the teeth of the four machine guns chattering from the *Lady Death.* On top of it came the boom of the three-incher from the deck.

The cutter rolled, seeming to groan under the charge. A spotlight flashed across the water from the *Lady Death's* bridge, and a snarl of red fire followed. Through the light, Tay could see the sailors falling overboard from the other cutter. He saw the bridge window smashed, the captain fall out of it and tumble headlong to the deck of his vessel.

The sailors in front of Tay, grunting, cursing under their breath, jerked open the breech of the gun again, jammed home the charge—the powder and bunting. The breech clicked on its hard jaws of steel.

"Mark!" Tay screamed. *"Fire!"*

He watched the salvo slice neatly into *Lady Death's* bow. But even as the shot hit, the kidnap cruiser was roaring with their three incher at the other cutter. They caught her amidships. The Coast Guard craft wallowed in the water, shaking, and swinging from side to side. Then it suddenly began to sink—rapidly.

Tay's voice was hoarse, desperate: "Mark—*fire!*"

Insane rage coupled with mad fury was seething through him. The *Lady Death*, snarling laughter bursting red from her porthole, chattered her teeth in the direction of the cutter still left afloat.

"Captain Trevor," Tay shouted, "bring us alongside. They outnumber us in artillery like a battleship against a tug. Their machine guns will chop down our crew. Maneuver us alongside. It's our only chance!"

Trevor, red face running with sweat, stuck his head over the side from the bridge. "But it's madness!"

"No more mad than this sea-going murder," Tay barked.

"All right," Trevor screamed. "Alongside we go!"

The gun was loaded again, and as Tay gave the order it screamed its steel death; its fire and smoke. The sailors, panting by now, wearily loaded again. Tay was looking through the darkness. The shot had again hit amidships. He could see the hole in the gleam from the spotlights. The *Lady Death* was lurching desperately. Two of the port-hole machine guns were silent.

But their three-incher wasn't, and the shot that thundered from it almost took off the cutter's bow. The whole vessel shook. Machine gun chatter followed in the wake of it.

"On your bellies, sailors!" Tay yelled.

THE seamen ducked down. The cutter kept creeping closer and closer to the crippled kidnap cruiser. Tay could see the three-incher bearing down on them for another shot. He ordered the sailors up on the cutter's deck gun. They loaded in record time, and their shot came simultaneously with the *Lady Death's* bid for destruction.

The deck of the cutter was shattered, and three of the sailors went down, two of them falling over the side. Screams burst from their lips, then desperate gurgles—as they sank in the water and were crushed by the moving wreckage of the cutter.

They came together sooner than anyone expected. Trevor made a neat, last-minute maneuver to swing the ship broadside to the deck of the *Lady Death* instead of hitting head on with his battered bow.

Tay was up over the deck in an instant. Trevor leapt from the bridge, gun in hand, crossed the deck, and swung onto the kidnap ship. Two of the sailors followed, guns in their hands.

Tay swept down deck, clipping off two of the porthole gunners by taking them with utter surprise. He opened the door of the cabin, swung inside. Trevor rushed in the direction of the bridge.

Tay looked across the room at one of Landers' lieutenants, a huge blond, nattily dressed. He lifted his gun. Tay's trigger finger worked faster, however. His automatic roared. The spluttering shot from the crook went splintering into the wooden deck as he keeled forward, his face gushing blood. Tay's bullet had taken out a chunk of his cheek.

He deserted the cabin to help Trevor on the bridge. But when he got there, the coast guard officer was standing, staring down at a man who had slumped by the *Lady Death's* wheel.

"I—I guess that settles things here," Trevor said.

Tay nodded. His blood was racing hot. "The craft will still run. Take what men there are left alive aboard this ship, and leave me a skeleton crew of Coast Guard sailors. You can ride your prisoners back in. I'll get a slicker and hat and go after Martha Mason."

"But don't you think a more centered attack would—"

"The element has to be surprise," Tay clipped, "or they'll kill the little girl. It's a job for a man alone. Go ahead, captain—" his voice caught—"I'll see you in Pedro after I bring the others in."

Sweat was still running from Captain Trevor's red face. He blinked in the glaring overhead light, stuck out his hand and shook Tay's.

"Okay, Trigger Tay," he said, not unproudly.

TAY and his sailors found the small channel between the rocks on Seagull Island within an hour. It was the only possible place where the kidnapers could berth. The *Lady Death* coasted in quietly, motors dead, lights all out.

Tay pulled a hat down over his forehead, clasped a yellow slicker tightly about his immense body. "No noise, no lights. And not a man is to leave the vessel," he said quietly.

Then he swung from the deck to the rock landing. He could see a large-sized cabin house not far ahead, lights glowing from the windows. The overhanging cliffs and bluffs of the island made the house invisible from the ocean. A boat would have to slip up into the hidden channel before it was in sight.

He had seen no one standing guard out front, and when he got to the door, he paused and then turned the knob. He stepped inside, closing the door behind him.

Sandra was directly across the room from him, and she looked up. Little Martha Mason was in a corner on the left, sobbing. Holtz, who had been skipper of the *Lady Death* coming out of the channel, stood with his back to Tay.

"It's only me," Tay mumbled.

Holtz paused for a bare instant. But it gave Tay time to get further into the room. He leapt suddenly behind Holtz, jammed a gun into the small of his back.

"Don't make a move!"

There was a moment of silence. Sandra Poynter, blue eyes wild, was reaching into her purse.

"You either!" Tay said.

He felt Holtz trying to pull his hand from his pocket. Saw, in that instant, the pearl-handled revolver in Sandra's hand, aimed toward Tay. And then Martha Mason cried out in a trembling seven-year-old voice:

"Please! Mr. Holtz don't shoot me."

Sandra Poynter screamed. "He's going to—"

Holtz lunged to move forward. He was holding a gun he had lifted from a breast pocket of his coat. A gun that was pointed at the child star. Tay knew that the code of this gang was to kill the victim if he or she were cornered.

And then, suddenly, there was the explosion of a gun. Tay started across the room, fear pounding in his throat. But Martha Mason had not been hit. Then he knew. Holtz was slumping from his grip, crumpling to the floor.

Tay let go of him and looked down. The kidnaper's bloody and unconscious figure did not move.

When Tay looked up again he saw the hay-blonde, the little smile—a hard little smile—on her too-crimson lips. Her watery-blue eyes flickered. The pearl-handled gun in her hand was still smoking.

"They—they promised me," she said jerkily, "that they wouldn't hurt her . . . ."

But Tay heard the door to the next room opening. He leapt across to it just as it swung back. For a cold fraction of a second, he stood face to face with Lou Landers. The gun in Tay's hand exploded. But Landers had moved, was out of the way. Even so, the bullet scorched his hip—and he was flung back into the room from which he had come.

As he stumbled backward, Tay followed him in, raised his weapon again. Snarling, Lou Landers gripped the edge of a table. His gun belched rapid fire.

Wham—Wham—Wham . . . .

Shoulder seared, Tay was spun about, his own shot going astray. He felt the floor coming up, felt his head bashing against the wall. Even then he was twisting around, straining his feverish eyes to get a line on the swaying figure of the kidnap chief. His vision was blurred. He held his automatic with both hands.

Wham—Wham . . . .

He did not know how well he had fared, for he could not see. He knew only that he heard a bullet splinter across the floor just an inch from him. He tried again to aim, as Landers' figure moved across the room. *"Shoot a little ahead,"* his mind told him desperately, *"a little ahead, as when you get a bird on the wing, or a speeding rum runner . . . ."*

He fired.

Rubbing his eyes, he stared across the room. He saw Lou Landers before he fell. Saw the awful hole in nis right temple.

TAY navigated the *Lady Death* back to San Pedro, and when he got as far into the channel as the Fifth Street landing, he stopped. Sailors loaded Lou Landers' body into the police barge. Holtz, conscious now, but handcuffed, was herded into the waiting craft. Ted Tay himself gently handed the beautiful little Martha Mason to her weeping parents.

He heard the child say: "Don't cry, Mommy, I'm all right . . . ."

And then Sandra Poynter came on deck. She was very composed, and her face was without expression. Tay looked at her impassively, and his eyes flickered. He said:

"You wait." And to the police barge coxswain: "That is all—shove off."

The barge chug-chugged off into the night. The sailors went back to their stations in preparation to taking the *Lady Death* on into Wilmington. Only Tay and the hay-blonde that was Sandra Poynter remained on deck. There was a strange, incredible look in her eyes.

"Why—why wasn't I taken with—" But she stopped short, seemed to choke a little.

Tay regarded her for a moment longer, then he said: "Can you swim?"

She began to nod, began to smile, but he gave her no encouragement, and in the end she did neither. She just stared at him as though he were something to be looked at with awe. Then she kicked off her high heeled shoes, climbed over the side of the *Lady Death*, and splashed into the water.

Ted Tay stood on deck, without moving, without even trying to think. The splashes of her even swim strokes grew fainter and fainter.

At last he looked down at her high-heeled shoes standing side by side on deck, and there was a flicker of a smile on his lips, and a light that was in his eyes . . . .

Will Fritz sat in on a dangerous game, in which men gambled with Treason. And Fritz was hoping desperately to be dealt a . . .

Traitor's Trump

By Henry P. Stevens

"TEN years behind bars," snarled the tall man from the side of his mouth. "Ten years for savin' my own life!" His drooped shoulders jerked indignantly as he paced the ragged carpet of the small living room.

Will Fritz leaned forward in his chair near the dirty window and, elbows on knees, stared wide-eyed at his cousin's gray face.

"John, not quite so loud," he said. "Betty—my wife, you know—is trying to sleep." He nodded to the bedroom door. "Poor kid needs all the rest she can get."

"Sorry. I was excited."

"But John, about this prison business—I thought you were in the army all the time."

John Fritz whirled around, his thin lips writhing in a leer.

"Army?" His slitted gray eyes smoldered with hatred as he stood there, clenching and unclenching bony fists.

"Yeah, sure I was—till a crazy-drunk officer sliced me with his saber!" He fingered a deep scar running from temple to chin. "I had to beat him up to save my own skin."

Will looked down at the carpet. "And you got ten years," he muttered. "But—but how about self-defense?"

John Fritz cackled. "Self-defense, damn' right! But with no witnesses. A private's word against an officer's." The growl sunk deep in his throat. "Then, ten years behind bars; and booted out with a dishonorable discharge. Haven't held a job since. People find out—" He laughed harshly. "I've been through hell since we were together on Uncle Emile's farm, Will."

Will looked up. "It's a damn' shame!" he choked indignantly.

"Worse'n that," rasped John. "Worse than the man without a country. But some day, I'm gonna get even."

"You say that people find out." Will lowered his head again. "That makes me wonder—"

"What?"

"Wonder about myself. Y'know I work in the Navy Yard, across the river."

"Yah," grunted the thin-lipped man. "For dear ol' Uncle Sammy, eh? What doin'?"

"I'm a junior clerk," mumbled Will apologetically, "in all those blue-print files."

"Hell, then, you're all set."

"All set!" exclaimed Will. "All set! Slaving for a few bucks a week? And my wife, lying sick in the next room, wasting away with T.B.? The only way I'd figure to be all set is to have a couple thousand dollars to take Betty out to Arizona so she can live again. The doctor says it's her only chance."

JOHN FRITZ'S agate eyes measured his cousin calculatingly. "You *are* in a hole," he agreed. "But —there's ways of gettin' out."

Will's lower lip drooped. He stared down at the frayed upholstery on his chair.

"There is no way," he sighed, shaking his head. "Just going on and on—"

John leaned forward stabbing the air with a forefinger. "I know one way," he snapped. "A way that'll get me part of what's due me, too."

The clerk looked up quickly. "How?"

John Fritz waved a protesting palm. "Wait a minute, now," he warned. "Keep your shirt on. S'pose I tip you off—and you don't want to play the game?"

Will blinked up. "I'll keep mum," he assured.

"Yeah," growled John ominously. "You'll keep mum. You'll keep mum, or else!"

"Go on," prodded Will nervously.

"Okay." John Fritz swung a chair close to his cousin's, dropped into it. He leaned forward earnestly, tapping Will's knee with a bony forefinger. "Now, you handle blue prints. All right. I know a certain man who'll pay plenty for blue prints."

The clerk stared at him with startled eyes. "What d'you mean?" he demanded, raking a nervous hand through his brown hair.

John slumped back in his chair and glared. "Don't be dumb," he sneered.

"You mean I— Oh, I—I couldn't do that!" Will was mumbling wildly. "Why—that'd be—treason! They'd shoot me!"

John's blue scar twitched rapidly. "Rats!" he snapped. "Nothin' to it, kid."

"I couldn't do it," Will desperately massaged a fist between his knees.

"Couldn't, eh? You mean you ain't got the guts!" The gray-faced man leaned forward once more. "Listen kid: One deal—just one deal, and you'll be out of a bad hole and walking down easy street. Easy street—for life."

He leaned back with a triumphant smile.

Will bit his lower lip nervously without reply.

"It'll be a cinch," goaded John. "And just think, inside of a month Betty would be up and enjoying herself in the sun. She's young, Will; she's got a right to live. And you've got a right to give her the chance. It's your duty."

Will heaved a lengthy sigh. For a while he sat brooding, as if in a trance. Suddenly he looked up.

"Where is this guy?" he demanded. "Take me to him!"

John's body relaxed. "Now you're talkin' buddy," he cheered, patting Will's knee. "But," he shook his head, "I can't take you. You'll have to arrange the deal on your own, so's he won't shy off. Best thing is for you to call him up; tell him about your job and all. I'll tell you his name: Bamberg. Call Berkley, seven-two-two-one. He'll probably make arrangements to meet you somewhere."

"But—this fellow—what do you know about him?" protested the clerk. "How'd you come to know him?"

John Fritz grinned. "Oh, a guy gets to know about things like that—in stir." His grin changed to a scowl. "Why? Gettin' cold feet? You going to sit around and watch Betty die by inches?"

Will jumped to his feet. "No!" he cried. "I'll do it! I'll call him tonight!"

THAT night Will Fritz's hands tightly gripped the wheel of his old brown sedan as he guided it through the ruts of a country road outside Parmouth. Then his headlights gleamed on a black car waiting in the roadside darkness. He pulled in behind it.

A thick-set man of medium height rounded the side of the black car and approached, carefully avoiding the beams of Will's headlights.

"Douse those lights," he growled.

Will recognized the guttural tones as those of the man he'd talked to on the phone earlier that night. He shut off motor and lights, opened the door of his car, and stepped out.

The thick-set man's right hand was in the side pocket of his coat as he advanced. "Will Fritz?" he demanded, craning forward. "Let's see your Yard pass."

"What for?" demanded Fritz uneasily.

The bulge in the other's pocket moved. "Are you the guy who called me?" he snarled. "Come on!"

Will fumbled in his breast pocket to haul out a card and hand it over.

The other stepped back. A ray of moonlight picked out the white pasteboard, which he scrutinized carefully.

"All right," he muttered at last and handed back the card. "Now, you know what we—I'm after, eh?"

"Plans—blue prints," gulped Will.

"Right. Ready to go through with a deal?"

Will nodded.

"Good! No need to say what it'll cost you to talk out of turn, eh? Now, there's one set of plans in particular: the new radio-controlled aerial torpedo that they've been working on lately. Get me the master blue print of that torpedo. It'll be worth $25,000 to you. Think you can do it?"

Will swallowed. "Twenty-five thousand," he murmured. "I—I can do it."

"How?" asked the man.

"Well, of course I couldn't get the print itself out. But that particular job has been microphotographed. I'm sure I could get a film—they're very small—and all you'd have to do would be to project it on a screen."

"Good. How soon can you deliver?"

"Tomorrow night," mumbled Will.

"Okay. Now, here's what we'll do—"

He arranged headlight signals for their meeting. They parted.

THE following night, William Fritz, junior file clerk number 6249, nervously scuffed back and forth over the frayed carpet of his cramped flat. His clenched fists were jammed deep in his pockets. Light from the bulb overhead shone on his white, pale face. The aerial torpedo plan was heavy against his chest. He licked dry lips, shot a feverish glance at a battered alarm clock on the dresser. Ten-thirty. A half hour more of this, he thought. He stopped prowling suddenly, to stare at his reflection in the mirror. His face worked nervously.

A cry burst from him. "I can't do it!" He turned, ran to the door, jerked it open, pelted down the dim hallway to a wall phone. His hand shook as he jerked the receiver from its hook.

"Navy Yard," he rasped hoarsely. "D u t y Officer's office? . . . Send some men over here, Monrose Apartments, right away! Spies! I—I was going to—"

He broke off, gasping in pain, as something hard jammed between his ribs.

"Hang up!" a steely voice clipped. Will's jaw dropped. Turning his head fearfully, his frightened eyes met John Fritz's hard ones gleaming from under a slouch hat. The receiver gave off crackling sounds as Will obeyed.

"Now, into your room." John prodded Will down the hall, belted him through the doorway, closed the door behind him and leaned back against it.

In the center of the room, Will faced about, thin shoulders hunched over, wild eyes staring at the menacing Army automatic John held drawn at his stomach. The latter's eyes burned in the gray mask of his face. The long scar on his cheek twitched in the harsh light.

"You yellow hound!" he snarled, his thin lips scarcely moving.

Will clenched his fists to his sides. "I can't do it," he gasped.

"Ain't that too bad!" sneered John. "But you're in it now—and so am I. And we're going to see it through. I figgered this'd be the only way you'd do it—with a gat at your back."

Will breathed in hoarse gasps as John stepped forward.

"You got the plans? Let's see—" His slitted eyes watched Will fumble inside his coat. The tight packet of papers trembled as Will passed them over.

John grabbed them in his left hand and thumbed them over expertly. "All right." Shoving the papers back, he added, "You keep 'em. If we get nabbed, I don't know a thing, see?" He backed to the door knob. "Come on." He motioned over his shoulder with the gun as he flung the door open.

The gun muzzle pressed hard between Will's ribs as he moved into the hall. It stayed there down the stairs and into the street.

Will's lips were quivering as he darted nervous glances around. A near-by street lamp showed no uniforms, only one ragged hobo slouching past. The gun forced him into his parked sedan. Settling behind the wheel he heard:

"Get goin'." The gun jammed into him between the seats.

DRIVING through town, Will clenched the wheel. His body was covered with cold sweat. At an intersection, he saw a cop leaning negligently against a lamp post. He made a clumsy attempt to stall the car.

"Nix!" snarled John, belting him a ringing clout on the ear.

The car leaped forward as Will pressed hard on the accelerator. They sped on through the outskirts of town, the lighted windows on either side growing more and more infrequent. At last they hit the Post Road and rolled into open country. The headlights shone on thick pine woods on either side. Deliberately he gunned the car to a breakneck speed.

Suddenly a siren started wailing behind them. Will tensed, his foot started for the brakes.

John's gun prodded. "Don't stop."

Will jammed the accelerator to the floor again. The engine labored loudly with a carbon knock. The wail of the siren rose in pitch. Will was crouched over the wheel waiting for the sound of shots when the black sedan eased alongside. He saw moonlight gleaming on the blue steel of a gun and the visor of the cop's cap as he leaned out, bellowing:

"Pull off the road!"

Will slowed down.

"No funny business," John was muttering in his ear. "I'm doing all the talking."

The big cop strode up to Will's open window, leaned an arm on the sill, poked his head inside.

"What the hell's a matter?" he bawled. "You deaf or somethin'?"

John was leaning over the back of Will's seat. "We heard the siren officer," he chattered excitedly, "but, y' see, we're in a terrible hurry."

"Zat so?" The cop grinned savagely. "Well, ain't that too bad?"

"But," gasped John, "he—he's taking me to my mother. She—she's dying! Can't you let us go this time?"

The cop gulped down a remark. His grin faded.

"Hell," he murmured lamely. "Hell, that's tough." He looked down at his sleeve. "Well, you guys go ahead then. But take it a little slower." He drew his head out of the window, moved back, and stood staring at Will for a moment.

The gun prodded relentlessly. Will shoved in the clutch, yanked the car back into the highway. They drove on in silence for three miles, then Will turned off onto a dirt road. The car bumped over ruts.

"Is this where you meet him?" demanded John. Then, as Will nodded: "You've got signals, huh?"

"I make two flashes," mumbled Will sullenly. "He comes back with four."

"Okay," snapped John testily, "be sure you make 'em."

Will's heart was in his mouth as the lights of an oncoming car showed around a turn ahead. He pulled over.

As the car neared, he flashed his headlights twice. The big black sedan's headlights flashed four times before it purred swiftly by.

"Hah!" grunted John. "What now?"

"I go a mile farther, turn and come back." The car bumped on. The headlights showed a clearing at the roadside.

"Turn here," ordered John Fritz. Will slowed, cramped the bus around, headed back. At last, his headlights revealed the black sedan drawn up close to the roadside bushes.

"That looks like it," advised John. "Pull up." He added grimly: "No monkey business. The gat'll be on you every second. Just go ahead as you planned it."

Will swerved his car behind the other and switched off the lights. He slumped back in his seat.

"Out with you," clipped John.

As Will slowly opened the door and climbed out backwards, John crouched down, easing out the other side.

THE same thick-set man loomed up suddenly in front of Will.

"Got them?" he demanded.

Will reached into the breast pocket of his coat and passed over an envelope.

"Hold it, you!"

Will froze and turned at the barked order.

"Reach high, Bamberg!" John Fitz's torso showed over the hood of Will's car. Moonlight gleamed on guns in both hands. "Caught you with the goods in your hands!"

Bamberg grunted angrily and raised his arms slowly.

Guns roared twin spouts of flame from the roadside bushes. Lead thudded into Will's car and ricocheted, whining. A slug drove Will back against the door.

He slumped down to the running board. John's 45's boomed a cannonade as he crouched low behind the hood.

The fusillade from the bushes quit suddenly. John ceased firing and straightened up. The only sound was Bamberg's noisy breathing grunts as he lay on the ground with one hand pressed to his side.

John Fritz whipped round the front fender, darting a quick glance at Bamberg as he leaped at Will. The latter was bent over with right hand pressed against his thigh.

"They got me," he said quietly.

John slipped his gun into his coat pocket and extended his hand.

"Hell!" he exclaimed suddenly. "I'm sorry you got plugged, but this was the only way to get these dirty spies red-handed. I faked that yarn about my going to prison. I'm in government secret service."

Will looked up at his cousin incredulously, gasped: "You—a secret service man?"

"Yes. I would've told you before, but I was afraid you wouldn't be able to act your part well enough if you knew it was all a put-up job."

Will still stared. "Thank heaven!" he muttered. Then he looked startled. "What—what's going to happen to me?"

John's face was grim. "I'll cover for you, because you *did* have a change of heart. You wouldn't have gone through with it except at the point of my gun. Still, I can't help feeling disappointed, kid. There are a lot of men who would have eaten lead rather than sell out their country."

"But John," said Will eagerly, "I didn't sell out—honestly I didn't. Remember that cop? Just as we pulled away from him, I slipped one of the microphotographs up his sleeve. You see, those plans were made in divided blue prints. One wouldn't be any good at all without the other."

In the shine of the headlights Will could see John's face soften in a smile.

"Good boy, Will! That sounds more like you." He patted his cousin on the shoulder sincerely. "Listen, I'll have a good deal of drag with the service after this. Maybe you'd like me to get you a post out West for a while—say, in Arizona?"

Assignment to Hell

A G-Man Mixes Printer's Type with Gun Lead

By Frank Gruber

It was a clever setup—Handsome Danny Needham, gangster supreme, using a little old tin-lizzie for his bank raids. It was clever, too, the way that tin-lizzie could vanish into thin air. But G-man Smith was banking on the chance that the robber-baron was so clever he'd give himself away. . . .

ELMHURST, IOWA, baked under a stifling sun. The townfolk had retreated to the shelter of their homes and business places, and Main Street was deserted except for a car or two that rolled listlessly along the street.

Tom Bedford, publisher of the *Elmhurst Clarion,* his shirt sticking to his back, turned to the big plate-glass window which faced the street, pulled a handkerchief from his hip pocket and mopped his perspiring forehead. At that moment the roar of a heavy-calibred pistol shattered the oppressive heaviness of the quiet street.

The pistol report had scarcely started to echo across the street when another gun blasted, then another and another. The town came to sudden life; a high-powered automobile motor roared up the street, a woman screamed and a man yelled at the top of his lungs. Glass shattered.

The handkerchief dropped from Tom Bedford's hand. For a moment he stood, crouched and flatfooted. Then he bounded around his desk and in two great leaps had caught up a double-barreled shotgun that stood in the corner of the little newspaper office.

"Bank holdup!" he cried, to the lean young man who was just springing up from behind the second desk in the office.

Bedford lunged for the screen door, crashed into it with his big shoulders and almost fell down the three concrete steps to the sidewalk. The young man, the reporter on the *Clarion*, hit the screen door as it rebounded and spilled out to the sidewalk after his employer.

A little flivver, seemingly vitalized by the devil itself, hurtled toward the newspaper office. Bedford said, "Ha!" and brought the shotgun to his shoulder. It spat fire and thunder.

The terrifically speeding flivver was less than fifty feet away when Bedford fired, and retaliation was instant. An ugly snout was shoved over the side of the car and began to spew fire, lead, and hell. Chips of brick from the building behind Bedford and his reporter flew like hailstones. The plate-glass window tinkled and crashed.

The shotgun in Bedford's hands roared again. More slugs chattered from the machine gun of the speeding car. Bedford yelped and threw himself flat on the sidewalk.

The machine gun stopped as suddenly as it had begun. The speeding flivver was past the newspaper office, roaring up the street in excess of sixty miles an hour, an amazing speed for such an old, dilapidated car.

Bedford climbed to his feet and shook the shotgun in the direction of the disappearing car. "Damn you!" he swore loudly.

"Handsome Danny Needham!" It was the reporter who spoke. He, strangely, had not thrown himself to the sidewalk when the machine gun was in action. Bedford, looking at him now, was surprised that this young man should be so unruffled by the thing he had just witnessed. The only sign of excitement the reporter showed was in his eyes, which were brighter than usual, and his chin, which was thrust out a bit more than ordinarily.

Cars began roaring past, on the trail of the fleeing flivver. People spewed from the buildings all around. In ten seconds a hundred people were running and milling around in the block between the newspaper office and the next one where the first shooting had started.

"Bank holdup!" was the cry. "Handsome Danny Needham!" Thus verifying both Bedford's and his reporter's guesses.

A crowd was gathering around the newspapermen. "Damn!" Bedford abused himself. "The champion trapshooter of Cedar Valley—and with two shots I score two complete misses, at fifty feet. Bah!"

"Lucky you didn't break the windows of the furniture store across the street," suggested the reporter at Bedford's elbow. "You were aiming right at them when you fired that second shot."

Bedford turned on his reporter, his eyes shining. "Smith! Hey! This is press day. We close in a half hour. Quick, inside, have Gliffe tear out the whole front page. Get at that typewriter. This is the best story of the year. Start it: 'Bank held up. Bandits make getaway under fire.' I'll get the details and give them to you as you write. Hop to it!"

Smith's eyes lit up. "I gotcha, boss." He whirled and dashed into the office. He bounced down into his swivel chair, ripped out a sheet of paper from his typewriter, hurled it to the floor, and, with quick, practiced fingers, rolled a brand-new sheet into the machine.

His fingers began flying over the keys; they clicked and clattered.

PRESS day! Let the townsfolk gab about the big event outside. Walter Smith was the reporter of the *Elmhurst Clarion*. He *wrote* the news.

He worked furiously. Doors banged, people dashed in and out of the office. Tom Bedford's voice boomed as he swore and stormed from office to press-room and out to the street. He shouted commands at Smith, gave him details of the bank robbery as he received them from people outside. A thing like this happened only once in the lifetime of a weekly newspaper publisher. The biggest story of the year, breaking on Thursday afternoon, press day, right in front of the newspaper office; and the publisher playing an important part in it. That was news!

Tom Bedford tore a sheet of copy from Smith's typewriter, dashed into the press-room. Smith inserted another sheet, tapped the typewriter keys furiously. Five minutes later Bedford tore it from his machine. Then another sheet, and it was finished.

Smith's weary arms dropped to his sides. He leaned back in his chair and was conscious again of the stifling heat that, in the fever of composition, he had forgotten. He extracted a limp package of cigarettes from his shirt pocket and damp packet of matches. They refused to light. He picked up a lighter from his desk and flicked it into flame. He was applying it to the cigarette, when Bedford came into the office.

"It's done!" he cried. "Be on the streets in ten minutes. An extra!"

Smith looked different now. Before, he had been the newspaper reporter, forgetting all else in the heat of writing a story. He had been young, alert, vibrant with life. Now, strangely, he looked older. There were stronger lines in his lean face, and the jaw seemed to stand out more prominently. Where he had looked scarcely twenty-five before, he now looked thirty.

"You're pretty sure it was Handsome Danny Needham?" he asked carelessly.

Bedford nodded vigorously. "Sure. They didn't wear masks. Jeff Miller and a couple of the boys at the bank recognized Danny from his pictures. They've seen them often enough. But even if they hadn't recognized them, that getaway car was a giveaway. It's figured in almost all their escapes. A little old flivver, looking like fifty others in any town they hit. But scooting off at eighty miles an hour. You saw them shooting by here."

"I guess you're right," agreed Smith. "You certainly had a narrow escape when they opened with that Tommy-gun."

"Brrr!" Bedford shuddered. "Don't I know it? I was a fool to run outside with that shotgun. Just a miracle that guy with the gun didn't cut me to pieces—and my plate glass window."

"Fifty bucks will buy you a new one," said Smith. "But what about the twelve thousand they got from the bank?"

"That's covered by insurance—for which I'm damn' glad."

Smith looked curiously at his employer. "You're president of the bank, aren't you?"

Bedford shrugged, and it seemed to Smith that his lips drooped. "I own about forty-five per cent of the stock. President of the Elmhurst State Bank, that's me." He laughed shortly.

Smith began picking at his fingernails with a nail file. "You don't sound very enthusiastic about it. I imagine I'd be if I were president of a bank."

Bedford looked at Smith. "Maybe you wouldn't be, Walter. I'm thirty-five years old. I own half the bank, this newspaper, the furniture store across the street, the hay, grain and feed business up by the railroad, the Bon Ton Restaurant, the Elmhurst Hotel and a few other odds and ends. I'm the richest man in town—in the county, in fact. When I came to this town ten years ago I didn't have a dime. That's what enterprise has done for me. I showed these hay-shakers a few things about business."

Smith forgot his nails. "If you own all those businesses, why do you devote practically all your time to the newspaper. You probably don't make as much off this in a year as you do, say, off the hotel."

Bedford chuckled. "Smart boy. You're right. I make very little off the paper—but—because of it I am able to make money from the other businesses. A small-town paper is a powerful weapon. It makes public opinion, controls the politics. The paper is my most important asset. I can employ some one to run the bank and the other things, but I prefer to run the paper myself."

Smith nodded. He rose to his feet. "If you don't mind," he said, "I'd like to file the news at the telegraph office for the Des Moines paper. I've been picking up a bit of change corresponding for the *Register.*"

"Okay, Walter," Bedford said. "I like to see a young fellow with some initiative."

SMITH left the newspaper office. Outside he regarded the shattered plate glass window, and shook his head. He continued up the street to the railroad depot a block away.

There he picked up a pad of telegram blanks, bit his lip for a moment, then wrote a brief message. But it wasn't addressed to the *Des Moines Register,* and nothing was said in the message about a holdup. It read simply:

PETER SMITH
343 Keosauqua
Des Moines

Uncle stopped over today.

WALTER SMITH

He shoved the telegram to the station agent, who scanned it.

"Forty-five cents," he said. "Didn't know you had relatives in Des Moines. I got a cousin—"

"My brother," Smith cut in. "I run down and see him now and then."

He paid the fee for the telegram, waved a hand at the station agent and departed before the man could impart to him confidences pertaining to his cousin. There were many things on Walter Smith's mind. His brother, "Peter" for example. Peter had a different name in Washington.

There he was listed on the records of the Department of Justice as Sanderson, and right below the name was the one of Walter Smith. A month ago Walter Smith had received his order from the head of the department:

"The Needham gang must be smashed! Since Needham made his break from the Indiana penitentiary, he and his gang have held up more than sixty banks in Iowa. He's been identified on several occasions. I'm sure his hideout is somewhere in Iowa. All the banks the gang has held up have been within a hundred-mile circle. Somewhere inside that circle is their hideout. We haven't been able to find it, but we've traced some of the hot money. It originates in the neighborhood of a town called Elmhurst, population three thousand. I've a hunch that the hideout is somewhere near that town. Go there, report to Sanderson in Des Moines. That's all."

Before he had joined the Department of Justice, Walter Smith had been a newspaper man. He wanted a legitimate reason for being in Elmhurst so he could work without being

SAX

suspected by anyone. By a strange coincidence—and the exchange of a hundred dollars—the boomer reporter who worked on the *Clarion* decided to try greener fields on the same day that Smith arrived in Elmhurst. Smith applied for the job and was taken on.

He had worked for the *Clarion* one month at the time of the holdup of the local bank. His job was an ideal one for his purposes. He was out on the street constantly, talked to everyone under the guise of getting local items. He learned some interesting things about townsfolk, but after a month he was as much in the dark concerning the whereabouts of Handsome Danny Needham and his gang as when he had first come to Elmhurst. Handsome Danny's career of crime continued meanwhile. He held up banks right and left. One day he would strike in Keosauqua County; the next day, a hundred miles north in Butler County. Sheriffs and local law officers set traps for Handsome Danny. He sprung a couple of the traps, but slipped out of them with such ease that law officers were chagrined.

After he filed the telegram at the railroad station Smith returned to the newspaper office and found it deserted. On Bedford's desk was a stack of newspapers, still damp. He picked one up, scanned the headlines: NEEDHAM GANG HOLDS UP ELMHURST BANK. He started to read the account he had written himself, when a box in the center of the page caught his eye, and he gasped aloud. He had *not* written this item. It read:

WHERE WILL HE STRIKE NEXT?

Handsome Danny Needham has, during the past four months, held up an average of two banks a week. He has jumped from county to county. No one knows where he will strike next. It may be up in Waterford or down in Mitchell. No one knows.

IT was nine-thirty the morning of Thursday, one week after Handsome Danny Needham had sacked the Elmhurst State Bank. Walter Smith, of the Department of Justice, sat in a car on the main street of Mitchell, Iowa, which was some fifty-odd miles from Elmhurst. The car was rather dilapidated, but under its hood was an engine capable of doing ninety miles an hour. It was patterned after the car he had seen hurtling past the office of the *Clarion* a week ago.

Up the street, two blocks from the Mitchell Bank, stood another car. In it sat Special Agent Maxton. South of town, in a cornfield, at the edge of the road, was Agent Cooper and his motorcycle.

Smith got out of his car now and then, stepped into neighboring stores and made small purchases. He dawdled over them, then returned to his car and read a magazine. Ostensibly he was a farmer waiting for his wife who was shopping in the stores. Now and then, he warmed the motor of the car.

Always he watched the bank in the next block. Cars stopped before it, a dozen or more flivvers of the same general vintage as THE CAR. Smith saw too, a burly, blue-uniformed figure sauntering casually in the next block, now and then chatting with townspeople.

Smith was playing hookey from his job in Elmhurst. This was press day, and he was committing a cardinal sin for a weekly newspaper man, being A.W.O.L. from the job on press day. Bedford would probably fire him when he returned. But if the plan today was successful, Smith wouldn't want to return to the job.

Smith watched the policeman in the next block. At eleven-thirty he left the bank block and came toward Smith's car. Smith started to read his magazine. The policeman passed him with a mere glance, turned right at the next corner. Smith put away his magazine. The cop had evidently gone home to lunch. Things could be expected to happen. Smith was sure it wasn't a coincidence that Handsome

Danny struck when local policemen were off duty. Some one "cased" these jobs for Handsome Danny.

Five minutes passed. Smith watched the cars stopping near the bank. He could distinguish nothing from them.

Ten minutes. Smith stepped on the starter of his car to warm the motor.

Then hell exploded in the next block. A machine-gun began to chatter like a giant riveting machine; screams of men and women split the air. The Tommy-gun roared continuously for ten seconds, stopped a moment, then roared again. Now and then its roar was punctuated by sharper, cleaner reports.

Smith roared his motor to life, began backing away from the curb. The gun up the street stopped chattering and a motor roared. Smith got his car out beyond the line of parked cars—and then a little flivver, motor roaring, fairly skimmed over the cobblestones and passed him.

Smith hunched low over the wheel, slipped the car into gear and stepped on the gas. The car leaped forward. The bandit flivver by this time was a block away and picking up speed. A mile ahead of it, in a cornfield, was Agent Cooper. Smith hoped that Cooper would obey orders, not try to mix with the gang, but merely try to trail them to their hideout.

Now Smith's car was hitting sixty; seventy in the next block. He was gaining on the car ahead. Behind him he heard the screaming of a siren. The town was sending up the alarm. In a few minutes the roads would be swarming with police officers, vigilantes. The G-man on the other side of town was no doubt pounding along in the rear. But, right now, all that stood between the bandits and Smith was a lone man with a motorcycle.

Handsome Danny Needham had one foot in a trap. Would the trap hold—or would Needham slip it?

Eighty miles an hour, and Danny saw the curving road at the edge of town. The bandit car, three hundred yards ahead would have to slow down a bit to take that curve.

Smoke began to puff from the rear of the bandit car. The wind-shield in front of Smith shattered to pieces. Slugs struck the hood of the car. A bullet in a tire, and he would be finished. Smith let his foot up from the gas a bit.

Then he saw Cooper up ahead. The G-man was on his motorcycle and had his gun in his hand; he was prepared to fight the bandits. Damn' fool!

SMITH stepped on the gas again, jammed the pedal down to the floor. He heard the Tommy-gun chatter ahead, saw Cooper's motorcycle jump from the road and hurtle into the ditch. Smith almost cried aloud. Well, now it was up to him alone. The trap had failed.

The pavement ahead suddenly lifted straight up into the air. A terrific detonation shook the road. Smith gasped and jerked his foot from the throttle. He knew instantly what had happened. The bandits had thrown a hand grenade into the road behind their car. Smith was so close behind, and coming so fast, that he knew it would be a miracle if he could stop the car before it hit the broken pavement.

He clutched the wheel wildly and set himself for the shock. The car hurtled forward. He'd released his foot from the gas, but he couldn't put on the brakes at the speed he was going. That would surely upset the car.

The broken concrete flashed nearer, and then, at the last instant, Smith saw that the shoulder of the road was fairly wide. He jerked the car to the right. He hit bits of concrete, lumps of dirt. The car dipped into the ditch, and Smith jerked wildly to the left. The car leaped out of the ditch, hurtled crosswise across the rough pavement and nosed into the ditch on the other side. The engine went dead.

Not even knowing whether his tires were still all intact, or whether the car would be able to get out of the ditch, Smith jammed his foot on the starter. Ah, the motor caught. He put the gear-shift into reverse and stepped on the accelerator. The motor roared, and the wheels churned round and round, but didn't grip. He cursed and reversed, shot forward a few inches. Into reverse— Ah, the wheel took hold. In an instant he was out of the ditch and on the road again.

Precious seconds had been lost. The bandit car was out of sight around the curve. But in a few moments Smith would be around it, then there was a long, straight stretch.

Smith took the curve at sixty miles an hour. Before him the road lay like a wide, gray ribbon. Smith's mouth dropped suddenly open. The flivver was gone. All that was on the road was a huge truck coming toward Mitchell. Was there another curve ahead? Had the bandit car already made it at its terrific speed? Or had it turned off on a side road?

Smith stepped on the gas pedal and cursed luridly. The truck lumbered toward him. Smith wondered for a moment whether it were best to stop and query the truck driver. But he would lose a two full minutes by that—more than two miles at the speed the bandit car had been going. The truck was a huge, ten-ton stake truck, loaded high with baled hay.

Smith decided against stopping and swung past the truck without losing speed. A quarter mile beyond he topped a slight knoll, and then his last hopes sank. The highway stretched straight for at least three miles, and there wasn't a single car on it. The bandits must have turned off on a side road. There was woods here, and it needn't have turned off very far for Smith to have missed it.

He stopped his car and turned around. Before he could start back, another car, coming from Mitchell, hurtled toward him. Smith waved to it and the car stopped. G-man Maxon leaped out.

"Lose you?" he cried.

Smith nodded. "Yes, they threw a grenade on the pavement and almost spilled me. By the time I got around, they must have scooted down a side road. There's a dirt road back a ways. I'm going to shoot up the right side of it for a mile or so and ask at some farmhouses. You take the left side. If you learn that a car passed, continue after it and leave word at a farmhouse. I'll be on your trail not less than ten minutes later. Good luck."

Maxon ran back to his car. A couple of hundred yards back Smith shot off the road to a narrow graveled turnpike. He had to throttle down his speed to less than forty miles an hour to hold the road. A quarter of a mile from the paved highway he came to a farmhouse. A middle aged man was cutting weeds beside the road.

"See a car pass here a few minutes ago?" Smith yelled.

The man shook his head. "Ain't seen no one pass for more'n a couple of hours."

Smith's spirits plunged. "Are you sure?"

"I been workin' here since breakfast time," the farmer assured him.

Smith let in the clutch again, stepped on the gas. He couldn't take any chances. A half mile beyond he came to another house. A boy in his teens was whittling a stick in front of the house. To him, Smith repeated his question: "See a car pass here a little while ago?"

"No, mister," replied the boy. "Ain't seen none all morning."

Smith cursed softly as he turned his car with difficulty in the narrow road. Needham had sprung the trap and slipped out of it.

At the concrete pavement he met Maxon, also just returning from a useless quest.

"But where could the car have gone?" cried Smith. "It couldn't have disappeared from sight down that straight stretch of road in the few minutes I lost sight of it."

"Maybe these farmers on these side roads are in cahoots with the gang and lied to us."

Smith shook his head. "That seems almost impossible. They've made these strange getaways from other towns. They can't have farmers in cahoots with them all over the state. There's only one other explanation possible—I wonder . . . ."

Suddenly he started. "Cooper! I almost forgot. He was hurt."

A DOZEN cars had already gathered at the spot where Cooper had been shot by the fleeing bandits, but Cooper had already been removed. Inquiry produced the information that the G-man was only slightly injured. A bullet in the left arm and some bad bruises from his fall. He was in the local hospital receiving first aid treatment. Smith wasted no time at the scene of the accident. He did not want to reveal his true identity. It would mean delay, criticism and perhaps argument. He had to make a report to the Des Moines division, and that would be difficult enough.

It was three o'clock in the afternoon when the truant reporter entered the *Clarion* office. Tom Bedford, sleeves rolled up and looking harried, cursed him.

"Where the hell you been? Don't you know this is press day?"

Smith winced. "I'm terribly sorry. I ran over to Waterford last night and got tanked."

Bedford leaned back in his chair. "I'll be damned. I just got rid of one souse reporter last month, and here I've got another. Well, lemme tell you something—" He stopped suddenly and snorted in disgust. "What the hell! You're all alike. Get at that typewriter and get busy. But I warn you, if you get drunk on press day again—"

Smith grinned. "Oke, chief. I'll do my drinking on Fridays hereafter." He stripped off his coat, threw it on a desk. Then he stopped. "That's funny," he said. "Hay in a newspaper office."

Bedford looked across his desk, saw Smith staring down at a small wisp of hay on the floor.

"What's so funny about it? You know I own a hay business along with a lot of other crazy businesses. One of my men was just in here."

Bedford and Smith got the paper to bed at seven o'clock, only a couple of hours late. Smith returned to his hotel then, washed up and had dinner across the street in the Bon Ton Restaurant—another Bedford-owned enterprise. While he ate, his mind worried over the puzzle of the vanishing flivver—and Tom Bedford. Bedford owned half of Elmhurst, had more than two hundred people working for him in his various enterprises. He probably didn't know half of them personally; certainly he couldn't investigate every man employed by his various managers.

Smith arose from his chair and sauntered outside. At the garage in the next block he rented a car for the evening. He climbed into it and drove up the street. The Elmhurst Hay, Grain & Feed Business was located beside the railroad tracks.

Smith parked his car in front of the office. There was a large yard beside the office. He peeped in and saw a couple of ten-ton trucks parked in it. A watchman came out of the yard.

"Hello there," Smith greeted him. "I'm Walter Smith. Work for Bedford."

"So do I. You'll be the newspaperman," replied the watchman. "What can I do for you?"

"Mr. Bedford asked me to check up for him. All his trucks here now?"

"O' course not," replied the watchman. "Only two in the yard. Two are upstate somewhere buying hay, and the fifth's out on the farm. Bedford knows about it."

So Bedford owned five of these trucks, and they were accustomed to traveling all over the state. That gave the truck near Mitchell a legitimate reason for being in that section—but it was still a coincidence that Smith should run into it there. A truck on "the farm"; that was something new. Smith hadn't known that Bedford owned a farm. But it wasn't surprising. He owned almost everything else.

"That's right," he agreed with the watchman. "Say, he told me to run out to his farm with some orders for the manager. I haven't been out there before, and I'm a bit mixed up in my directions."

The man stepped out to the sidewalk. "Go straight up this road to the first fork going left. Take it and continue about a half mile, then turn right on the graveled pike. 'Bout a quarter mile on it—then you can see it."

SMITH climbed into the car again. It would be dark in a half hour or so, and he wanted to get a glimpse of Bedford's farm while it was still light.

He had no difficulty in following the watchman's directions, but he was surprised to discover that Bedford's farm was in a rather remote section. He passed only one other farm-house until he came to the Bedford farm, and he saw then that the buildings were almost a quarter-mile from the road. He stopped the car before a lane leading in to the buildings.

"Lookin' for something?"

Smith started. A man had stepped out from behind a clump of trees. He was holding a double-barreled shotgun. Smith carried a .25 caliber automatic strapped around the calf of his right leg. The bigger gun he'd carried that afternoon was in the bottom of his trunk at the hotel.

"This the Bedford farm?" he stalled.

The man with the shotgun spat out a stream of tobacco juice. "It shore is. Who are you?"

"I'm Walter Smith. Work on Bedford's newspaper."

"Yeah? I s'pose you got some instructions from Bedford for Hank Barnes. Well, go on right up to the house."

Smith didn't want to see Barnes, but the man stepped on the running-board, holding his shotgun in the hand that he held away from the car. Smith cursed inwardly and started for the farm-house. He'd have to do some bluffing and stalling.

Then as he approached the farm-house Smith saw something that interested him; a big hay truck standing *inside* the barn, with the doors wide open. Why drive the hay truck inside the barn on a hot summer's night? Smith stopped the car and climbed out. The man with the shotgun dropped off the running-board and yelled. "Oh, Hank, some one to see you."

A man inside the house came to the screen door, but did not open it. Smith could see the vague outline through the screen, but could not recognize the man.

"Whaddya want?" came the brusk query.

"Mr. Bedford sent me out to ask if you got back all right with the hay?"

There was a slight pause, and a chill ran up Smith's spine. He had a hunch that he'd guessed the wrong thing to say. But then Barnes answered: "Yeah, we got it all right, and I got something here for Mr. Bedford. C'mon in and get it."

Smith climbed up to the veranda. The screen door opened—and Smith looked into the black muzzle of a huge .45 automatic. "C'mon right in, Mr. Smith," snarled the man behind the gun. He backed away, giving Smith room to enter.

Smith walked forward, and then his eyes lifted from the gun to the bearer's face. His heart seemed to turn a complete somersault — Mr. Hank Barnes was none other than Handsome Danny Needham. Smith had never met him in person before, but he'd looked at that face so often on reward notices and prison photographs that he knew it almost as well as his own face. Well, this was the end of the trail.

Then he looked behind Barnes and saw—Tom Bedford himself!

No wonder they'd been suspicious of him. He'd told the man on the road that he had a message for Barnes, had told Barnes a minute ago that Bedford had sent him out here—and here was Bedford himself.

FOOTSTEPS sounded behind Smith; rough hands felt his clothing. Smith held his breath. Ah, the hands missed the automatic strapped around his calf.

Bedford stepped forward, his eyes snapping. "You've been snooping too much, Smith."

"A reporter's habit," said Smith.

"You're the guy who almost sprang that trap on us near Mitchell today," snarled Handsome Danny Needham. "You're a damned G-man!"

Bedford growled: "And you told me you were on a binge over in Waterford. Well, you were a good reporter, but as a copper you've been a washout. You made too many mistakes."

"I dunno about that," said Smith, drily. "You made too many mistakes yourself. Last week when you fired those blank shotgun shells, for instance."

"I wondered about that," said Bedford. "When you kept repeating how lucky I was in not shooting out the windows of the store across the street."

"And the hay in the office this afternoon," said Smith. "And advertising your next holdup on the paper. Your newspaper blood was too much for you. You couldn't resist the temptation to predict the news."

Bedford's eyes glinted. "Ah, you guessed from that."

"Of course," said Smith. "I'd worked for you a month. You made two similar predictions. No one paid any attention to last week's news, but I did. The hay truck was a good stunt though—but too perfect. A flivver can't vanish into thin air, so it had to be in the hay truck. Danny held up a bank, scooted out of town to where the truck was planted with the tailboard let down. It was simple for Danny to run the flivver up into the truck, slam up the tailboard and stack three or four bales of hay in back to conceal the flivver. Sixty seconds was enough for the disappearing act."

Bedford's lips were thin. "You figured it all out, didn't you?"

"Not quite," replied Smith. "I don't know how you got lined up with Danny."

Bedford laughed shortly. "You may as well know that too. Well, I arranged Danny's break from the Indiana jail. Danny's really a native of Elmhurst. His real name is Powers. He ran away from home as a kid, changed his name to Needham. I went through the Indiana Penitentiary with some newspaper men a couple of years ago and recognized him."

"And your small-town empire was toppling, because of financial difficulties, so you got Danny out of jail, planned his jobs and split the swag—which you used to bolster up your business here?"

"T'hell with all this!" snarled Handsome Danny Needham. "Bedford, let's get this over with. I'm honin' to clear out."

"What!" Bedford was really shaken. "You're goin' to light out?"

"What the hell!" exclaimed Danny. "How do I know this G-man didn't tip off some one? There's a hot seat waiting for me somewhere, and I ain't anxious to sit in it, so I'm playin' safe. We bump him off, and I clear out."

"But what about me?" exclaimed Bedford. "I can't clear out. My money is tied up."

"That's right," agreed Handsome Danny. "It wouldn't be safe for you—or for me to leave you here."

For a moment Bedford didn't grasp the significance of Needham's words, but then he suddenly gasped: "You—you wouldn't!"

Handsome Danny's eyes were cold as a snake's. "Money doesn't mean a damn thing to me, Bedford. Nothing does—except my life. I can't take any chances with that."

Smith's spine tingled. In one moment hell would break loose here in this room. Handsome Danny Needham had three henchmen, every one of them armed. On Smith's side there was only himself—and Bedford. Smith had a tiny .25 calibre seven-shot automatic. A mere pea-shooter.

He saw Bedford's face working. "You can't kill me, Danny," he pleaded. "I won't—" In the middle of the sentence he whipped out his gun. The move caught the gangsters by surprise. They leaped back wildly and clawed for their own guns.

Smith threw himself to the floor and jerked at his trouser-leg. The gangsters, believing him unarmed, were concentrating on Bedford, and the publisher received the full brunt of the initial attack. Guns exploded, and Bedford cried out in anguish.

Then Smith began shooting, the little gun making spiteful cracks that punctuated the reports of the bigger guns. Handsome Danny was in the fight with two guns. Bedford across the room, was down on his knees, firing his gun mechanically.

A slug almost lifted Smith from his feet, hurled him back on his knees. His left shoulder went completely numb. A body tripped, fell on him. He jammed the little automatic against the body, squeezed the trigger. The body went heavily limp. Smith shoved it off him, clawed frantically at a big gun that lay in loose fingers. He dropped his little pea-shooter, began firing with the big gun.

Something exploded in his head; he was sightless for the moment, but continued to pull the trigger instinctively. Fire seared along his ribs, and that returned his vision. A blurred figure staggered into focus. Smith fired the gun at it.

Then suddenly there was no more firing. Smith wiped the back of his left hand across his sticky face and looked around. Bodies lay all around the room, limp, huddled. One was crouched on hands and knees. Smith, looking hard, recognized a face with part of the jaw shot away. Tom Bedford. Pain-stricken eyes looked into Smith's.

Compassion swept over Smith. "You made up for it, Bedford," he said softly.

Bedford's tortured eyes widened for an instant, then the head fell forward, and the body collapsed to the floor. He was dead.

Pert young Rosa O'Mara flirted so much with excitement that she was slated for lead-slug wages when she played cashier for a . . . .

Hijacker's Payoff

By Henry F. Church

GAZING through the lunchroom doorway in rapt admiration at the swanky blue roadster with its Illinois plates, Rosa O'Mara thought that the towering black derricks of this Texas oil town formed a sorry background for such beauty and elegance. Immediately she decided that she and the car were in the same category.

Fifteen minutes ago the three occupants of the car had come in for lunch, and already, by alert listening, she had picked up their first names. The stout, red haired one was Jake; the darkly handsome man, with the close-clipped mustache, was called Duke; and the sandy, insignificant fellow answered to the name of Spud.

She cast a disapproving glance down the counter, where leaned Johnny Carson, his lengthy frame encased in muddy corduroys, and his rowdy blond bang hanging thatch-like over his freckled face. She wondered why nature had not endowed him with black hair and a close-clipped mustache.

The big man was mopping his brow.

"This Texas heat becomes unbearable at times," Rosa said. "You gentlemen headed south?"

"Yeah," growled Jake, "the car's headed that way. What's it to you?"

"The heat isn't the only thing unbearable around here," Johnny Carson drawled, speaking to no one in particular.

The little man choked on his coffee, and the others spun on their stools to face the speaker.

"Meaning who?" asked Jake, and leered in a manner that made Rosa worry about Johnny.

"Nuts," said Johnny enigmatically, and straightened up in all the glory of his six-feet-four of brawn.

Jake turned back to his meal, but the evil grin still flickered about his lips.

"You shouldn't have butted in like that," Rosa told Johnny when the three were gone. "It isn't good for business."

"Neither are you. What the heck do you know about running a lunchroom, anyhow? Just because your uncle left you the joint, it doesn't follow that you've got to run it personally. I've got a far better job for you."

"Being Mrs. Johnny Carson would be a job all right," she told him, and would not further discuss the subject.

THE three came back for supper, and while they waited for their orders, Jake talked in low tone with Duke. The little man, left out of the conversation, seemed not to mind it at all, so Rosa figured he was probably only the chauffeur.

Pausing behind the coffee urn to smoothe her fair hair and touch up her lips, Rosa was in a position to admire Duke's profile and pick up fragments of the muted conversation. Not that she was given to eavesdropping; she just relished a bit of outside talk occasionally. However, their talk seemed to center on the local bank and other uninteresting financial matters, so she concentrated on the handsome profile.

Duke seemed inclined to argue on some point, and Jake, in a sudden rage, thumped his huge fist on the counter. "Hell," he growled, "I can tilt it myself, if you haven't got the guts."

"Sh-h-h-h!" warned Duke, and threw a nod in the direction of Rosa, who colored violently.

When they were leaving Rosa was almost sure that Duke flicked her a wink. She wasn't quite sure about it, but she decided to stay around a little longer, anyway. Her hunch was good. In fifteen minutes he came in alone.

"Come back for something?" she asked pertly.

"Yes—you."

"Oh," said Rosa, and blushed. She hadn't expected such quick action. "As a rule I don't step out with the customers," she informed him coldly.

"I haven't asked you."

"Oh," gasped Rosa, getting redder.

"Forget it," he told her, and leaned on the counter. "Just how much did you hear when you listened in on Jake and me?"

"Enough to make me believe that a bank robbery is being planned," she told him flatly. As a matter of fact, the idea had just occurred to her.

Duke laughed heartily. "I was afraid of that," he remarked. "Well, that's exactly what brings us here."

"Oh, gee, gosh!" gasped Rosa, clutching at the cash register.

"Now don't get Jake and me wrong. Did you ever hear of the F. B. I.?"

"Is it a gang?"

"John Edgar Hoover wouldn't like that," replied Duke gravely. "No, the F. B. I. is the federal office that wipes out gangs. *Spup-pup-pup-pup!* Just like that. Can you keep your pretty mouth shut?"

"Oh, yes, indeed," assured Rosa, flattered.

"Then I suppose I'll have to let you in on the secret, since Jake couldn't keep his trap shut. We're down here to *stop* a bank robbery. Where can I talk to you alone?"

"I've got a car of a kind," she told him reluctantly, hoping that he might have the blue roadster near-by. But he didn't have it, so, shortly, they were rolling along in her car, out beyond the line of derricks, where vegetation was again in evidence.

"HERE'S a good spot," said Duke. He reached over and turned off the ignition. "Romantic, too, what with that dyspeptic moon and the oil-laden zephyrs. Now, what I'm about to tell you must be held strictly secret. Cross your heart?"

He took her hand.

"Listen, mister," Rosa told him crisply, "I can cross my own heart without any help from you. If you've got business, spring it; otherwise—"

"Ah, yes. Indeed yes," sighed Duke, and released her hand. "Ever hear of the Kavum mob?"

"Everybody has heard of those hyenas."

"Jake would love that," said Duke, and laughed. "Now, the spiel is this. The district office got a straight tip, by grapevine, that the Kavum mob is coming up for air, after a year's hideout. And, on top of that, a hot lead that your local bank is scheduled for a touch. So the chief sent Jake and me down here to stand by, thinking that maybe Kavum would put on his comeback here.

"Now, listen closely. At the Oklahoma line we ran into one of Kavum's 'lieuts' thumbing it south. Since we recognized him, and he didn't know us, we figured if we could stick with him long enough he'd lead us to Kavum. So we pretended we were big shots in oil and offered him the job of driving us here. His eagerness to take it convinced us that our hunch was right."

"You mean the little one? Why he seemed harmless."

"Spud Banning, himself. Right-hand man for Kavum. Calls himself Spud Brown now, but he has eighteen notches on his gat, nevertheless."

"My, you must be awfully clever," sighed Rosa, and made only a few futile attempts to withdraw her hand when he again took it.

"Only average. The real cleverness must come from you. You've got to help save this bank in spite of itself."

"I don't get you."

"Well, we're up against a snag. We laid our cards today before old Colonel Jason, who runs the bank, and he told us to go roll our hoops, as he wanted no federal interference in his affairs."

"But where do I help out—cleverly?"

"I'm coming to that. Naturally, we expect Kavum to come in on the flood tide. He may be planning to catch a peak payroll; or he may be waiting for a certain silver shipment rumored to be coming up from Coahuila—around a hundred grand in ingots. Or maybe he's out to cop both."

"But what could Kavum do with all that silver?"

"Lady, you'd be surprised. Now, the point is, if old Jason would give us the low-down we could lay our plans for Kavum accordingly; but the old sour-puss says if he gets in a jam he'll call in the rangers."

Rosa began to get his drift. "But I don't know Colonel Jason well enough to get familiar about his banking affairs," she told him.

"Do you bank with him?"

"I'll say so. I've three hundred dollars in savings."

"Then you owe it to yourself to protect it. A girl of your looks and brains should be able to get the dope for us."

"Oh, gee, gosh! Maybe Johnny Carson would know about the payrolls and the silver. Johnny knows a heap."

"Banker?"

"Heavens, no. He's the one who was rude to your friend."

"So that was Johnny. I thought it was a guinea fowl. Your boy friend?"

"Well—er—yes, I suppose so—but we're not engaged."

"Don't apologize. I know exactly how you feel. Pump him, by all means, but don't let him in on the know. And remember your *new* boy friend is counting on you."

"I guess we better be rolling," said Rosa in a small voice.

ROSA didn't see Johnny until the next evening, when he dropped in for a plate of pork and beans.

"Why should I know about any silver coming up from Mexico?" he countered her roundabout questions. "And as for payrolls, they've got a habit of popping up on Saturdays. Gone in for financial research?"

"I was just asking," said Rosa, pouting prettily.

"Why not ask old Jason for a financial statement or a bill of lading, or something? That ought to serve your *new* boy friend better than word of mouth."

"I don't know what you're talking about, Johnny Carson!" flared Rosa, but she didn't sound convincing, even to herself.

" 'Romantic spot, what with that dyspeptic moon and the oil-laden zephyrs,' " said Johnny, balancing the last bean on his fork.

"Johnny Carson, you snooped on us!"

"Nope. I snoozed on you. How did I know when I crawled into the rumble seat of your car to wait for you, that I'd wake up in the middle of the balcony scene from Romeo and Juliet?"

"Oh, how I hate you! I hope you heard him refer to you as a guinea fowl. Now, I suppose, you'll blab all over town that he's a F. B. I. man and spoil his whole plan."

"No, I'll leave that to him. He made a good start, confiding in the first strange girl he met."

"I think you're horrid."

"Before I answer that, let me ask you a personal question. Will you marry me?"

"No!"

"Okay. Now that you've at last made a definite statement, I know where I stand. Well, never let it be said that Johnny Carson is a poor loser. If it will help your new boy friend, tell him that the Mexican silver shipment is due to arrive at the bank early tomorrow evening. I know, because the stuff is already as far as the border in our company trucks, marked 'Machinery.' The colonel is a canny old soul."

"Johnny," said Rosa, "I didn't really mean to say such a big 'No,' and it's awfully sweet of you to help out like this, and you don't really look like a guinea fowl."

"Aw, forget it. It's all for a noble cause," said Johnny, and strolled out.

Later that evening, in the blue roadster, she told Duke how she had sounded out Johnny, but neglected to say that he was already in on their secret.

Duke suddenly became serious. "I don't want to break up a beautiful friendship for you, Rosa, but just how long have you known this—er—Johnny person?"

"Two months and four days. Why?"

"It clicks! Kavum was reported headed south just about that long ago."

"Look here," said Rosa, her small chin protruding belligerently, "don't you try to hang *that* on Johnny Carson! Why—"

"Okay, you asked for it," Duke told her sadly, and took from his pocket a Federal Bureau of Investigation bulletin. Ten fingerprints, each in its separate rectangle, were on it; and, under the inky whorls, grinned the unmistakable likeness of Johnny. In heavy black letters the name of Steve Kavum and the offense of bank robbery struck out at her.

"Oh, Duke!" Rosa sobbed on his shoulder. "Do you reckon his tip about that silver shipment was a trick?"

"I wouldn't know. It would be just like old Jason to resort to Old West methods to handle that shipment. On the other hand, it may be a trap of Kavum's, or a blind. I'll have to ask Jake."

"Oh, gee, gosh!" moaned Rosa. "To think that I almost became a gangster's moll!"

SHE certainly didn't intend to sleep a wink that night, she told herself; but her young and healthy body took matters over, and she awoke next morning refreshed and fully convinced that the resemblance between Johnny and Kavum was mere coincidence. She had a nice little speech of reproach all planned for Duke. But enroute to the lunchroom, she got another shock. Seated in his car and headed south, was Johnny, and leaning in the window, in deep conversation, was the little man, Spud.

"That settles it!" she declared, and returned to her lodging place, where she spent the balance of the day whimpering. Never again did she want to see Johnny Carson—or whatever the hyena's name might be. But she felt more cheerful when Duke called that night and invited her to ride in the blue roadster.

The moon was not yet up, but she could see the dark bulk of the car parked at the curb, and was puzzled when a cigarette glowed from the driver's seat.

"Jake wants to talk with you," Duke explained, and hoisted her into the rumble seat.

At close range she saw that the cigarette was in the lips of Spud, and that the big man was seated beside him. Well, she thought, these operatives were certainly sticking close to the little gangster. She wondered how she was going to let Duke know that she had seen Spud and Johnny together. The car, gathering speed, turned southward on the main highway. It certainly was exciting to be helping out the G-men like this.

"We're going through with it, trick or not," Duke told her. "We've got word that the trucks are really rolling. We've got the bank covered, also."

"But, Duke, you're not taking *me?* I don't want to get in any fight."

Jake looked back and laughed. "There won't be any fight with you along, sister. You're going to be plenty up in front if it comes to a pinch, and if this guy Johnny is sweet on you, there won't be any fight. He's supposed to be riding the lead truck."

That didn't make sense, thought Rosa. If Johnny Carson was Steve Kavum, and had managed to get in on the hauling of the silver, why should he be bringing it in at all? Lots of other things didn't make sense, come to think of it. Why would this little gangster be allowed to accompany them if they were bent on taking Kavum?

A great light struck her, and it wasn't the moon, which was just beginning to peep over the horizon. "You know, Duke," she said with a calmness that surprised her, "I believe that you're a big bum."

"Aw, go to hell," Duke told her gallantly.

"This ought to be about right," said Jake.

The car turned into a side road and came to a stop. The big man climbed out with a sub-machine gun in the crook of his arm.

"Watch your step," warned Duke. "Those damned rangers know how to shoot."

"It's a pipe," sneered the big man. Then to Spud he said: "Go down to the road bend, punk, and watch for their lights. Step on it."

ANOTHER car drew up, as though familiar with the rendezvous, and four rough-looking fellows climbed out. "Time you were here," growled the big man. "You birds have got your routing and know your jobs. You'll take the trucks when we make the touch, and me and Duke will meet up with you later, along with the bank gang. Duke, you'll drive the blue car."

One of the new arrivals interrupted. "Sorry to tell you, Steve, but there ain't no more bank gang. They were waitin' for 'em with Tommies!"

"Now ain't *that* hell?" said the big man, and shrugged. "Well, we can't have everything. As I was saying, Duke, you'll drive the blue car."

"Aw, give me a break with my new moll," protested Duke.

"*Your* new moll!" sneered the big man, and laughed in a manner that caused Rosa to shiver.

"Oh, have it your own way," grouched Duke; "but what's the matter with Spud driving?"

"We ain't taking Spud no farther than right here. He doesn't know it yet, but he's going to drive the other car out from that side road to block the trucks. We need men in this outfit, not runts!"

Left alone with her troubled thoughts, Rosa had no doubt, now, that the big man was Kavum, himself, and that Duke had used her as a silly dupe. Even the little man had acted well the part assigned him. Why, he'd even fooled Johnny. At that moment Spud came racing back, and, while he was yet reporting, the lights of the trucks flashed around the bend. Rosa, knowing what was planned for the little fellow, felt suddenly very sorry for him. She was still feeling sorry when she discovered that her feet were not bound.

Off to the side of the highway Kavum was hurriedly placing his ambush, so, with some difficulty, she climbed out of the car and went quietly down the side of the road until she came to a protecting ditch, where she could run without being seen.

She kept to the ditch until it became shallow in a dip in the road, and then, forgetting her own danger in her great eagerness to save Johnny from the waiting trap, she took to the road. In the full glare of the oncoming headlights, she raced to meet him.

Back of her a sub-machine gun clattered. *Spup-pup-pup-pup!* Just as Duke had told her on their first ride. The leaden bullets screamed past her on the concrete road.

"Oh, gee, gosh! Maybe I'm hit!" she mumbled behind the tape, and fainted.

THE lead truck hesitated while Johnny picked her up, and then the convoy moved warily up to the ambush. Johnny and a group of armed men leaped out.

"All down, Spud?" he called.

The little man stepped forward, a smoking sub-machine gun in his fists.

"Full bag," answered Spud, and struck fire to a cigarette.

"Boys, meet Spud Kerney of the G-men," invited Johnny. "The F. B. I. calls him the one-man gang buster, or something sissy like that." He remembered Rosa, and went back and found her recovered from her faint.

The trucks with their load of honest oil machinery, and nothing else, lumbered on their way, and Johnny helped Rosa into the blue car beside Spud, who was at the wheel. She was crying softly, so Johnny untied her.

"But you couldn't really blame me for believing him when he showed me your police picture," she told him. "I still don't understand that."

"Darling, your up-to-date gangster has his own gallery of who's who in crime detection. He simply pulled my mug and pasted it over Kavum's to fool you."

"Johnny!" said Rosa, and put her arms about his neck.

"Hey!" protested Johnny Carson. "Wait until you wash your face. I don't like the taste of adhesive tape."

Murder Junk

By Charles Molyneux Brown

Narcotics Inspector Gil Grady followed the treacherous trail of a hated menace, dope, straight into a dead-end trap. And his only hope of life lay in the dumbest of all creatures—oysters.

THROUGH a broken chink in the dirty glass of a back alley door, Gil Grady watched the three men in the shipping room of Dominic Sansone's small wholesale fish house.

The stocky little narcotic agent was taking a chance at his spying in broad daylight, but taking chances was part of Gil Grady's everyday routine.

Vince Lido was in that shipping room, and the narcotic division suspected the man of being a big dealer in illicit narcotics, but so far he had been too clever to be caught handling junk.

Lean, swarthy, nattily dressed in a gray suit, Vince Lido was examining carefully in turn the five barrels of shell oysters just delivered by an express wagon.

Pudgy, fat-faced Dominic Sansone, Vince Lido's uncle, looked on worriedly, fidgeting with his dirty smock.

The third man, a brawny, stupid-looking porter, seemed a little puzzled by Vince Lido's interest in the oysters.

Gil Grady guessed Vince Lido was looking for a secret mark, and the guess proved good when the lean man hissed an exclamation of satisfaction, snatched a marking crayon from the porter's apron and marked a big "X" on the side of one barrel.

The agent could hear as well as see through his chink. The smell wafting out was terrible, but he didn't mind that.

"Take 'em all down to the basement refrigerator room, Frank," Vince Lido ordered the porter sharply. "Put this barrel I've marked on one side. It's for a special customer, so don't let it get out on an order."

The porter rolled the five barrels onto a freight elevator, and the thing descended creaking to the basement.

Vince Lido turned to his uncle then. "We'll leave it lay till tonight," he announced briskly. "I got to go see some guys now and tell 'em to get their money together for a delivery."

Dominic sighed gustily, his fat face unhappy.

"Me, I wish I never listen to you!" he blurted. "I'm sorry I get into this business. Somebody talk, somebody find out, and then Dominic Sansone is in big trouble."

"Stop squawking," his nephew snapped impatiently. "You're in now. You'll be happy enough when you get your cut of the big dough. Anyhow, who's going to talk? Nobody knows anything but you and me—and the oysters. Oysters are dumb. They don't talk."

He pushed through swinging doors to the front of the store. Dominic followed, wagging his head worriedly. The shipping room was temporarily deserted.

Gil Grady tried the door, found it unlocked and pushed it open a little way. He eeled through, closed the door softly and streaked silently for the entrance to the basement stairs he had spotted.

He stole down gummy treads into a dimly lighted, smelly basement. He crouched behind a pile of cases and impatiently watched the slow-moving porter roll the five barrels of oysters into a refrigerated room.

Two greasy bulbs made hazy light in there. Barrels, boxes and hampers of fish and sea food littered the room.

The porter rolled the last barrel inside, snapped off the lights at an inside switch, closed the massive, insulated door and dropped a latching bolt in place. He clumped to the elevator, and the thing creaked upward.

THE moment the elevator reached the upper level, the agent darted from his cover and reached the door. Carefully he lifted the latching bolt, pulled the door open and reached inside, snapping on lights.

Eagerly he popped inside the refrigerated room, pulling the heavy door not quite shut.

He saw the X-marked barrel at once, standing a little apart from others, and pounced on it.

With his pocket knife he cut away the burlap covering over the unheaded top of the barrel. Beneath chunks of dirty ice, shell oysters glistened wetly.

Grady turned the barrel on its side and began raking out the ugly lumps of shell oysters. When a good third of the barrel's contents lay strewn at his feet he uttered an elated grunt and pounced on four shiny tin cans disclosed.

The cans, about the size of condensed soup cans, were tightly sealed and unlabelled, moist from ice drippings and a little muddy from contact with shell oysters.

Eagerly he took one beneath a dangling bulb, punctured the top with his knife and shook into his palm a little dab of whitish powder.

He touched the tip of his tongue to the stuff, then spat quickly and wryly.

Heroin, pure and uncut! Enough in those four cans, when illicitly sold, to bring the big dough Vince Lido had mentioned.

Pocketing the punctured can, Grady cut an express shipping tag from the barrel. He read the smeary writing on it. The shipper was shown as a "J. Martinez," of New Orleans.

Gil Grady knew that a lot of heroin from the Honduras had been run into New Orleans recently, past vigilant agents there. Official warning bulletins had been sent other offices.

Any shell oysters shipped into Bluff City would likely come from New Orleans. Grady had known that, and heroin had popped into his head when he had seen the expressman deliver those five barrels to Dominic Sansone's fish house.

His hunch had been good. He slipped the express tag into his pocket with the shiny can. Agents at New Orleans shortly would be looking up J. Martinez, and Grady himself would take care of Lido, Sansone & Co.

The heavy door squeaked. Grady whirled to face it, and shot up his arms when he stared into the ominous muzzle of a big automatic pistol held steadily in the hands of Vince Lido.

Behind him in the doorway, backing up the play with a rod in his hands, was a ratty-looking skinny man with the feverishly bright eyes of an addict. Dominic Sansone's scared, white face looked behind them.

"Hold it, mug," Vince Lido snarled.

His swarthy face was contorted with rage and suspicion. He saw the spilled oysters and the three shiny cans and cursed savagely.

"Just what I thought," he rasped. "A narcotic dick. It's lucky for us Moke told me about seeing you duck into the alley while he was waiting in my car. And me having the hunch to come back for a look around."

None of the dismay the agent felt showed in his square face. He eyed the savage junk runner steadily.

"Get in there, Moke," Vince Lido snapped. "Frisk him good."

The ratty man eeled past his boss, circled to get behind the agent and deftly went over him. Eager fingers removed an automatic from a shoulder holster and plucked a blackjack from a hip pocket.

MOKE made little mouthing noises as he worked. Patting over waistline and pockets, he felt the lump of the shiny can and drew it out. Vince Lido cursed afresh, advancing and snatching the can.

The ratty addict pocketed the lifted weapons, shuffled before the agent and pointed his rod at Grady's middle.

"Shall I let him have it, Vince?" he squeaked eagerly, finger twitching at the trigger of his gun.

"Not here, you fool," Lido snarled hastily. "Later on—after dark—we can take care of him. If he starts yelling clout him down."

Moke crouched, eyes glittering. All he needed was an excuse to shoot or clout.

"You can't get away with this, Lido," Gil Grady warned coolly. "Even if you bump me, there are others to get you before I'll be good and stiff. We've been watching you. My chief knows I'm tabbing you, and where."

"I know where I've seen you before now," Vince Lido spat at him. "You've been tailing me."

He stared hard into Grady's ice-blue eyes, then a cunning leer spread over the contorted, swarthy face.

"I'm guessing you're playing a lone hand," the junk runner snarled. "If you'd had a buddy with you he'd have been in on the play. I don't know how you tumbled to the oysters, but being smart has cooked you, G-guy."

"You'll find out differently, Lido. You'll never get away with the heroin." Grady spoke with confidence he hardly felt. The man had guessed too shrewdly. "You'd better call it a day and take your rap for illegal possession."

"Nuts. I'll get away with the junk and everything else. Think I'm passing up six or seven grand because a lousy narcotic dick throws a bluff at me?"

Vince Lido was cooler now. Shrewdness and nerve were cropping out again.

From the doorway Dominic Sansone waved fat hands and bleated a scared inquiry:

"What you do with this man, Vince? Already the big trouble comes. I knew it!"

"Shut up," Lido jerked over his shoulder harshly. "We'll take care of this bird, all right."

Quickly he picked up the other three shiny cans and pocketed them. His gleaming dark eyes made a quick survey of the refrigerated room.

Helpless, with Moke's gun inches from his stomach, Gil Grady watched the swarthy face.

"There ain't no other way out of this place but the door," Vince Lido announced with satisfaction. "A guy yelling in here couldn't be heard outside. It's made to order to hold the dick."

He backed to the entrance doorway, and, at his signal, Moke backed away too. Both rods covered Gil Grady unwaveringly. The agent watched them ease out of the refrigerated room, and his heart sank a little.

Dominic had a belated thought, and business instinct overcame uneasiness.

"Hey, I got orders for two barrel oysters to go at four o'clock," he yelped. "How I fill those orders, huh?"

"I'm leaving Moke out here to watch the door," Vince Lido told him. "You can get your oysters any time you want. The dick won't make no trouble."

The heavy door swished shut with a soughing sound. A dull clank announced that the latching bolt had gone home.

"WELL, anyhow, I've got light," Gil Grady muttered grimly. Unless they can turn 'em off from outside, somehow."

The lights didn't go off. After a five minute searching prowl of the refrigerator room, Gil Grady knew there was only one way out, and it would take a battering-ram or dynamite to spring the door.

The concrete ceiling and cement floor; the thick, insulated walls, would muffle any shouts he might make from being heard outside on the street.

Grady had been in tight spots before this, and worked out. He realized fully the danger of his predicament now, but he wasn't panicky. He sat down on a box of smelly smoked fish and lighted a cigarette, thinking swiftly.

Come dark, and Vince Lido and more of his crew would appear, to take care of the grim business of escorting a lone narcotic agent on a one-way ride.

There wasn't a chance of the chief or any of the boys looking him up down here. They didn't know in the office about the wholesale fish house connection he'd been tabbing.

Grady threw down his cigarette and paced as he thought. He glanced at his watch. A quarter of four. Pretty soon now, Dominic Sansone or some one in his employ would be coming for those two barrels of oysters to fill the orders.

Vince Lido had probably gone to arrange for dope deliveries tonight. There might be a chance to stage a desperate break when the door was again opened. But there was Moke and his rod. The little rat would welcome a chance to use it.

Grady paused and stared into an open barrel of shell oysters. It was one of an older lot than the five just received. The burlap from this one and others near it had been removed for re-icing.

Staring aimlessly down at the oysters, Grady saw that some of them had their shells open a little. He didn't know it, but they were drinking melting ice water.

He jarred the barrel, and the shells all closed up as quick as a wink. A sudden flame of interest burned in the blue eyes.

Grady remembered reading in a newspaper once how a rat, prowling in a barrel of shell oysters, had gotten his foot trapped in a big bivalve.

He eased up to another barrel and glanced into it. He could spot a dozen oysters with shells a little open.

Resourceful brains lay under the red thatch of Gil Grady's head. He had a plan now, a slight one, but a forlorn try was better than no try at all.

He got out his knife, broke a thin piece of wood from a crate and for eight minutes was a very busy trapped narcotic man.

At four o'clock by Grady's watch, he heard the door latch clank. Cautiously the door opened. Moke's gun appeared in sight first, and then the cautious, ratty face.

Grady, sitting humped on his smoked fish box, met the leering eyes dully. Moke shoved the door wide and made a beckoning gesture, keeping the agent covered.

Pop-eyes uneasy, the fat of him quaking, Dominic Sansone came into the refrigerator room. Gil Grady could hardly restrain a sigh of relief when the man seized on the barrel of oysters the agent had thoughtfully rolled nearest the door.

Quickly Dominic got that one out, and then the one just behind it. He seemed relieved to get that part over.

Moke waggled his rod and pointed a finger at his own belly. He let his jaw go slack and rolled his eyes suggestively.

"Tonight, mug," he mouthed evilly, "I hate narcotic dicks. One of 'em sent me up once, for a long rap."

He backed out, and the heavy door swung shut. Grady regarded it a little glumly. Maybe it would have been better to have taken a chance a few moments ago, swinging the short iron bolt he had found, and was sitting on now.

Still, his plan might work, and there was always tonight left for a desperate chance.

PACING most of the time, to keep his muscles from growing stiff in the cold, dank room, it seemed to Gil Grady that minutes had never crawled so slowly on his watch.

Since six o'clock, when he knew it would be dark outside, his ears had been anxiously attuned for the sound of that door latch clanking again.

At four minutes past seven the sound came.

He whirled and faced the door, tense and alert. The short iron bolt was shoved down in his waistband, hidden by his coat.

The door opened with a rush this time, wide. Moke appeared in the opening, rod levelled, ratty eyes wickedly alight.

"Come on out, G-guy," he ordered, retreating a little. "The boys are waiting for you upstairs. We're going places."

Stiffly Gil Grady marched out of the basement. Every sense tingled alertly. His little scheme hadn't worked. He'd have to try and take Moke, and battle past the mob upstairs. There probably wasn't a chance that he could succeed.

Moke halted him with a gesture, standing three paces distant, his rod pointing at the agent's belly.

"Listen, guy," the addict mouthed, "Vince says if you'll come along nice and quiet, he's promising you you'll never know when a slug takes you. Make us trouble and you get it when you do, and where it'll hurt the most. Get me?"

"You'll never get away with it, Moke." Grady grinned without mirth. "Remember, I told Lido that!"

Moke blinked. Nerve like this got him a little. He snarled to cover his uneasiness.

"We'll see how good your nerve is when the time comes," he husked.

Without warning, there floated down from above the sound of battering on doors, booming dully.

Moke froze, his jaw dropping, his eyes turned up.

Somebody bleated a scared yell upstairs. It sounded like Dominic Sansone's voice. Gil Grady's eyes gleamed with hope and exultation.

"It's the cops, Moke!" Vince Lido's yell came faintly. "Get the dirty G-guy!"

Moke didn't have that chance though. The moment he had gone off guard, Gil Grady's hand flashed to his belt and plucked out the iron bolt.

He struck for the sloping forehead, leaping sidewise as he did that.

Moke's rod cracked belatedly. The slug merely twitched Grady's fanned coat tails. The bolt crashed over the bridge of Moke's thin nose, crushing flesh and bone.

The skinny addict slumped. Grady wrested the automatic from a slackening grip and raced to the stairs.

Splintering sounds mixed with the battering noises now. Bounding up the stairs three treads at a leap, the agent popped into the shipping room.

Vince Lido and a man something like Moke in appearance faced the shipping room entrance doors, crouching with rods in their hands, ready to blaze when the doors gave.

Dominic Sansome huddled against a wall, fingers stopping his ears, eyes tightly closed, his fat face dirty gray in hue.

"Drop those rods, you two!" Grady rapped out the order, bracing his feet and bringing up his weapon.

Both the armed men whirled, startled consternation on their faces. Lido's pal dropped his rod and shot his arms up, but the junk runner snarled and whipped his gun up for a try.

Gil Grady let him have one neatly placed in the shoulder.

Lido's rod blasted, but the slug went wild. He staggered from slug shock, dropping his rod and clutching his spouting shoulder.

Gil Grady was coldly ready to give either of them lead where it would do the most good.

THE big, stoutly-made shipping-room doors crashed down. Blue-coated, husky men with big guns in their hands barged in.

Right in the van of them was Gil Grady's chief, Dan Arnold. His anxious eyes lighted up at the sight of Grady standing there grimly, covering his prisoners.

The cops made short work of shackling Vince Lido, the other gunman and the terrified Dominic. Dan Arnold bounded over to make sure that his agent was unharmed.

"There's another rat down in the basement," Grady told the cops. "He's in a pretty bad way, I guess. I slugged him."

Cops darted down there after Moke. A grim captain of police and other officers holding the prisoners, ringed about Grady then. Tersely he told his story, omitting some parts of his experiences in the refrigerated room.

"The heroin," he wound up, "is in Dominic's safe up front, I imagine. How about it, Sansone?"

"Yes, mister," Dominic nodded eagerly. "All of it. Vince Lido, he get me into this big trouble. I make big mistake."

"You'll have a long time to think it over," Dan Arnold assured him grimly, and turned curious eyes on the agent.

"Now I want you to tell me how you worked the gag with the oysters, and got your message out," he demanded. "The chap who opens oysters at the Stag Café oyster bar found this thing in one he opened up a little while ago."

He fished a little celluloid slip, not much bigger than two postage stamps, from his pocket. Vince Lido stared curiously.

"This thing reads," Arnold went on briskly, *"Call eight-five-five-two-*

nine. Tell Arnold Agent Grady held basement Sansone fish house. The manager of the Stag called me, and I hustled the boys down. It looks like we made it just in time."

"Vince Lido and his men were just about to take me places," Grady grinned. "I told him though, that he'd never get away with it."

Then he told his chief and the astonished cops about observing the oysters with their shells open, and getting his idea.

"I whittled some little pegs and popped 'em in half a dozen of the big boys before they could close up," Grady explained. "Then I cut the celluloid leaves in my notebook in slips and wrote messages like that—six of 'em. I shoved the slips into the oysters and pulled the pegs. Then I salted my messengers in the top layers of two barrels of oysters Dominic obligingly delivered for me around four this afternoon."

"Well!" the red-faced police captain boomed. "I'll be damned!"

Dan Arnold, who knew how resourceful Gil Grady was, merely grinned.

"You told Dominic that oysters were dumb, this afternoon, Vince." Gil Grady's blue eyes danced at the gaping junk runner. "But oysters are not so dumb—when you put words in their mouths!"

Anne Marvyn's heritage was a bitter one—that of a lawman's woman who knew that men of justice must ever fight against outnumbering odds. And her fear for Ben Swanson, the F. B. I. agent she loved, made their marriage impossible—until she was forced to be . . .

Satan's Chauffeur

By Charles Marquis Warren

Author of "Torture Tryst," etc.

ANNE MARVYN sat alone in her car at the Yuma Airport. Her face, as she lifted it to the blue expanse of sky, was tired and drawn, as though from an incessant weariness. Her eyes, clinging to the tiny Fairchild that circled the airport, were dark with an expression of dread that had, at last, taken firm root in her mind and heart.

The Fairchild banked sharply, nosed down and came streaking for the field. Anne closed her eyes, leaned forward a little and inclined her head. She didn't want to see him get out. She had a queer, empty feeling that this time something had happened to him, and she didn't think she would be able to stand seeing him hurt, shot up.

A Heart-Gripping Drama of the Grim Handicap a G-man Always Accepts

She tore her eyes open, and again the telegram on her knees swam before her vision. It was from Ben.

IMPORTANT YOU MEET ME AT AIRPORT STOP HAD PARTY WITH SAM BUT SAM LEFT PARTY STOP THINK SAM INTENDS STOPPING BY YOUR PLACE STOP LOVE TO YOU AND JIM STOP

Each word of the wire had seared into Anne's brain as she had been waiting for the last two hours at the airport, watching with a cold void in her heart as each plane came in.

Ben was coming in—her Ben. And somehow she knew he had been hurt. That "party" with Sam—she knew what that meant. Special Agent Ben Swanson had finally met up with Sam Ciro. Ben had been trying to catch up with Ciro ever since that public enemy had broken loose from the tin-horn rackets and started casting his sinister shadow of big shot with the first slug he had fired into a victim's back.

Sam Ciro had risen rapidly in the last few months. His power had been felt, first in gangdom, then in the overcrowded annals of the local police wherever he happened to be, and finally he had come to the attention of the Department of Justice as a man who was slick enough to look before he leaped, a ruthless killer upon whom the killings could not be pinned.

Anne knew all this. She knew that Ciro, tracked doggedly by Ben, had finally lost his head. He and the three bodyguards that made up his mob had killed openly in Los Angeles, when a police lieutenant who refused to be either bribed or intimidated, had cracked down on Ciro's protection racket. Ciro himself had shot down the lieutenant and then headed out of the state. And his crossing the line had made his capture an F. B. I. job.

All this Anne knew in a vague, general way. What sent her mind spinning with fear was the fact that Ben had had his "party" with Sam Ciro, and Ciro had "left the party." That meant

Ben had caught up with the killer and Ciro had shot it out and escaped. That Ben was still alive and well enough to send a wire and give chase, Anne knew she should be thankful. But it wasn't over. It would never be over. If Ciro didn't get Ben, then the next one would—or the one after that.

She wrenched her thoughts away from the hopelessness of it and forced her eyes to gaze at the Fairchild, which had landed and was standing with idling motor at the end of the runway.

ANNE MARVYN saw him get out, saw the queer, hunched way he carried his left shoulder, and the way he held his left arm close to his body with his right hand. Then she was out of the car and running to meet him.

He nodded, and smiled gently to her, and said: "Hello, Anne. Glad you could make it."

She didn't cry out at the sight of his white face, the rumpled suit, the wet, sticky mess around the tiny hole in the cloth of his left shoulder. Ben wouldn't want her to make a scene. It was part of his creed to ignore his hurts, just as it was with her father.

Ben and Jim were part of what they called the Law, and their job entailed the risk of bloody shoulders. They didn't complain, and they didn't expect her to. That was the way of it; her father had adjusted her mother to it —and now Ben, the man she was to marry, was adjusting Anne to it, or thought he was.

Her lips pressed tightly together, she linked her arm through Ben's right arm, and walked with him to the car. Silently she drove along the road that led to her father's gas station. She stole a look at Ben and saw that he was leaning back, eyes closed, lips as tight as her own. Finally she could stand it no longer.

"Ben, does it hurt much?"

He opened his eyes and smiled at her.

"Ciro couldn't hurt me, honey," he said softly. "He happened to throw a lucky shot while I wasn't looking."

She didn't believe him. The Arizona sun heat relentlessly down upon the chapperal dotted plains on either side of the highway. Soon the heat would reach the broiling point and become intolerable; but a cold shiver ran through her trim body as she gripped the wheel.

"What's going to happen, Ben?" she asked in a level voice.

He sat up and tried flexing his wounded arm. With difficulty he managed to straighten and bend it.

"I don't just know, honey," he muttered. "I caught up with Sam on this side of El Centro. I didn't use my head and was driving a department car. Sam and his three gorillas had drawn off the road and were waiting for me. It was my own damn' fault. They let me have it. I managed to get a couple of them—and I think I winged Sam. But they drilled my car, and then Sam picked me. The last I saw of 'em they were tearing down the road."

She didn't take her eyes from the macadam. She felt as though her heart were being picked to pieces. In a minute she knew she was going to scream.

"I know how Sam Ciro's mind works," Ben was saying softly. "He knows how to drive the roads and elude the dicks. He and his gorillas have had a lot of practice at it. They pick up the radio warnings in their own car and then drive accordingly. He knows the easiest route to Chicago is the northern route—up by Flagstaff and on through Kansas. Therefore he's going to take this southern way— to Phoenix, through New Mexico and up through Texas. That's the hard way. I figured that. When I managed to get back to El Centro I wired you and got a plane. It took me some time to get the plane, so Sam's had a head start. But I figured I could overtake him here."

"Here?" Anne's voice was breathless, almost hysterical.

"Yes, honey." As usual, Ben seemed to be oblivious to the fact that he was knifing her leaden heart with every word. A long time ago, Anne's father, Jim, had knifed her mother just like that, when he was town marshal and was tracking desperate, renegades. Anne's mother had survived that gnawing, unceasing, cold fear. But Anne told herself that she would never go through what her mother had gone through before her. She couldn't stand it.

"You see, honey," Ben was saying, "Sam has got to get to Phoenix. Your father's station is the last spot where he can get gas for a stretch of almost a hundred miles. That stretch is flat country, dry and parched when the sun beats its hardest. He won't take a chance of running out of gas."

"And you—" her words stuck in her throat, and tears were misting in her eyes—"you'll meet him there?"

"That's right. He's due any time, and this time—"

"Stop it, Ben!" Anne cried.

SHE ground on the brakes. The car was over to one side of the highway. Not far down the road, were the pumps and the small stucco house of her father's gas station. She didn't see it. She was blinded by desperation and the fear that had always gripped her.

Ben was leaning toward her, startled, anxious. She didn't see him. Tears had welled in her eyes, and her words spilled out like a torrent unimpeded by Ben's attempts to soothe her.

"Ben, you can't do it. I won't let you! It isn't fair to you or to me. We love each other. We want to marry. But how can we—*how can we!* Ever since you've been—been tracking down men, I've lived in a constant nightmare of fear and dread. You know that. Every time you write me, every time you see me, my mind is half-crazed with the constant fear of learning you've been shot. Ben, I can't stand it. I can't!"

"Honey!" Both his arms were around her, and his voice was soft. She would not listen.

"No, Ben. I won't let you explain it this time. I know too much of what you'll say. But what do I care about the F. B. I., or the government? The men in Washington don't love you—they don't want to marry you and live with a cripple the rest of their lives. But I do. And I want you well and strong. I want my man to live a normal life."

"Anne," his voice was even and softly persistent. "Anne, this isn't like you. I have a job, and that job is a fine thing. It's fine to protect life, isn't it; to clear the place we live in of a class of animal that kills on sight; that steals and kidnaps and menaces society? It's a comforting thought to you, isn't it, Anne, to know that the persons close to you are safe and that the things they love and regard as sacred are safe. Somebody's got to keep them safe, honey."

"Yes, I know." Anne's voice had now calmed. It was as though she had suddenly made a decision. "Yes, I know all that. Jim was like you are now. He told Mother the same things. She lived in a constant terror, the way I live now."

"And Jim is all right now, Anne. He served his job—he came through. He's got his gas station now, and he's happy."

Anne's face was set, grim. She dabbed at her eyes, then resolutely turned on the ignition, pressed the starter.

"This great department of yours!" she muttered. "You believe in it. You trust it. But does it help you? No. Why do they let one man go up against four killers? Why, if it's such a good department, does it permit you to risk your life without any help?"

"If they put two department men on every dangerous thug in the country, Anne, they would have to employ millions of men. One G-man is expected to do his job, and with favors from no one."

She headed the car for the gas station.

"You've made your choice, Ben. I

won't go through with it. It's not that I blame you for wanting to do your job. It's just that I want you as you are. I love you, Ben, and I want you to be safe. You can understand."

"Yes," he said softly, "I think I understand."

BEN'S WOUND was bathed by Anne and her mother. It was a fresh tear, painful but not serious. Besides a slight stiffness in his arm, it would not bother him.

Jim Marvyn, tall, stately, gray-haired, came in at intervals from attending the pumps, and talked to Ben as the G-man rested in the small living room. They had a lot in common, those two: Jim, a proud representative of the old Law; Ben, the eager, resourceful exponent of the new. Once Jim said:

"Don't worry about it, Ben. Anne's like her mother. She'll get over it. She'll see the right."

But Ben shook his head. "No, I don't think so—not this time."

Anne heard, and she bit her lip to keep back the tears. She turned her head slightly, so as not to see Ben's frowning face.

"What good is your law, your department?" she asked huskily. "What do they teach you that will take care of you?"

"They train you to be alert," Jim said kindly. "They teach you to take advantage of every opportunity—and in that way you protect yourself and others."

"It didn't save Ben from being wounded," Anne said quietly.

"It saved him from being killed." Jim smiled indulgently.

Ben got up. "I'll need my gun," he said. "I figure they ought to be along pretty soon if they're coming. Where'd you put my .38, Jim?"

"Out in the kitchen. Had to wash some of those stains from it—it was hanging under the shoulder that got nicked." Jim turned and went outside.

Bent went into the kitchen. It was now hot—broiling—probably a hundred and twenty or more out on the highway. Sam Ciro would certainly have to stop. He'd walk right into the trap. The heat would bring him in, gasping. Ben picked up his gun, reloaded it.

Anne's long, horrified scream brought him running through the house. He heard Mrs. Marvyn sobbing. Gun jutting from his fist, he threw caution to the winds at Anne's second scream. An ugly sight met his eyes in the fleeting second before he flung his shot, and before a bullet tore into him.

SAM CIRO had managed it sooner than Ben thought was possible. The long touring car was drawn up beside the pump. Jim had just finished filling the tank with gas. But Jim was lying in the dust and the sweltering heat now. He was lying beside the car, where he had fallen when one of the gorillas in the car had leaned out and cracked him when Jim had suddenly given them a grunt of recognition.

Sam Ciro, swarthy-skinned, black-haired, big and broad, was getting out of the car, automatic in his hand. One of his men was already clutching the figure of Anne Marvyn. He was trying to drag her away from where she leaned over the still figure of her father.

In the back of the car, from where he stood on the elevated level of the porch, Ben Swanson could see two men, their bodies sagging stiffly in the seat. Those two, he knew, were dead. He had gotten them early that morning in the gun fight.

Even as his mind fleetingly took in these points, the G-man's gun slapped up and kicked his palm as he threw lead into the man who was struggling with Anne Marvyn. He had to be careful not to hit Anne, and he took longer to aim than he would ordinarily. When he fired, the man spun clear around, a round hole in the back of his head. He sprawled across the inert figure of Jim Marvyn.

The special agent whipped around to fire at Sam Ciro. But the swarthy killer had taken advantage of the extra split second Ben had required to aim, and the swarthy man sent a slug ripping into Ben's thigh.

Ben fell forward. Ciro turned and grasped the stooping figure of the girl.

"You're gonna drive me to Phoenix, baby," he rasped. "Get in quick before I—"

Ben had risen to his feet, his gun gone, and was limping toward the gunman. Ciro swept the girl in front of him, and his automatic came up again. He had the G-man on a dead line between the eyes. But Anne's arms suddenly lashed out, and the killer's wrist was deflected. The bullet splattered into the roof of the porch.

With one motion, Ciro's heavy arm raised his gun, brought it down on a sweep for Anne's head, and at the same time, he leaped out of the way of Ben Swanson's charging body.

The gun grazed Anne's temple, stunned her. She gave a sharp gasp, was conscious of Ciro closing in with Ben, the swarthy man trying to bring his automatic into play, and then she slumped against the running board of the car.

Through a dazzling blur she saw the figures of the two men as they rolled in the dust beside the car. Once she thought she saw Ben get up and stumble out of the reach of the huge arms of Ciro, saw him roll about the front of the car. Then Ciro catapulted his big body into the figure of the G-man. They were in the front now, and she could not see. But she heard the sickening sound of fist against bone, and then there was silence except for the heavy breathing of one man.

"Ben!" she called, trying to stagger to her feet. "Ben—are you all right? Ben—"

She gasped and sank back as Sam Ciro stumbled to his feet and lurched toward her. He had found his gun and was prodding it into her neck, bruising her flesh.

"In the car, skirt," he gasped

(*Continued on page* 124)

The MAKERS of MARLIN GUNS

famous since 1870 — bring you

Guaranteed Quality

10-Day FREE TRIAL

80 Blades $1

Regular $4 Value

Marlin

FIRST QUALITY, DOUBLE-EDGE

BLADES

40 *for* 50¢

160 Blades $2 *Regular $8 Value*

Marlin has found a way to give you as smooth and delightful a shave as you ever enjoyed in your life and save you a lot of money too.

It's selling in wholesale quantities instead of driblets that does it. Packing 40, 80 and 160 blades in a box instead of 3 or 5 And passing the savings on to you.

Swedish Surgical Steel

That's the way Marlin gives you for 1¼c each blades made of finest Swedish Surgical Steel, scientifically hardened, ground and honed, and guaranteed by a reputation of 66 years' standing.

Faces Clean, Healthy, Attractive

Faces shaved with Marlin Blades have that clean, healthy, attractive appearance that every one admires. Nearly 500,000 men testify to this fact. And no wonder! Marlin Blades cut clean and smooth at exact skin level. No unsightly skin blemishes, nor turned under hairs caused by the jagged edges of poor quality blades.

An Amazing Price

You get this sensational 1¼c price because Marlin performed a major operation on the spread between the cost to make and the cost to you. Original blade patents have expired. With Marlin you pay only for blades, not patents.

Shartenberg's one of New Haven's leading stores, reports, *"We sold 400,000 blades in 10 months. Their high quality is bringing repeat business."*

Money Back Guarantee

Use Marlin Blades for 10 days at our risk and then if you do not agree these are the best blades you ever used, we refund the purchase price. Plus postage.

FRANK KENNA, President

Order Now — Send No Money

Pay the postman $1 for 80 blades or $2 for 160. (40 for 50c plus 18c for C.O.D. and M.O. fee.) We pay the postage. Or, send stamps, money order, check or currency and save 18c fee.

THE MARLIN FIREARMS CO.
2710 Willow St., New Haven, Conn.

Please send me..........boxes of Marlin Double Edge Blades at 40 for 50c; 80 for $1; 160 for $2.

ENCLOSED AMOUNT

Name..

Address..

City..

(Continued from page 122)

harshly. "I got to get to Phoenix, an' you're drivin' me. I'm too fagged to try it in this heat."

THE drive was a nightmare for Anne Marvyn. Ben's still body had been directly in front of the car, and she had had to maneuver it carefully so as not to run over him.

The sun was beating down, and brilliant shafts of its heat struck the macadam of the highway as she drove. Breathing was difficult, and the glare seemed to reflect from the dry plains and come under the hood of the burning-hot car and scorch her skin.

Sam Ciro sat gasping by her side, his gun sticking in her ribs. He didn't talk. His labored breathing and the pressure of the automatic were enough. As though he had spoken to her, she realized that when she drove him near enough to Phoenix, he would callously kill her and drive on.

For one reason, Anne Marvyn was glad of that harrowing ride through the terrific heat with the swarthy killer at her side: her change of mind that came too late to benefit her or Ben or old Jim.

She had now actually seen killers at work. She had seen her father mercilessly beaten down. She had seen Ben shot and beaten. The man beside her was a killer. She knew now what they were, what hideous menaces, what warped animals they could be. And Ben's words came back to her—the words that she had ridiculed.

It wasn't fear for herself that changed Anne Marvyn's mind. No, not that. She didn't mind dying so much now. She had nothing for which to live—with those still figures lying back there by the gas pumps. It was the sickening sensation that she hadn't realized that what Ben and old Jim had said was true. Men like the man beside her were unleashed savages—and decent people needed protection from them.

She knew now what her mother had gone through in the old days when

(Continued on page 126)

(*Continued from page* 124)

Jim had maintained the law as a town marshal.

Tears were in her eyes, her mouth was parched, and there was a lump in her throat. She was wishing only that she had let Ben know that she believed in him—even if his law didn't teach him how to protect himself while he was protecting others. She was wishing those things, sobbing softly to herself—when it happened.

There was a loud, hissing explosion, and she was suddenly blinded by a cloud of white that rose in front of her, covered the windshield. The car shrieked to a lurching halt.

Steam—the radiator had burst—the sun had been too hot for it here on this inferno of a prairie.

Cursing, Ciro jumped out of the car—loped around to examine the front of the engine's hood. Realizing it was hopeless to consider driving the car farther, the gunman smashed at the burst radiator with his automatic. In a fit of rage he swore at the heat, at the car, at the burning sun.

He came around to where Anne sat at the driver's seat. She saw the look in his eyes that had been there when he shot Ben Swanson. She saw his gun come up and level at her—and she looked at it impersonally, unafraid. She kept thinking of Ben, lying there in the dust. They hadn't taught him how to cope with these mad dogs . . . .

"I got to get to Phoenix, sister," Ciro was gasping through the sweltering heat. "I got to start walking—an' I can't be bothered by a skirt. You're gonna get it, baby. Here it comes."

As though in a trance, she watched the muzzle of the gun train on the bridge of her nose between her eyes. She knew it was coming, and it didn't matter. Ben was back there . . . .

Not until Ciro had turned and started running down the highway did she notice the sound of the motor. When she could get her frozen muscles to work and could turn around, she saw the car—*her* car. Jim was driving and Ben Swanson leaning over the door.

ANNE MARVYN didn't remember much about it afterwards. Vaguely she saw Sam Ciro turn and fire wildly at the G-man. She saw the answering spurt of flame from Ben's gun, saw Sam Ciro clutch at his face and slump back, off the road—into the dust . . . .

She was in Ben's arms—she remembered that. Ben's thigh was bleeding, and he had to sit on the running board of her car. She didn't care. She wanted to mend his wounds, make him sound again; and then she had a lot of things to tell him before she sent him out once more into that never-ceasing war that would always fill her with harrowing dread, but yet would make her proud of him when he came back.

"Ben," she said, "I understand—now. That sun coming down, causing the water to boil and burst the radiator—that was an act of God, a miracle. But as long as there's miracles, Ben, you'll be all right. I know that. You've *got* to be all right."

Ben Swanson looked at her, an indulgent smile on his lips. He started to speak, but changed his mind and kissed her instead.

Anne didn't remember old Jim Marvyn scratching his head, muttering to himself, wandering down to the big touring car with the broken radiator.

"Miracles," Jim murmured to himself. "Ben told me something about his managing to roll under this radiator while he was wrestling Ciro. I've never heard of a car boiling over along this stretch, unless the radiator was empty. Let me see—"

Jim bent his old body down, gazed underneath the radiator of the car, to where a small spigot valve to the radiator tubing had been turned, permitting the water to drain.

"Well, it may be a miracle," old Jim grinned to himself, "but it sure takes a heap of G-man to work one!"

Made in the USA
Monee, IL
30 November 2025

36961609R00076